TROLLEY RIDE IN
MANHATTAN

4.00

FERGAL
O'BYRNE

MENTOR BOOKS

This Edition first published 2000 by

Mentor Books
43 Furze Road
Sandyford Industrial Estate, Dublin 18
Ireland
Tel. (00353 1) 295 2112/3   Fax. (00353 1) 295 2114
e-mail: admin@mentorbooks.ie
www.mentorbooks.ie

ISBN: 1-84210-010-6

Editing and Layout by Mentor Books
Cover Illustration: Ted Turton
Cover Design: Slatter-Anderson
Printed in Ireland by ColourBooks Ltd.

1 3 5 7 9 10 8 6 4 2

contents

This book is dedicated to Maiken Kromann . . . my very beautiful and very patient Danish princess.

Also to Dermot McCormack who wore a cravat one day and started the whole thing off. To William Morgan Jnr who acted out some of the early words and kept the momentum going.

. . . There are many, many others but it would take a small Scandinavian forest to include you all. You know who you are . . . and your exclusion has done a little bit for the environment.

prologue

Cadumphff.

The others tease him about it.

Cadumphff.

They do not mean to be malicious in any way but it's just every time he falls off a rock that is the sound he makes.

Cadumphff.

And Cadumphff has fallen off many rocks in his time. It is something that he is very good at. He doesn't care ... he rather likes specialising in something.

He is the only one among them who can tell the future. This is not a peculiarity of his species or a genetic or scientific aberration ... it is due to the fact that after falling off one particular rock he damaged the part of his brain that deals with the normal passage of time and memories and things like that. It all got a little bit screwed for Cadumphff and now he can tell the future. That's just the way it is.

Most of the faces looking in at him are happy. One in particular is a snotty-nosed kid in chocolate brown shorts, an orange and lemon striped tee-shirt and ox blood two strap sandals ... who is clutching perilously to the remnants of his Loop the Loop ice pop. This kid has a big chocolate, lemon and lime smile ... like some African country's flag ... that will be wiped away in forty-three minutes by his mother using a lipstick-stained hanky wetted by her own saliva. Cadumphff knows this. This is not what makes him sad.

Cadumphff is not a big <u>armadillo</u>. He is not small either. This is what it says on the front of his enclosure in the zoo.

<u>armadillo</u>
The peba, or nine-banded armadillo, is found in South and Central America and in Texas, Oklahoma, Louisiana, Arkansas and Mississippi. The six-banded and three-banded armadillos are found in South America.

Despite short legs, the armadillo moves relatively quickly and with its strong feet and thick claws it can burrow with considerable speed. Armadillos make up the species *dasypodidae*.

Please do not feed the armadillos. Nothing. Not even a square of chocolate or a single crisp. Especially the one sitting there on his own that looks like he can tell the future. He is spoofing . . . he cannot tell the future and even if he could the Management of the Zoo do not wish this to be turned into a pleasure park packed with sad individuals looking for enlightenment . . . that's assuming he could tell the future which of course he can't so let us desist from idle speculation here and now.

We are serious about the chocolate and the crisps though.

Signed: The Management & Staff of the Zoo.

Cadumphff is of the six-banded variety. Most of what is said about them is true. Except the part about being able to tell the future. This bothers him not.

He has been well fed . . . about an hour ago . . . and he is not in the mood for doing anything right now. He could get up and move to another part of the enclosure but that would be too much effort. He knows exactly what part of the enclosure that would be, what the ground temperature would be and how many young children would point at him and say . . . 'Oh, look at that one there, he seems so removed from the rest of the armadillos so maybe he is different from them and maybe he can tell the future.'

Cadumphff always knew he would be captured and put into a zoo and that he would be well looked after. What makes him sad now is the snotty-nosed kid with the melting ice cream. This makes him very sad.

Cadumphff knows that this kid will be shot three times exactly twenty years sixteen days and ten hours hence . . . on a street corner in New York City . . . while holding a laptop computer in one hand and a Guinness bag containing a large amount of narcotics in the other . . . while his girlfriend Becky is in buying cigarettes . . . Marlboro Lights to be exact and a packet of Lifesavers which is a bit of a joke . . . and that on his way to the hospital he will accidentally be thrown out of the ambulance while still on a hospital trolley . . . and that there will be a virus on his computer playing havoc and spewing random pages from the Internet onto the screen as the injured man hurtles along on his trolley . . . and that maybe it all could be so different if the snotty-nosed kid could understand that the rapid movement of Cadumphff's left eye is a genuine coded warning containing a detailed Gantt Chart Life Plan of how to avoid this doomed chain of events.

The snotty-nosed kid is not able to interpret these signals unfortunately . . . and his mother takes his hand and leads him off to see the penguins . . . none of whom incidentally can tell the future . . . but they are very cute which is often a much better survival attribute.

This . . . the thing about the snotty-nosed kid . . . is what makes Cadumphff sad.

He also knows that feeding time is not for another five hours and forty-seven minutes. This also makes him sad.

Another thing he knows is that he will never mate. That is what the others say . . . stay away from Cadumphff they say . . . 'He is not right that one and the way he keeps falling down off the small rocks. And the way he always seems to know exactly when feeding time is and gets to the food first. Suspect that one . . . stay well away from him.'

This makes him sad.

But he has learned to live with it. Feeding time is in five hours and sixteen minutes . . .

1

Shem and the badumphff noise

Badumphff.

The first sound my ambulance trolley makes . . . as a direct consequence of when it hits the ground.

Ooouff.

The first sound I make.

Tucked inside the trolley. Arms inside the sheets but not for long. One sheet to the wind. The ambulance speeds off in one direction . . . I in the other. Straight down Fifth Avenue. <u>Newton's Third Law</u> at first hand. Third time lucky. This is not the first time I have had a brush with one of Newton's laws. Too many numbers to deal with. Brain hurting.

I crane my neck back . . . no easy feat let me tell you . . . to see a startled paramedic inside the ambulance looking with gaping mouth back at me. We are now travelling in opposite directions from each other, which is somewhat troubling. The doors of the ambulance are swinging back and forth like shutters on a house in Kansas before the onset of a serious tornado.

The paramedic is still holding a mobile phone . . . oh, I'm sorry I mean a cell phone . . . to his ear, though judging by the aperture of his mouth and the fact that his lips have not moved in the last few shocked seconds, it is highly likely the person on the other end thinks that there is serious fading on the channel. That is technical talk . . . fading on the channel don't you know. Very impressive. When someone goes silent on the other end of a cell phone . . . then blame it on shock or fading on the channel. Both have the same effect.

Newton's Third Law

For every action there is an equal and opposite reaction. There is no getting away from this. It is true. Newton, Sir Isaac (1642–1727), born in Enniscorthy so he was. He was a fierce man for running up to the top of Vinegar Hill and then rolling all the way down again. Some say he was mad but they were the jealous ones. He said that rolling down the hill was his way of proving that there was some universal force controlling the movement of all things. It was not until one day when a small boy, who was rolling down the hill for entirely entertainment based reasons and landed on Newton's head, that it struck him just what all this up and down the hill stuff was really about. He called it gravity. The parents of the small boy called it a travesty and demanded equal royalties on the discovery.

All the shops are closed . . . moresthepity. This is unusual for Manhattan. I suspect that something is not right.

One of my trolley wheels is a bit dicky. Okay, Okay,

Okay and Dicky . . . pleased to meet you all . . . the four wheels of my chariot . . : I've just named them that now and I think it's bloody hilarious. A lonely feeling. If I had the inclination I would do something about the wheels and their little periodic shimmy every twelve rotations. Given enough time I would eventually come full circle . . . given a big enough parking lot, and all other things being equal . . . *ceteris paribus* . . . I would eventually end up back where I started from . . . something about the size of <u>Nebraska</u> should do it. But I am given none of those things. Moresthepity.

What I am given however is a very nice television set on the end of the trolley. Top of the range. No messing. If you have the insurance over here they really look after you. TV on the end of the bed on the trolley . . . with a hypo-allergenic pillow just in case you happen to be allergic to hypos . . . all a bit much and what with my guts spilling out all over the place . . . but there is a remote control on the side of the bed which is dead handy and I will probably try it out just so I can say I tried it out and got my money's worth. You are expected to get your money's worth over here. It is considered the thing to do. There are home courses you can do all about Getting Your Money's Worth which cover all the essentials.

Nebraska

There is a barley farmer in Jutland, Denmark, who has a field exactly the same shape as Nebraska. This is true. This is no accident or fluke of nature. The farmer is Lars Pedersen and he is a direct descendent of the first man who ever drew the Nebraska State boundaries on a piece of parchment. The memory of this shape is so indelibly ingrained

on Lars' brain patterns that he has fashioned the
field into this shape. You can only notice this from
the sky.

Lars himself is unaware of the fact about the shape
of his field and he will go to his grave in exactly ten
years' time without ever having known about this. He
will be buried in a corner of the field right beside
where the town of Scottsbluff would be in the real
State. – *Cadumphff*

I drove through Nebraska once on my way from
St Paul, Minnesota to San Francisco, California. I thought it
was going to be very cool. I was enthralled by the cover of
a Bruce Springstein CD called *Nebraska* but it was round,
flat and hot and not very exciting. So was Nebraska. I really
believed there was a town called Buttfuck in Nebraska but
there wasn't. I remember phoning my dad . . . who
coincidentally was born on 1st March, the same day
Nebraska joined the Union . . . from the middle of nowhere
and asking him what the weather was like back home. It
was raining in Ireland but it most certainly was not in
Nebraska. On that day I wished it had rained because I
missed the rain and I thought the Nebraskans would like
some rain. Or maybe some SNOW. The ground sure looked
like it could use it. I said as much when I pulled in to a little
gas station to the old man working the pumps and he
asked me where I was from and I said Ireland and he
looked at me earnestly and said . . .

    – Is that upstate somewhere?

    – Eh . . . it's in Europe.

He sloshed the clump of tobacco around in his mouth
and spat a large wad out onto the asphalt. It sizzled on the

scalding surface and gave off a wondrous aroma. He squinted his eyes and spat again. It landed in exactly the same place. The little puddle spread out into the shape of Nebraska which was too spooky for me so I went to leave as he imparted his final gem of wisdom to me.

– I knew a guy from Finland once.

I did not stop driving until I had crossed the border into Wyoming.

❏ SNOW

The TV tunes itself into some movie or other. It looks like I've seen it before. Camera pans in. It is late at night. NYC. New York City. Fade in background city sounds.

A sidewalk.

A trickle of blood. There is some residual slush on the ground and the red and the white blend together like raspberry ripple ice cream.

I presume it's blood . . . it's hard to tell sometimes . . . the light isn't great. Director going for the sinister look. Succeeding.

A neon sign across from the street is winking like some varsity girl on the night of her final exam results. A huge poster underneath . . . Hilfiger . . . Hilfiger . . . lovely girl in nano-precision jeans and white tee-shirt. Smile. Teeth. Smile. Teeth. Smile.

Teeth like stars. Miss America. Prom Queen. Slow motion dance . . . the high school band is churning out some tooones . . . cheerleaders twirling their twirly things. You can almost smell her the TV is so realistic. She is drinking one of those trendy teen alcopops . . . and smiling . . . and drinking. I can smell her. And the alcohol. Honestly. She smells like teen spirit.

God . . . my own TV . . . these hospitals must have budgets to burn. But sorry, the movie . . .

A yellow cab whizzes by . . . spraying the man lying in a pool of roaring red blood with rain and sludge and grit and salt . . . the snow chains biting into the succulent snow. The gauche redness of the blood on the TV screen is quite impressive. Momentarily you can see my reflection in the dull hubcap . . . convex face horribly distorted in the metallic reflection. I sure as hell don't look too good. I am confused. The man in the movie is me.

A caring hand puts a coat under my head. The camera zooms in, generous Samaritan or bastard that maybe takes my sneakers and does a runner . . . that would be the end of the night and make no mistake about it. Maybe I could get the money back off my medical insurance. It is important to claim for these things and Get Your Money's Worth.

The director of the movie does not show the face of the good Samaritan yet but you can see his hands. Nice watch. He was holding a cell phone but he placed it on the ground while he attended to the injured man. The camera zooms in and on the small cell phone screen we can see the word 'Susan' and that the call is still active. Seconds ticking away. All paid for by the company anyways. But my medical would probably cover it as well. They cover everything over here. If the seismic disturbance of my body falling to the pavement had caused an earthquake in Tokyo then my medical would cover it . . . that's what the guy in the red braces and Jets tie said to me as he closed his briefcase and shook my hand and said I wouldn't regret opting for Maximum Cover. He didn't quote this very example but I knew what he meant. When he had finished selling me the policy he snapped his braces twice and said

. . . 'That's another soul saved so I'll sleep easy tonight.' He gets 8% of every policy he sells. ❑

The whole world claims off medical, that's why you have it in the first place coz if you don't have it you can't claim. Dub told me that in The Scratcher one night. The Jets were losing so people in the bar were taking solace in their drinks and we were wasted anyways so it made no difference.

- Remember Shem, fuck them first before they fuck you.
- Yeah Dub.
- That's the only way to survive.
- I hear you Dub.
- Now you remember I told you that.
- I will Dub.
- How's the game going? I can't see too good.
- We're still five down . . . middle of the fourth.
- Fuck 'em.
- Before they fuck you, I know Dub.
- You're learning kid . . . you free to do a message for me?
- I dunno . . .
- I'll make it worth your while Shem.

Get your claim in even before you get injured that's my philosophy . . . I have a philosophy . . . I might be leaking away into oblivion here . . . the very substance of my being melting away like an ice pop in a heat wave but let me tell you this much . . . I have a philosophy. Dub always said that that was the basic trouble with me . . . that I had a philosophy and that I always thought before doing things. Dub was fucked up in the head and had no philosophy about anything or anybody.

- You think too much Shem.
- I know Dub ... you're right of course.
- So you'll run this errand for me then?
- I'll think about it.

He is now propped beside me on the trolley as I travel down Fifth Avenue ... ubiquitous white Marlboro dangling from his ruby lips. Everyone knows that Dub uses some light lipstick or make-up or some kind of thing to make his lips appear more luscious but no one ever mentions the fact.

He shouldn't really smoke around the hospital bed but you have to make exceptions especially when technically speaking we are not in a hospital or an ambulance for that matter but are in fact out on Fifth Avenue where it is still legal to smoke. Dub would just tell you to fuck off if you asked him to stop anyways.

His white full-length leather coat blends in with the sheets ... it is as if we are joined at the hips ... inextricably intertwined at a molecular level. Perish the thought. The only molecular bonding I've ever had with Dub was an initial handshake and that was so brief that the molecules would have had to have been smart to have melded with anyone. He doesn't like to be touched.

Dub should really be dead himself. He lives out in that five per cent region of the bell-shaped curve of life and has never put much belief in statistics. Statistics are for dead people he always says and he means it.

He has spent his life skewing the statistics and surviving against the odds. Maybe it's because there are stupid assholes like me that will take the chances for him ... still he's not the worst and it wasn't his fault that I got shot.

- And they left you with nothing ... I told you ... fuck them first ...
- Before they fuck you Dub.
- Incidentally kid, what did you do with the stuff? You know ... there was a lot of money riding on this deal.
- I can't remember too much Dub ... maybe if you come back later I'll be more rested and I'll be able to ... I think it's still in the ambulance.

At this point the trolley goes over a sizeable pothole. Dub falls on his arse and smudges his white leather coat in the process. He will sue the city and all its citizens for that little upset and make no mistake about it. Fuck them before they fuck you.

2

the trouble with Santos

Trouble.

It is the one thing that has always followed him around. Even looking out from the swinging doors of the ambulance he knew that T had once again found out where he was and decided to tap him on the shoulders to turn him around, then punch him full in the face.

This time Trouble was in the guise of little old me.

When Santos arrived screeching in the ambulance I was on the sidewalk. The proper chain of events seems fucked up and I am zooming in and out seemingly at random. I cannot seem to control this. I wish there was some button or knob I could twist to realign it all. Maybe there is a clause in my medical insurance cover but I'm damned if I can remember it. Just have to work with it. Could ring your man with the two snaps of his braces and tell him one of his souls needs saving. Maybe not.

The paramedic was very efficient and in control. There was another paramedic, Louie, who was also the driver.

A saline drip was hastily assembled and a needle stuck into my arm. I was man-handled onto a trolley. The Santos guy had a Rican accent.

- You got medical insurance buddy? Hello, can you hear me . . . have you got medical insurance?

A sweaty hand rifles through my wallet.

- Yeah, he's covered. Come on we better move along. Stand back there now people give us some room. Please lady, can you back away there please, thank you, thank you, coming through, coming through . . .

I remember thinking that Santos was probably from out Belmont or Wantauk way or one of those areas . . . wooden house with the flag fluttering on Columbus Day . . . God bless Hamayrika he always says and . . . way to go my man . . . what about that John Travolta guy, eh . . . you gotta love him, man . . . what with his comeback and everything, man. His great granddad coughed to death six hours after landing in the promised land. Welcome to Hamayrika.

Santos looked down at my bloodstained wallet and pulled a fake ID card from it. All he could see was half the name Shem O' something and a few details about date of birth and stuff.

This is the genesis of Trouble for Santos . . . you see the owner of the card, Me, is now hurtling through the streets of Manhattan on a trolley . . . after falling out of the back of the ambulance while he and Louie were engaged in other things. They did not hear the click clack of the door, strictly contrary to the manufacturer's specifications it might be added, opening. Santos would have to face the music on this one.

Neither of them, Santos nor Louie, noticed as the trolley sailed out into the night.

Badumphff.

The first time they really took note was when the said trolley bounced off the ground and made a noise that Santos would later describe to his wife on the phone as 'Badumphff'. And after they heard the badumphff sound they also got the sickening sensation that they were travelling in the precise opposite direction to that of the trolley and its occupant. Santos remembered something from high school physics about Newton's laws but couldn't focus on it right at that moment.

Louie was transfixed . . . which was ill-advised considering he was the driver and his neck should not be craned around at that particular angle and that gazing out into the <u>Manhattan</u> night and just shaking his head from side to side was not the best course of action needed. Stopping the ambulance and retracing their journey would have made more sense but Louie was in a state of mild shock and so his foot would not respond as required and so they continued onwards in a straight line, increasing the relative distance between themselves and the trolley with every passing second.

Louie was not bright. He only got through high school on account of the credits he picked up due to his acumen at throwing the discus. He had been State Champion once. That state was Nebraska. His mother once confided in her sister that as a child he had fallen off some rocks in the back garden and banged his head. 'Cadumphff' was the sound he made when he fell, she said. Ever since that day she had known he would not be super intelligent so she bought him a Frisbee and later a boomerang, although she put it away in the attic as he had a habit of throwing it and forgetting that it would come back to him.

There were so many times that his mother would shrug her shoulders and just say, 'That's the way it goes'. People brought up in Nebraska are famous for saying, 'That's the way it goes.' The State should be called Stoicska instead.

Santos could only tolerate Louie . . . just about. He despised the slow drawl and the way he always said 'That's the way it goes' . . . whenever they picked up people from a car wreck or had to scrape someone's remains from under a subway train.

But right now Santos was rapidly figuring out how he could lay the entire blame on Louie. There was sure to be an investigation conducted and a report ordered . . . and heads were guaranteed to roll. Santos was a paramedic trained to save peoples' lives but when it came to the preservation of his own skin he was definitely number one.

Manhattan

The name Manhattan is derived from an Algonquian term for 'island of hills'. Circa 1524 the island was sighted by the Italian navigator Giovanni da Verrazzano. He had no idea at the time that there would later be a bridge erected in his honour. In 1609 the English navigator Henry Hudson made an extensive exploration of the area. He had no idea at the time that they would name the river in his honour. In 1624 a Dutch trading post, called New Amsterdam, was established on southern Manhattan Island. No one at the time had any idea about what the Dutch were up to. There are still people who are unsure, most notably the Dutch.

To secure the Dutch claim, Peter Minuit, the

director general of the Dutch colony, purchased the
island from the Native Americans for goods valued at
about 60 guilders, or some $24. He also had no idea
at the time that they would name a steak after him.

And anyway Santos' wife would kill him if he got the sack.

This is true.

Santos was a statistic. He was one of the few but
growing percentage of modern American males who are
the subject of wife beatings and his wife, Clarissa, was one
of this particular crime's greatest exponents. It was handy
for Santos being a paramedic. Sometimes he had to work
at home on the weekends.

Louie was still craning his neck around at that
unbelievable angle . . . years of discus throwing paying off
. . . staring out the open door like some scene from
The Exorcist. He was not married and thought he would
never get married.

Louie will die in a plane crash in exactly twelve
years, eight months and twenty-seven days time.
The cause of the crash will be cited as faulty Kapton
wiring. He will leave behind a wife and two kids. She
remarries . . . a reformed alcoholic who preaches
about abstinence but who tragically dies in a bizarre
coffee related incident. – *Cadumphff*

When we were all in the ambulance I felt like hugging and
holding Santos for all I was worth but I knew it would break
some ethical work code or something and he might misread
the signals and give me a dig in the head or something,
which would definitely be breaking his ethical work code.

Under Santos' beard you can still see them. *Rian na bolgaí*[1]. Never get rid of them. Maybe laser surgery but I don't think so. Didn't have that back in the days of *Peig*[2] though . . . all her brothers died and she had to wash them and put pennies on their eyes, God bless each and every one of them.

I told Santos all about *Peig* in the ambulance when they got me in there. How we had to read all about her in Irish class when we were in school back in Ireland and how it was possibly the most boring book in the entire world. I could tell my story was boring Santos which lent some credibility to what I was saying. It was just that the little crater marks etched into his skin reminded me of something she said in her book. The book that single-handedly turned learning the Irish language into torture. *Rian na bolgaí*. Go figure.

Santos seemed upset.

- What? Ring no fucking what? Jees, isn't there no English-speaking people left in Hamayrika?

I tried to correct him about his use of the double negative 'isn't there no . . . ' but my lips translated the brain waves into gibberish. Durbel frummpelly frump. That's what it sounded like in hindsight. And hindsight is a great thing. Ask any trucker as he's reversing into an alleyway over on the Westside and that's what he'll say to you . . . hindsight is a great thing.

Hamayrika. That's what Santos actually said. I think I laughed or coughed or splurted at the time.

God bless Hamayrika. Ham Er Eecca. Ham and Eechca.

[1] The mark of the pox. The marks left over after a smallpox attack.

[2] *Peig*, an autobiographical story, widely regarded as the most boring story ever told. Up there with *Great Things to do with Food Processors* and *Light – An Architect's Tour of Ireland's Best Street Lights*.

Ham and eggs. Ham and eggs. Hmmm, foooood. So hungry now ... but they probably won't feed me ... waste of time when you can actually see it going into your stomach and coming straight out again. Comedian I once saw over in Astoria in some fuck-off Irish bar ... what is a bran diet says he ... it's when you swallow a piece of rope and just yank it right through.

Worse-off people than me need food and let them have it, I say.

But ham and eggs all the same ... you're an awful man Santos ... you have put the craving on me now ... and maybe a few Belgian waffles ... oh yeah, and an order of hash browns on the side. Mmm. That would be nice now ... down at The Greek Diner on Queens Boulevard.

- Sure honey, I'll bring it right over to you.
- Thanks Daisy.
- You got it.
- Oh, and maybe I could get a steak. Bloody.
- Sure, do you want sauce with that? We have a special this week, pepper and garlic.
- Sure, bring some of that too ... and better put an order of fries on the side as well. Oh, but hang on, I'm running out of sides here ... maybe you better bring me a side as well to put all these orders on.

Blank expression. Pencil held steady on paper order pad. She has another stuck into the back of her hair should this particular pencil cease to function for any spurious reason. Daisy is corpulent. Eating the profits of the diner on her breaks and fair play to her, I say. Cheeks ripple independently as she talks ... two different sets of instructions ... <u>Sperry's Theory</u> of the brain taken far too

25

seriously. But what can you do? Her right hand does not know what the left hand scribbleth.

Sperry's Theory

Dr Roger Sperry won a Nobel prize for his ground-breaking work on brain disorders. Epilepsy used to be treated by severing the corpus callosum . . . a little bundle of nerves joining the two halves of the brain. This may be where the phrase 'a little bundle of nerves' originates from . . . but maybe not.

Sperry studied people who had undergone this treatment . . . the severing of the corpus callosum that is . . . and observed that they exhibited 'two-brain syndrome' . . . where they appeared to have each half of their brains corresponding to distinct functions. Sperry was ambidextrous.

– Do you get that one Daisy? Running out of sides?
– I didn't think it was very nice.
– Ah, relax girl . . . I'm only kidding you.
– Sure honey, whatever . . . I'll bring you some coffee right away.

I think about asking her for some honey on the side as well, but I know there will be trouble.

She has seen it all, this one. Name tag Ethel but she's a Daisy . . . they all are.

> Daisy that works in the diner
> At weekends a water diviner . . .
> Her hair in a bun, two weeks in the sun,
> On retirement her cousins will mind her.

– Sure thing honey.

3

Dr Klinowitz's trolley

I am starting to trust my trolley now. Like getting a new car and not really knowing how you like it until you have to swerve or avoid some obstacle by braking suddenly. And then you know how the car handles and you feel better. I have no brakes on the trolley but judging by how well she is handling these wet streets of Manhattan I would say I am reasonably secure. The amount I'm paying for medical insurance you think they'd have ABS as standard. The TV and ABS. That's not asking too much.

The model of the trolley is called a *Klinowitz Lune*. I smile at that . . . calling a trolley a lune. Surely this is a misnomer . . . designer with a sense of humour. Many a lune has been a passenger in it I don't wonder.

Big pothole this time. *BADumphFF.*

It was caused by a meteorite hitting the street when everyone was in bed. The only one who saw it was Ed the Drunk . . . he's been to Vietnam and when Ed told the authorities about it, they took one look at his records and saw that he had been one of those administered with <u>Xinlyzendrine</u>, as part of the US army's attempt to make their soldiers more aggressive . . . and they dismissed Ed the Drunk's claim.

Ed was most vexed and in the days when he was receiving daily doses of Xinlyzendrine he would have smashed up the place and boxed a few of the army guys senseless. But he is weak and feeble now and most of his muscle is atrophied and he couldn't give a flying fuck anyways. In fact, these are some of the classic side effects of long-term exposure to the drug. One army report actually cites that 'muscle atrophy results and the patient displays all the signs of not giving a flying fuck'. Another side effect is the messing that goes on with the perception of time. I think someone has Micky Finned my saline drip with Xinlyzendrine. But I cannot be sure of this. To be honest I couldn't give a flying fuck whether they have or not.

<u>Xinlyzendrine</u>
This does not exist according to official records. If it did exist it would be used by the US Marines to increase aggression. A leaked report from the mayor of New York's office stated that this drug could be given in small doses to the city's construction workers to encourage them to work harder. The side effects, especially the one about not giving a flying fuck, would be hard to validate and maybe the city could benefit. And some of the roads need some serious attention what with the YUCATAN CRATER type of things. No messing.

They gave Ed the Drunk $50 to shut him up and he spent it on Wild Turkey. He only managed to drink half of it because his hand went into spasm, he dropped the bottle and it smashed into fifty pieces. By a complete aberration of the laws of probability each piece of glass had split into an exact replica of one of the fifty US states. This is highly improbable but not entirely impossible. The makers of Wild Turkey could have gained major capital out of this but none of the representatives from the company were around when Ed smashed the bottle. Moresthepity.

Years later the makers of Jameson whiskey will produce a bottle that is pre-moulded in such a way that, when empty and hit gently on the neck with a hammer it will break into thirty-two pieces . . . each one an exact replica of one of the thirty-two counties of Ireland. After many complaints they have to recall all the bottles because the piece for the six counties of Northern Ireland will not break apart no matter how hard they are hit. – *Cadumphff*

As Ed looked down at the shards of glass and the liquid scampering away he realised that he didn't give a flying fuck one way or the other.

And that night when he saw the meteorite crashing into the street . . . well he really didn't give much thought to it.

Ed the Drunk will eventually clean up his act, marry a young widow and go on to become one of America's leading advocates of reinstating prohibition. He will become known as Ed the Not-So-Drunk and will travel all over the Bible Belt states and will be accidentally killed when he drinks a cup of scalding hot coffee that causes him to have a massive heart attack. – *Cadumphff*

I feel sorry for Ed the Drunk and I tell him that as he sits on the end of the bed.

- What about that meteorite Ed?

He shrugs his shoulders.

- Was it really as big as they say?

Again he shrugs his shoulders. He is looking longingly at the saline drip. Thankfully the words 'Alcohol Free' are written in relatively large letters on the front of the pouch. He says nothing and we sit and watch a documentary that is just starting on the TV.

❑ YUCATAN CRATER

The narrator has that voice on ... the hushed 'don't disturb the animals even though this is all in a studio' voice. Camera pans on a beautifully exotic forest scene. It seems to stretch for hundreds of miles. Digital computer effects but so what. PhotoShop eight point two.

Cut to a happy dinosaur munching on some exotic leaves. He would prefer to be chomping on some exotic fruits but the leaves will do for an appetizer.

The Tyrannosaurus Rex is happy . . . that much is apparent. The words 'Tyrannosaurus Rex' literally mean the tyrant lizard king. I am the tyrant lizard king and I can do anything. The narrator told us that. Ed the Drunk knew that as well.

Ed says he has seen this before and that this particular T-Rex is called Dan and he is well respected in his community. Dan does not think he is a tyrant . . . a bit of a joker certainly . . . but no tyrant. Like the time he told the others that some Pterodactyls had taught him how to fly but only when no one else was watching. The others spent weeks tracking him to see if they could catch him off guard . . . but they never did. I haven't the heart to tell Ed that this is a documentary.

So Dan is munching.

The narrator is whispering.

Dan doesn't hear him. A few million years and a couple of thousand miles separate them. This is of no importance to Dan.

Dan giggles to himself. He has just thought of another practical joke that he can play on his buddies. It is very funny. It is probably the funniest thing he has ever conjured up in his whole life ... this is going to be the big one ... no doubt about it.

Off in the distant sky he hears a rumble. Not like the rumble before the heavy rains that he usually hears. This one is much more troubling.

He munches away ... keeping vague attention on the rumbling ... and concocts his master joke further.

The clouds over near where he has heard the rumbling are turning a funny sort of red. The redness has spread quite far across the sky and the rumbling is getting louder and nearer. This causes Dan a small amount of concern. There is already one sun in the sky so why should they need another one ... it seems a little bit pointless really ... and especially one that is coming so near and making it all get quite warm and sticky. Dan decides that he would like the red ball to go away and that he should really concentrate on his master joke.

The rumbling is getting beyond an irritation now.

Dan stops munching.

He knows that the others would surely see it and if he was to say anything they would just think it another of his practical jokes ... which it most certainly was not ... but if it was it would be mightily impressive. And anyway his mate, Stella, is expecting their first and he doesn't want to annoy her as she is particularly moody of late.

He decides to start munching again and does so more

deliberately and intensely now. They are good leaves . . . even if they are warmer than usual which is not caused by, or does not have anything to do with, that enormous red ball that is most definitely not hurtling towards him at a very alarming rate.

Dan munches.

He is thinking about what he and Stella will call their newborn when it arrives.

The narrator's voice cuts in over the scene. The voice annoys Dan. He does not like it one bit. Even less than he likes how hot it is getting now. The tree in front of him bursts into flames spontaneously from the intense heat and Dan realises that now is perhaps a good time to go off and find Stella. ❏

- These National Geographic people spare no expense.

I say this to Ed but he is sniffling and is too engrossed in the programme.

Ed suddenly blurts out:

- I was there when that all happened.

I nod courteously. I realise that the Xinlyzendrine is still residing in Ed's system somewhere. 1,687 ex-Viets have all reported side effects similar to Ed the Drunk's . . . meteor spotting. By a remarkable coincidence all of the sightings have been real.

Daisy from the diner comes skating alongside the trolley with the pepper and garlic sauce. She seems to be defying gravity by the very fact she is upright. Ed the Drunk looks her over once and appears to approve. She looks at my bloodstained shirt and tut tuts . . . the neighbourhood ain't what it used to be. Daisy has seen it all . . . even the meteors. No big deal.

- You know it's them meteors that got them poor dinosaurs too you know. And that's a fact. That was on one of those National Geographic programmes that my cousin Alma does always be watching.
- Is that a fact Daisy?
- It most certainly is young man.

She tut tuts again as if remembering the dinosaurs as some long lost customers. 65 million years ago the diner was in the middle of a lake and where her coffee pot is now is where the roots of a beautiful mangrove tree had stretched its tentacles into the marshy swamplands.

Progress.

- Yep, you work in this place long enough and you get to see it all. Here one night and a big meteor crashed right over there by the sidewalk.

Ed the Drunk is nodding his head in acquiescence while sneaking a quick sconce at her boobs, hidden somewhere within the folds of the white blouse and the apron.

- Caused an awful lot of racket. Lots of them firemen came over afterwards for coffee and pie . . . pecan with toffee sauce was on special that night and we darn near ran out of the stuff. You finished with that sauce coz others are wanting to use it?
- Sure Daisy thanks.
- The name's Ethel honey.
- Sure thing honey.

Her right hand taketh away and her left hand giveth to someone else.

Coincidences have a certain way of being contrived. But by forces beyond our control for sure. Take Uncle Bob. He is a really nice fellow . . . or at least he was until he was pounded into the ground by the nose section of a McDonnell–Douglas MD88 one beautiful calm day as he was fishing up in Canada. Now that is just plain tragic if you'll forgive the terrible and irresponsible pun. But Uncle Bob was big on puns so it's kind of in his honour. A memorial.

He used to say, while moving a toffee around in his mouth, that puns are what make us different from all other animals. He looked like the guy from the Werther's Original advert.

But is all of this mullarky with Uncle Bob and the plane really coincidental? No.

The really coincidental part is when they found out later that the pilot of that ill-fated plane had been in the same school as Uncle Bob.

They had been fierce rivals in the school chess club and one day Bob had beaten George . . . that's not his real name . . . and as the crash is still under investigation it wouldn't be fair to prejudice the hearings . . . using the formidable Sicilian Defence with the TARRASCH VARIATION. George had sworn vengeance and never truly got over that defeat in front of the girl whom they both loved . . . Nancy Pickett . . . not her real name either, same reasons as cited earlier . . . who also, much more coincidentally, was on the plane and would survive the crash.

George did not know Nancy was on the flight he was piloting.

George did not know Bob was fishing peacefully that day (luckily he had caught nothing) . . . at least that's what we have to assume until proven otherwise.

Ed the Drunk hops off the bed and wobbles unsteadily on his feet.

- Listen Shem, I'd love to stay a while and talk but I kinda have this notion about cleaning myself up and going to ask that lovely waitress for a date and maybe go around schools and universities preaching about the evils of drink. See ya.

He winks at me and asks me to wish him luck. Then he turns and looks at my wounds and advises that I keep the luck for myself and that he will survive which or whether. He looks sober all of a sudden. And then he is gone. The trolley is slowly wheeling along and there is a movie starting on the TV.

❑ TARRASCH VARIATION

It is a huge cavernous chamber made of marble from the four corners of the universe. It is vast . . . exactly one mile square. Exotic birds flying around chirping gaily . . . they live in the natural canopy overhead but never ever shit on the marble floor. They have been chamber trained and they know better. The camera roams around and gives a brilliant sensation of the expansive geometry.

The person down below in the exact centre of the room is Hod . . . creator of the known universe and Omnipotent Person in general. We know this because there is a small italic caption flashing the words 'Omnipotent Person' in the bottom left corner of the screen.

He is in a mad mood at the moment because he is losing a chess match. This rarely happens but he is losing this one. More interestingly from my point of view is that I am his opponent. The whispering commentator is explaining that this is the match of a lifetime . . . my lifetime, he wryly elaborates.

I feel I am really there. Maybe I am, maybe I am not. This is heaven, this is hell, who cares, who can tell, oh Lisdoonvarna . . . anyone for the last few drops of my blood now?

But seriously.

Chess is serious.

And there has never been a more serious game for me. I am wearing a plush bathrobe with 'Heaven' embroidered on it . . . the surly angel at reception said I could take it with me and $45 would be charged to my plastic. He then ushered me in to meet Himself . . . who they all respectfully refer to as Hod.

He does not even look up at first as I sit opposite him on the onyx chair that is proffered. He immediately starts playing. He is white of course. I try to start a conversation but he waves this attempt away with impunity.

He plays the Tarrasch Variation of the Sicilian Defence. The sequence of the moves comes up on the bottom of the screen in algebraic notation:

1.	e4	c5
2.	Nf3	d6
3.	Nd2	Nf6
4.	e5	Nfd7
5.	Bd3	c5 . . .

Hod is drinking a glass of Solpadeine. He seems to have a hangover. He swirls the glass around and the sediment in the bottom of the water spins around, forming an exact replica of the Milky Way galaxy. Maybe this is how it all began.

One of the exotic birds floats down and leaves a silver tray of various fruits and chocolates on our table. Hod selects a peach without looking up from the board and eats it in one go, stone and all. His mood seems to improve. Camera zooms in on close-up as the peach travels down his throat.

- Ahhh ... that's better. Now, you were saying?
- Eh, well ... your holiness ... (I have no idea what to call him) eh ... I suppose if I lose this game I'll be sent down to hell.

He sniggers ... and I could be mistaken but some of the tweety birds twitter and laugh as well.

- What? What did I say? I only mentioned hell.

They laugh again.

- Of course you did Shem. Concentrate on the game.

And so we pit our wits against each other. I presume The Almighty One is going to whip my ass ... although I am unsure if such abuse has reached to the upper echelons ... and let's be honest, as upper echelons go this is The Uppermost. I know he can read my mind and so I do not play my usual game but instead make random moves that I do not even think about ... in fact I actively do not think at all. The commentator is going into apoplexy which is hard to do when commenting on chess.

One thing ... while in the presence of The Almighty One my wounds have stopped bleeding. I suppose it is like an inverse stigmata effect.

A PA system goes bing bong and a beautiful sonorous voice announces ...

- Hod, you have your next appointment in ten minutes.

Hod grumbles and makes some hurried moves.

He has made a mistake. He was beating me but now there is a chance and I go for it. Five moves later it is stalemate ... a draw.

I try not to be patronising.

- So eh ... you let me draw there.

Nervous laugh from me.
- You played well. I made mistakes.
- Mistakes . . . you?

Nervous laugh from me again.
- Well, yes . . . a few . . . got the genetic programming
  wrong for the dodos.
- Well, yes . . .
- And the name.
- Dodos? I kinda like dodo . . . and it's catchy.
- No . . .

He is putting the pieces away in a gold box with a
separate section for each piece, though he
surreptitiously puts the white bishops into a pocket of his
sprawling robe.
- . . . I mean my own name. It's actually Hod but there
  was a typo in the business plan for Earth and I just
  never got around to correcting it before launch date
  . . . he explains further as I look bemused . . . the G and
  H are beside each other on the keyboard.
- Of course.

And he is gone. The surly angel from earlier sweeps into
the room and ushers me out into the streets of Manhattan
again. He is beside me on the trolley.
- So a draw . . . where does that leave me?

My wounds have started to bleed again.
- I am not at liberty to say. ❑

And my temporary guardian angel whooshes off into the
cold night air. Swoosh.

Another coincidence as we pass 42nd Street and Fifth
is that my trolley is now travelling exactly 42% faster than
it was designed to do. This causes me some moments of
concern. I never was a big speed freak but this is pushing

it. Somewhere in Pocatello, <u>Idaho</u> . . . the trolley's designer is fast asleep . . . he is one Dr Raymond Klinowitz and he is a nice person generally.

I am passing the New York Public Library and I think about popping in and checking on the performance stats of the trolley but I'm not sure whether they have ambulance trolley access. They cater for wheelchairs of course but this is different. Should write a letter of complaint to the mayor and claim I am being victimised.

Dr Klinowitz sleeps every night beside his lovely wife Siobhan whose parents were both from Galway. She was born in the States and is very much an American woman. She has been to Ireland twice and thought it was 'very pleasant except for the smoky pubs'. She thinks Raymond is a genius and looks forward with great anticipation to his next invention because they always have great sex on those particular nights. Raymond seems fuelled by his own creative potency. He finds it difficult to get aroused normally but the inventive buzz sends him wild. He can last for hours and is very passionate and loving.

<u>Idaho</u>

Joined the Union on 3rd July 1890 and the state tree is the white pine. It is the 14th largest state. One of the coolest names ever used in a sci-fi book is Duncan Idaho in the novel DUNE. This is true.

Another thing that is true about Idaho is that the State's name is an acronym for I Danced And Had Oranges. The meaning for this has been lost over time but it is supposedly related to an ancient Native American festive dance celebrating the medicinal benefits of vitamin C.

The film *Dune* is now showing on the TV at the end of my bed, which is on a trolley that has fallen out of an ambulance and is currently hurtling along through the streets of Manhattan with only three properly functioning wheels and a saline drip that is not really working according as it should be and all of this motley crew travelling at a speed that is well in excess of what these types of Klinowitz trolleys are designed for. Phew!

❑ DUNE

The camera pans slowly around the hall of a futuristic castle . . . the detail is impressive. Sting has just turned up and is looking cool in his leather one-piece. He is doing a bit of fencing . . . the camera work is great and I almost feel like I'm there. And actually I am there as I just walk in . . . in some minor role. It can be very disconcerting seeing yourself on the TV.

In this scene there is the really hideous Ugly Harkonnen Guy (UHG). The word 'Baddie' is flashing surreptitiously in the bottom corner of the screen just above the website address www.dunethemovie.com . . . all of which is bordering dangerously on subliminal advertising.

There is also a cow in the room who in fact is called Daisy in real life although Ermatrude is her given stage name. The UHG goes over and salivates over the cow. He roars that he wants a steak and Sting just smirks in the background.

I stand there like a gobshite.

UHG goes over to Daisy and literally tears a piece of her hindquarters away and starts to eat the bloody flesh. This is all in lurid gloss. I try to adjust the colour control but there seems to be some sort of molecular anomaly due to

40

the fact that I am actually in the picture as well and we all know that you can never turn down your own colour.

- Don't fuck with the molecules.
- Thanks for the advice Flann, I won't.
- It's very important.
- Oh, I know Flann, I know.

UHG offers the bloody tranche of meat to me. I decline. He seems nonplussed by this for about ten seconds and then he rounds fully on me so quickly that little globules of meat and blood spray onto my face. Not pretty.

Sting is smirking in the background.

UHG is still masticating the clump of meat. He stops suddenly and expectorates on the floor . . . that's the thing about baddies in movies like this . . . you never quite know what to expectorate from them.

I laugh at this to myself . . . the me on the trolley that is . . . and I think it is hilarious and that Uncle Bob would genuinely appreciate it if he was still around which he is not due to that unfortunate aeroplane accident.

UHG is now staring intently at me.

Sting is smirking in the background still. He seems to have very few lines.

UHG suddenly lets out a mighty roar.

- DAISY!

I think he is denigrating the poor beast that he is currently disassembling muscle by muscle when who should shuffle in from the left side of the screen only my Daisy from the diner. She nods me a surreptitious, knowing glance but says nothing . . . and this is a woman who is not known for her prodigious nodding capabilities. I nod back.

- Daisy dearest, can you possibly bring me some sauce
  to help me digest this leathery excuse for meat?

She shuffles off and returns with the plastic bottle of
the pepper and garlic sauce. UHG takes another chunk of
meat and squirts a wad of sauce into his gob . . . all the time
keeping his eyes firmly focused on me. This is an unsettling
experience believe me.

Sting smirks in the background.

Daisy shuffles out again and returns with a napkin,
which UHG ignores with impunity and wipes his mouth
with the back of his doublet . . . the nearest fashion item I
can associate with his garment. He then lets off a rather
sonorous fart, which causes Sting to smirk in the
background. UHG speaks again.

- Daisy, can you take this horrible beast away from me
  please?

I am about to remonstrate that that is no way to treat
the poor animal when I realise he is talking about me. Poor
directing work here I think. The blocking is wrong as well
and sometimes you can't see what the actors are doing
which is a bit amateurish. DVD will sort this angle shit out.

I have had enough of UHG now and I am about to
protest when the piercingly sharp point of Sting's épée
plunges into my torso. He repeats this three times. Once is
never enough with a man like Sting. The wounds look
remarkably familiar.

Big chance in the movies and I blow it . . . I can see my
mother all annoyed and saying to my father, 'Would you
look at the cut of him and his insides not even tucked in
properly.' ❏

Dr Raymond Klinowitz and his wife Siobhan never have kids. It is his fault but they don't know that yet. When they do find out he will dedicate the rest of his life to finding a solution to his impotence problem. He never succeeds and eventually his creative genius dries up.

Siobhan will fall in love with a young woman she meets at a temperance rally. The young woman's second husband falls down dead from a sudden heart attack brought about by drinking super-hot, microwaved coffee. A request goes out for a doctor and Klinowitz attends to the patient even though it is out of his area of expertise. Siobhan and the widow run away and live out the rest of their days in Seattle.

Dr Klinowitz does find the only <u>guaranteed cure for hiccups</u> however. – *Cadumphff*

But for me, in the here and now, hurtling along on one of Dr Klinowitz's successfully patented ideas . . . I just wonder that maybe there's a little alarm button going off in his subconscious . . . 'What if someone were to fall out of an ambulance travelling at high speed? Must run that one through the R&D tomorrow.' Tomorrow. Fuck sake Raymond my man . . . I need you to be here for me now.

<u>guaranteed cure for hiccups</u>©
This involves blocking all air passages and then drinking a glass of water in one go. The ear and nose areas must be covered tightly so it is highly probable that you will need someone with you to assist which can be really useful at parties . . . otherwise it is damn near impossible . . . and it is not much fun on your own. But it is guaranteed to work.

©Dr R Klinowitz – Patent Pending. Use only under advisement. The Surgeon General has decreed that this practice is not medically sound and should only be used as a prank to impress people at social gatherings and the like.

4

the truth about Becky

Rustle.

The wind whips over the water causing small white
ruffle lines like the remnants of some hurried cocaine deal
on a mirrored lake. It gently brushes against Becky. She
moves slowly and rhythmically to it.

It feels nice.

It feels very nice.

She is in <u>Kylemore Abbey</u> . . . a beautiful serene place in
the west of Ireland.

She is happy.

<u>Kylemore Abbey</u>
Nestling at the base of Duchruach Mountain on the
northern shore of Lough Pollacappul, in the heart of
the Connemara mountains, in the picturesque
setting of Galway, the abbey is regarded as one of
Ireland's most romantic buildings, with possibly one
of the longest holiday brochure descriptions.

Today the abbey is the monastic home of the Irish Benedictine nuns and a girls' international boarding school. It was built in the 1860s by Mitchell Henry, whose young bride was charmed by Connemara while on their honeymoon. She had a lot of spare time and had read about it in a holiday brochure.

Tragically, in 1874, Margaret contracted Nile Fever while touring Egypt and died. Mitchell had her body brought to Kylemore and laid to rest in a mausoleum in the grounds. The stunning and unique Gothic church was built as a memorial chapel to her memory. This has to be one of 'the' love stories of the millennium.

Becky is content. She is happy. There is nothing to trouble her here . . . all is bliss. Each day comes and each day passes and Becky more or less stays the same. It is the consistency that she adores . . . the knowledge of what the next day will bring.

Becky is staying where she is for a while that's for sure . . . she likes it here . . . no in fact she loves it here. And why not? There is nothing else for her anywhere else . . . there was once but that seems like aeons ago.

Becky is content.

Becky is happy.

Becky is an <u>oak tree</u>.

She sways slightly from side to side letting the wind take her. She is, after all, exceptionally happy . . . happier than the word 'happier' can ever possibly mean . . . except of course for that one Thing that keeps nagging at her . . . that keeps trickling up through her xylem right out to the tips of her leaves and down through her phloem to the tips of her roots. It is not annoying, it is just nagging.

oak tree

Oaks make up the genus *Quercus* of the family
Fagaceae. Repeat Fa-ga-ce-ae ... easy. The oak genus
contains about 450 species. Name them please. They
have all been counted and it is true. Oaks are
distinguishable from the other ten or so genera in the
beech family by various technical characteristics of
their minute, clustered flowers, but they are readily
recognized by their distinctive fruit ... wait for it ... the
acorn.

They grow in a variety of habitats, from sea coasts
to high mountain slopes and from wet lowlands to
high, dry mesas. And we have all known a few
mesas in our time. Flowering occurs in the spring-
sprong, before the new leaves appear and large
quantities of pollen are shed into the wind. The
trees may be deciduous or evergreen.

Summarise the above in 50 words or less.

Becky shrugs as best she can and surveys the scene. It is
breathtaking. So calm, so peaceful, so serene. She likes
being a tree. She knew she would. And what was it Shem
always told her ... the one good thing about being a tree
is that you don't have to dye your roots anymore.

It couldn't really get any better than this ... definitely
not. Except of course the Thing ... but other than that it is
Utopia. The wind rustles her leaves and the feeling could
almost be described as sensual. She questions this feeling
in her deepest consciousness. Yes. Sensual. Bordering on
sexual even.

Becky is glad of the feeling ... it seems so long ago now.
So far away.

The wind rustles her branches a bit more as if reminding her of its presence. There is a hint of moisture in it now. Hmmm ... Becky thinks about moisture.

A lone Labrador approaches and looks her up and down with his big sullen eyes. Becky knows this procedure and has experienced it a hundred times. When the dog is finished he saunters off. At least there are some useful nutrients in the urine anyway.

The dog is called Blinkie and will be run over by a car exactly 64 days later by an American tourist visiting the abbey in a rental car which he has not been able to control properly since collecting it at Dublin Airport ten days prior to the incident. The tourist – Raymond Klinowitz – told the police he was trying to cure a bout of hiccups and he seemed to lose control of the vehicle. When he gets back to the States he has regular nightmares about running over the dog. Raymond will die in a rundown hotel in Florida at the age of 64 while flaccidly getting a massage from an ex-porn queen named Jacklyn who will die of a sleeping tablet overdose at the age of 51. That's the way it goes. – *Cadumphff*

These things matter little to Becky. She is so happy now ... except for the one Thing. And that one Thing is starting to drift back to her now. Her surface bark temperature drops a few milli-degrees. Her outer sheath contracts imperceptibly and she can feel the internal pressure building up. Her boughs creak and moan and not a gust of wind about.

The image rises again in her subconscious ... she is becoming swamped by it ... Shem lying there on the sidewalk with those holes in him ... and she running towards him letting out a tremendous cry which seems to happen in slow motion.

The plaintive cry that she now . . . Becky the oak tree that is . . . lets out is at such a low frequency that no one hears it except for the sonar operator of a US nuclear submarine just off the edge of the <u>Mariana Trench</u>. The operator, Ensign Stewart, reports into PALP (Pacific Anomaly Listening Post) about a possible seismic anomaly.

<u>Mariana Trench</u>
A depression in the floor of the Pacific Ocean, the trench is the deepest part of the world. It is located just east of the Mariana Islands in the western part of the ocean basin. Hence the name. The Mariana Trench is an arc-shaped valley extending generally northeast to southwest for about 2,500 km and its average width is about 70 km. Near its southwestern extremity, about 338 km southwest of the island of Guam, is the deepest point on Earth. This point, the Challenger Deep, is estimated to be 11,033 m deep. Drop a penny and make a wish . . . it will have come true before the penny reaches rock bottom.

The Challenger Deep was named after HMS *Challenger II*, the vessel of those who discovered the point in 1948. They were quite bemused to find an orange Fiat 127, an abandoned shopping trolley, some empty cider cans and a rusted sign saying, 'No Dumping Here – By Order.'

The image comes to Becky again.

Pushing her way through the crowd and Shem lying in the pool of blood and the bag of stuff that he had been carrying and the laptop computer that had bounced open and was now lying quite pathetically by his head and was pumping out random pictures and files.

The website for Kylemore Abbey was on the screen. Shem had cached it earlier as. they had talked about getting away from it all and going to the west of Ireland to escape from all the hassle they were in.

It all looked so ridiculous ... the pictures of the beautiful flora and fauna ... and it said you could sponsor a tree and it would be looked after in this beautiful peaceful haven and that no harm would come to it. There were little Shockwave animations and a midi-file of soothing animal and bird sounds ... Becky wished that they had gone yesterday but they had not.

Right there and then ... with the crowd milling around her ... and her boyfriend lying in a pool of purple blood beside her . . . and she already down on her knees ... she prayed like she had never prayed before and then as she was praying the face of a smiling Old Black Man was looking at her and she asked him if he could whisk her away to the abbey and forget all of this . . . and the paramedic with the beard was trying to push by her and she was staring intently at the Old Black Man and he just smiled genially and nodded and then she looked at the computer screen and then she was actually inside the computer screen looking out at the street scene and then when she looked around inside the computer it turned into a three-dimensional landscape ... and then the wind blew and there she was an oak tree and she was so happy.

It starts to rain lightly.

Becky is happy about this.

The water will nourish her and replenish any lost moisture. A Little Brown Jobbie rests on one of her branches, calls out to a mate and then is gone just as quickly.

All will be well again ...

5

another thing about Becky

Janice is having her photo taken. She is thirty-nine and has the look of the surgeon's knife about her. To be cruel she is not good-looking . . . to be kind she is plain . . . to be neutral she is neither.

The photo is finished.

Janice will show this to the husband and kids back in St Paul, Minnesota much later. Just a pleasant photo of her standing in front of the massive oak tree . . . and the abbey in the background and a rather relieved-looking Labrador just about making it into the panorama version of the photo. She could scan it and then zap it via e-mail but she knows Chuck won't remember to show it to the kids . . . he has a weird thing about his computer and the kids and doesn't like them to touch it and her friend Marcie reckons that Chuck is looking at porn too much on the Internet anyways.

Janice came to Ireland on a whim . . . she had met two Irish guys at her high school reunion and they were the only Irish people she had ever met but that was enough for her. They had gate-crashed the party and by the end of the night they had them all dancing jigs and reels and having great *craic*[3]. Later one of the guys wrote her a poem and she thought it was the most romantic thing she ever read.

He had not made up the poem himself. It was the lyrics of a song by The Waterboys but it seemed to fit the occasion perfectly. She thought that he had written it and he never said that he hadn't. God bless the Irish.

And later in the car park they sneaked an illicit kiss and that was the end of that. It was the first and only time Janice had ever done anything like that on her husband though she was sure he had been up to no good a few times. The Irish had conquered her . . . the Irish had conquered America. There are the railroads to prove it. And U2.

She never heard from him again but she kept the poem and she has it with her now standing under the oak tree in Kylemore Abbey all those miles away from home and she reads the crumpled up piece of paper aloud to herself . . . and she sighs and the tree beside her moans . . . and then Janice says . . . 'Oh, Shem, you silly man, why couldn't you be here to read it for me now?'

This last line was never actually uttered. I added that in myself. I am the guy who wrote the poem . . . don't really need to explain that . . . but it is kinda embarrassing. It's being on this trolley with the wounds and remembering stuff like this. That's what's bringing all this on. I know about Becky being a tree . . . I was there when it happened. And that is why I have decided that I have to get over

[3] Gaelic word for Fun. American word for majorly messed-up drug that will kill you stone dead in about 12 seconds. Irish craic can kill people as well but it is far more subtle and likely to last longer.

there, to Ireland, as quick as I can. I want to see her again. See if there are any openings in the tree department. Fancy myself as a beech. There is something I have always wanted to say and mean it and here it is . . . Life's a beech.

The oak tree behind Janice shakes even more and the branches shudder even though there is no wind. A small branch falls off and hits her on the head. She looks around and up at the magnificent tree.

– What's wrong . . . you don't like poetry?

She laughs at the madness and liberating experience of talking to a tree all these miles from home. Her shrink said the trip would be good for her and she is starting to believe him.

The answer from the tree was at too low a frequency for Janice to interpret and she went off to play with the Labrador dog.

Far out in the Pacific Ocean US <u>sonar</u> operator Ensign Stewart decides to run a complete diagnostics check on his system software.

<u>sonar</u>

An acronym for SOund NAvigation and Ranging . . . a detection system based on the reflection of underwater sound waves. A typical sonar system emits ultrasonic pulses by using a submerged radiating device . . . it listens with a sensitive microphone, or hydrophone, for reflected pulses from potential obstacles or submarines. Peachy.

Modern submarines rely on sonar for detecting the presence of enemy vessels. The most advanced system, called a towed array, uses a long cable to which hydrophones are attached. At sea, the submarine deploys this cable so that it trails far behind. Please refer to *The Hunt for Red October* for more specific information.

But all this talk about Becky. It is because of the saline or the Xinlyzendrine that they are putting into it. I am lost without her ... actually to tell the truth I am lost. I seem to have slowed down considerably and wavered off course, although I still appear to be heading Downtown. I ask the guy on the street corner with the sandwich board. I have seen him around the city many times ... he is known as the POD ... the Prophet of Doom. He looks at me and just shakes his head as if to say I told you so.

- I seem to be a bit lost here ... can you tell me where I am?
- You are lost sinner ... and the path to finding yourself is difficult and fraught with danger.

He must mean that I have to go down through Washington Square Park.

- Yeah, but is there a safer way to go? ... I am kinda restricted here.
- Follow the easy path and great sadness will befall you.
- Great ... thanks for the help.

Fuck me, that guy is a barrel of laughs.

He is trotting alongside the trolley now ... the sandwich board knocking off his knees at a steady if somewhat laboured rate.

- The end of the world is nigh.

Actually it is not.
An invading alien race from the planet Rongagen, in the Paxo Quadrant, will come and wipe away the

planet bit by bit like a child with an eraser. There is nothing any human being can do about this and quite a few of them who will be asleep at the time will not even notice. A guy with a sandwich board standing on a street corner in New York City will say 'I told you so.' – *Cadumphff*

The POD is shouting and spitting at the same time. It is like driving through a car wash. A small flake of paint falls from the sandwich board and lands on the ground . . . nothing to worry about there. I pass a street corner and realise I am on Fifth Avenue and 38th Street East. So I know where I am, thank you very much.

6

the Old Black Man

Morgan Wholesome Jnr is not his real name.

Far from it, in fact.

Morgan was his real first name. But Smith was his given family name. And there was none of that Junior or Senior messing either. He added that himself.

His name used to be Morgan Smith . . . and it remained Morgan Smith until his 25th birthday when a walk-on part in the <u>Arthur Miller</u> play *The Crucible* convinced him that something a bit more catchy was needed.

He ogled for hours at his name in the lower rankings of the programme for that play and decided that he did not stand out enough.

The lighting technician was called Leah Freight-Copper and he thought that it sounded memorable . . . in fact Morgan still remembers it today and if you asked him who the rest of the cast were he would probably shrug his shoulders.

Arthur Miller

Born in New York City, Miller was the son of a coat manufacturer who suffered financial ruin in the Great Depression of the 1930s. You don't think too much about coats when you are depressed. Miller's major achievement was *Death of a Salesman*, though he denies any involvement. It won the 1949 Pulitzer Prize for drama and the 1949 New York Drama Critics' Circle Award for best play of the year, but what do they know?

It is true also that Miller was married to Marilyn Monroe but they were divorced shortly before she died. There is no truth in the rumour that he was writing a play called *Death of the Maiden* before they split up.

So his stage name became Morgan Wholesome Jnr. This is how he decided on his name. He had written ten possible first names and surnames that he liked the most on pieces of paper then rolled them up into small pellets. He wetted them slightly by chewing and flung them at a picture of the Rolling Stones that was hanging in his bedroom . . . the one from each pile that hit Mick Jagger's mouth would be the chosen one. No arguments or discussion and no turning back.

He smiled at the time, imagining how often he would be able to tell this tale over and over again on the *Jay Leno Show* or whatever.

His aim was slightly off and none of the names from the first pile hit Jagger's mouth but some of those from the second did so he decided to keep his own first name. From the pile of second names he had a direct hit with shot number six, which turned out to be the name Wholesome.

The other options were as follows . . . some of them
Morgan thought he might have been more fortunate with.

FIRST NAME	SURNAME
Alf	Rankin
Shaun	Drexler
Mark	Cobatte
Colt	Ecche
Constant	Arlew
Jacob	Wholesome
Rory	Fern
Eye	de Gauche
Stanley	Rubix
Al	Formosa

He added in the Jnr bit on the advice of his agent
Stanley Nife . . . whose name is actually his own.

None of this matters now. Water and bridges.

Years later and a ream of off-off Broadway productions
. . . his friends quipping that some of the shows were so far
'off' that they might as well have been in Nebraska . . . and
none of this seems to be that important anymore.

Stanley Nife was a tiger.

He was not a tiger, in fact he was an agent, but he was
a tiger when it came to getting parts for Morgan. He tried
everything. He often quipped to Morgan that it would have
been a lot easier if he had been born Black . . . he'd be able
to get him more parts. And Morgan's riposte was always
the same . . . but I am Black . . . and Stanley would feign a
surprised face . . . so you are my man, so you are. This is
true. Stanley Nife was not a racist, he was a realist . . . comes
from being born with that name.

You just gotta be realistic sometimes, Stanley would say ...look at me...and people would quite often look at him ...it was his way ...his main advantage in life was that people looked at him.

Stanley Nife was not White or Black but he was a kind of yellow.

Morgan Wholesome Jnr was not Black, but more a type of earthy brown.

These subtle distinctions were lost on the Broadway producers of his day who regarded the whole issue as somewhat of a grey area. Broadway can also be a grey area on the occasions when it is raining heavily and there is a power cut in the area and all the flashy lights have gone out.

There is no recorded race of grey people anywhere on planet Earth although some have said this of the Austrians.

Even so ...Morgan Wholesome Jnr had eked out a few parts and managed to make a living. His major claim to fame was featuring in two different episodes of *Starsky & Hutch*. Indeed, he had a signed copy of David Soul's album saying, 'See you around the set next time, Morgan. Regards, David.'

This was somewhat ironic as Morgan and David had never actually been in a scene together at the time he wrote that . . . but that was mere semantics, which is another grey area.

The first time he featured as a stool pigeon with the character Huggy Bear and had no lines although the camera did zoom in on him once in a sort of face-off with Paul Michael Glaser.

Morgan liked PMG a lot.

PMG had spoken to him on the set a number of times and seemed like a genuinely nice guy. To the best of

Morgan's knowledge PMG never released any albums but if he had he would definitely have had a signed copy.

In that episode he was given the credit 'Black Man #1'. There were two other actors with him but the director had chosen him to zoom in on ... it was a singular honour.

Stanley had been ecstatic ...

- They zoomed in on you Morgan baby ... on National TV baby ... this could be the big time. They zoomed ... Jees, I think you are the first of my clients that ever got themselves zoomed in on ... I could be wrong but this is the sort of thing you remember in this business, you know what I'm saying?

Morgan knew what he was saying. Stanley reckoned this was it ... the big break that would make it all happen. Morgan was sure he would be recognised everywhere he went and maybe even get laid out of it all.

Neither of these things happened ... although sitting in a Manhattan café once the waitress gave him the look a few times and when she enquired she was delighted to learn she was right ... she had never missed an episode. Said her name was Daisy. *Starsky & Hutch* was her favourite programme and make no mistake about it. Said that PMG had come in once with his wife and they had the pecan pie with the toffee sauce.

- Is David Soul really a good singer?
- I suppose so ... I have an album of his but I don't play it much.
- I was just wondering. So Morjane (for that is the way Daisy pronounced it even though it was not on the list of the original ten names that were thrown at Mick Jagger's mouth) ... you gonna be in it again?
- I dunno.

And he was.

And this time a speaking part ... lord be praised. Stanley nearly having a coronary.

And here were the words that Morgan had to say in his second episode of *Starsky & Hutch* ... 'AND THEN YOU DIE, BROTHER ...'

Stanley was most excited about this development. In rare, quiet moments in his office his arteries could be heard closing, such was the excitement and all the stress and him with a weak ticker and everything.

This episode pops up on the TV at the end of the trolley. *Starsky & Hutch* and *The Rockford Files* all sort of melded and mixed into the one show. Interesting.

The timing is either hugely coincidental or all part of the service with the Premium Medical Insurance ... which is even more impressive.

❏ AND THEN YOU DIE, BROTHER ...

The camera pans into the interior of a parked car and obviously on a stakeout ... Starsky and Hutch are sitting and waiting. Rockford pokes his head through the gap in the seats, slurping loudly on his cup of coffee.

Rockford: Shouldn't we really go in now?

Starsky: No.

Hutch: We'll wait for the signal.
(Starsky and Hutch exchange looks and raise their eyes to heaven.)

Rockford: And what's the signal?

Starsky: • What were you doing when the Captain was telling us the deal earlier on . . . huh? Out getting coffee and doughnuts no doubt. Haven't you been listening at all?

Rockford: I was, I have, I wasn't . . . oh, but just remind me once again, ha?

Hutch: (sighs) When we see the light in the abandoned warehouse window flash twice . . .

Rockford: That's the signal . . . gotya.

Hutch: How did you ever get your own show?

Rockford: I have a great agent.

Starsky: I must say I love the one where you and Angel are stuck in the . . .

Hutch: Hush . . . there's the signal.

Rockford: Where, where . . . I didn't see nothing . . . are you sure? Was it our signal? Did it flash twice or just once?

Hutch: It just is, okay?

Rockford: Okay, okay, fine with me . . . you go right ahead and deviate from the script . . . see if I care.

Hutch: Are you coming or not?

Rockford: Count me in.

Starsky: (*sotto voce* to Hutch) Maybe you should think about cutting the guy a little slack . . . he is James Garner, you know what I mean, and he does have his own show which is more than you or I have, okay?

Rockford: (outside car) Are you guys coming or do I have to solve this one on my own as well?

Starsky: Hutch . . . promise me.

Hutch: Okay, okay.

Camera pans into the interior of an abandoned warehouse. A drug deal is going down. Huggy Bear is nervous and is clutching his fake fur coat to himself more than normal. He is waiting for the boys to burst in.

Camera pans around to the face of a moustachioed youth and three Black guys standing around Me! . . . What am I doing here? I look pretty cool actually . . . in my brown leather jacket, flared jeans and cowboy boots. Dare I say it, but I look the part.

Suddenly the doors burst open and the boys burst in. Huggy Bear dives for cover. I try to scramble for the drugs and the Black Man fires at Rockford puncturing a hole in his coffee cup. This is serious. In all the times I ever saw *The Rockford Files* no one ever survived if they messed with his coffee.

Rockford: Oh man . . . now look what you've gone and done.

Black Man #1 beside me takes one in the shoulder and I take three in the gut. I fall forward onto a makeshift table and spill all the drugs and stuff. There is cocaine all over the place and some of it lodges itself in my hair and for a few moments I glimpse myself as an old man . . . and they say drugs age you prematurely.

In the melee Black Man #1 comes over to help me even though he seems to have been hit himself. He drags me behind some empty oil drums and cradles my head in his lap. He looks down at me and knows there is not much time left.

Me: Shit . . . we were so close and . . . and we could've gotten away with it . . . and we could maybe and . . . and then . . . and then . . .

Black Man #1:   . . . and then you die, brother . . .

He pushes down my eyelids just as Rockford comes around the corner . . . the styrofoam cup leaking onto his shoe. ❑

Daisy was so impressed. Morgan hadn't paid for coffee ever since, though the pie was always billed. She even wrangled a picture out of him and she had it framed and displayed on the walls with the other actors who had dined there.

Stanley nearly had a heart attack he was so pleased with the performance. Morgan was pretty pleased with it as well.

I thought I sucked to be honest.

Stanley did have a heart attack five weeks later. He had been in the office purring like a cat, while looking over some still promo shots from the show. The phone was not ringing and there was a moment of bliss and tranquillity for him. There was the sound of something slamming shut . . . his artery in fact . . . and that was it, he was gone. His face fell forward onto the photos and when he was discovered hours later, it looked like he had been trying to kiss Morgan on the knee which raised a few eyebrows here and there but mainly above peoples' eyes. Some of the photographic print had stuck to Stanley's cheek and so he had the singular privilege of being the first person ever buried with a David Soul tattoo on his face.

And then you die, brother . . .

The most recent gig Morgan Wholesome Jnr played was one where he was simply called Old Black Man . . . that's what the advert had said . . . 'Old Black Man wanted. Must have genial appearance . . . for advert.' Morgan was delighted when he got the call saying the job was his if he wanted it. It was one week's shoot for a decent amount of money.

All he had to do was to hold a saxophone (which he could not play) and smile and look like he was having a really good time ... the director insisted that there be a real saxophone player there to coach Morgan about how to hold the instrument properly. And the director himself showed Morgan exactly how he wanted him to laugh.

The ad was a great success and shown all over the States and Europe ... billboards, TV, posters, the works. Morgan was delighted. Daisy was ecstatic. Stanley was dead.

Morgan finds it weird walking around Manhattan and seeing his face on giant billboards. He tries to walk as much as he can to try to get rid of his limp although doctors said he could be stuck with it for the long haul. The night of the assault pinches him as a bad memory ... he is still frightened.

Sometimes Morgan passes by a billboard with the advert displayed and he'll stand there and stare at it until some passers-by stop to look and then it slowly dawns on them that they are beside greatness.

He is alongside the trolley now. He does not seem to be walking or running or hovering ... he is gliding along effortlessly. He seems embarrassed.

- Listen, about the shooting . . . thanks for the help . . . and the thing you did with Becky and all . . . that was real nice. I am going to go to see her if I can work out how to get there.

Morgan just nods quietly.

- Jees, you don't say much.

I start to giggle.

- Listen earlier on when you bent over to help me I
  could see you in the poster across on the other street
  corner and it was really freaky seeing you and your
  advert as well. I was seeing double. I thought it was
  some kind of a joke. Boy, you sure look like you are
  having a good time there and the saxophone ... can
  you play it?
He shakes his head.

7

first date with Becky

I remember the first time I met her. Becky says she remembers the day I called in to the bar . . . there were two of us actually.

- One of them was tall and handsome with wispy flicks of black curly hair . . . and then there was you Shem.

She pokes me and laughs.

Brendan and I sat at the bar and ordered two Coors Light and smoked our Marlboros. It was the way I laughed that caught Becky's attention. My face all scrunched up as if in pain and she making the Bloody Mary mix that she was famed for.

And the way I inhaled the cigarette as well . . . up through my nose and out again. Must have looked like a right prick. It looked almost feminine she said and she liked that. It turned her on for some inexplicable reason. No arguments from me.

She paid so much attention to me, albeit surreptitiously, that she put too much Worcestershire

sauce into the Bloody Marys . . . a fact that Annette and
George, the two barflies, would comment on later. George
never spoke. Annette did for the both of them.

- Jees Becky dear, what did you put in those BMs last
  night? Poor George here was up all night in the
  bathroom and the duvet was up if he wasn't . . . if you
  know whattimean.

And then the laugh. She had a cackle that could crack
glass so she did. And George would smile and nod and
Annette would cackle some more. They always sat in the
same place and put their pack of Marlboros on the table
between them. They made a big show of doing this each
time they came in . . . praying that someone would
notice and ask them eventually why they never smoked
them.

- Did you remember to bring the cigarettes George?

And he would nod and rummage in his pockets like
some nervous best man and finally find them and produce
them as if a long-lost passport or something and she would
clap her hands and tell him what a good boy he was. And
George would beam.

- We both gave up five years ago when we moved back
  to the city from Florida. I know most people move
  back there but there were so many old people
  around it got kinda depressing, didn't it George? So
  there was so much smog here that we said to
  compensate we'd give up the cigarettes and so we
  bought this last box and we said we'd never smoke
  them until the air in the city had cleared up.

This will happen in the year 2175. Unfortunately
neither George nor Annette will be around for this
momentous event. He dies in a subway mugging
incident and she smokes herself away in one

prolonged bout of loneliness. The autopsy report will comment that her lungs looked like carburettors.
– *Cadumphff*

Becky nodding, for she had heard this story over a hundred times but they were good tippers and basically nice people and they never caused anyone any harm so she could live with the ennui of this daily ritual.
- So what can I get you folks today?
- Two of your finest BMs please sweetie.

Brendan was off making a few calls so Becky made sure she had to replenish the peanut jar in front of me . . . and managed to spill them all over the counter and the floor.
- One hundred and ninety eight.
- Pardon me?
- One hundred and ninety eight . . . the number of peanuts . . .
- Oh . . . eh . . . really?
- You know . . . *Rainman* . . . when the waitress spills the cocktail sticks and Raymond knows exactly how many are there because he's autistic and he has a gift.
- Yeah?
- Sorry don't mind me I'm just babbling on and on. I'm not here long.
- I know . . . I saw you come in.
- I mean in the States . . . in New York.
- Oh right.
- I'm from Ireland. Shem. And you?
- Eh, Becky. St Paul.
- Oh really, and what brings you here St Paul?

We both laugh at the mix-up and the ice is broken. The ice is also broken in Annette's Bloody Mary mixture.

- Seriously, what brings you to New York?
- You ever been to St Paul you wouldn't ask.

Then she laughs and I laugh and I wanted her right there and then.

- So Ireland eh?
- Yes ma'am. Over here to be building the railroads if you don't mind.
- But haven't you heard everyone flies now.
- Oh, blessed be to the saints and angels above and me after travelling all those miles in a rickety old ship and me family at home starving.
- I am sure you can find work building airplanes or something.

I am now passing the bar where Becky and I first met. The trolley seems to sense this and slows to a mere crawl. Dub actually got her the job. . . . I remember this . . . it is clear and lucid and it appears as if these memories are my own.

Brendan returned and appraised the situation pretty quickly. He vaguely knew Becky from being around the Irish bars.

- Hi.
- Hi.
- So, what are you two talking about?
- *Rainman.*
- *Rainman?*

Brendan smiled.

- I thought you were asking the lady out.
- Oh, eh . . . yeah, well I was gonna do that . . .
- So how about it . . . will you go out on a date with my friend here?
- I don't usually date customers.

- Well then if I start a fight and you bar us then we won't be customers anymore and you can go on a date with him . . . say Thursday night at eight?
- Does he always make all the running for you?
- Sure, he's my agent.
- So . . . like . . . does he get ten per cent?
- Not if I can help it.
- Hey . . . you guys let's wait until the date and see what happens then okay . . . come on Shem let's get you the hell outta here.
- Excuse me sweetie, could we have another two of these?
- Sure Annette.
- He's cute.
- He sure is Annette.
- And that other guy has a nice smile.

And that date . . . it is so clear . . . the chemistry between us was so apparent that when I slipped my hand into hers when we left The Tramway Bar going down to the Village it felt so right. When I dropped her back to the apartment I wouldn't go in even though she wanted me to and I wanted to so badly . . . but I scraped my foot along the ground and gave her the sheepish lost boy look which we both knew was an act but such a convincing and charming one and I said that I would prefer to see her again first and that maybe we could go see a movie during the week or something . . . and she said 'sure' before I had finished the list of alternatives and so she laughed and I laughed and it felt good.

She was cute in an earthy sort of way. Bundles of long curly hair, sometimes tied up with a Spanish clasp. Cute button nose and a look that left a feeling of 'you'll never really get to know me but it will be worth trying to anyways'.

Then sitting in Central Park one day and the sun beating down and the two of us in shorts and tee-shirts and the half-empty bottle of Chardonnay lolling around on the grass and the quarter-eaten sandwiches from Polski's ... fodder for the flies.

- What do you want to be in the next life?
- I never really thought about it.
- You should.
- I don't really believe in all that crap.
- I don't either but you should still know what you want to be just in case all the afterlife stuff is true and you have to make a snap decision.
- You're not well ... you know that, don't you?
- I know ... so?
- I don't know.
- I'll tell you then ... I always wanted to be a tree.
- A tree? And what type of tree exactly?
- I dunno ... something big and strong and one that grows for ever ... an oak.
- I suppose.
- Trees are dead on the inside. Did you know that? All the life happens at the surface.
- You are fucked in the head girl.
- Come on (gentle poke in the arm), say something.
- Okay ... a dragon.
- A dragon?
- Well I'd say the chances of you coming back as an oak tree are pretty slim.
- But it is possible. Dragons don't exist anyways.

- Sure they do . . . we used to have them back in Ireland
 . . . they even helped us fight a war against the Brits.
Silence.
- Well I want to be a tree and that's that.
- And I'll swoop down out of the sky some day and
 breathe on you and reduce you to cinders.
- You breathe on me now after that garlic chicken on
 rye and you could do that.
And we laughed.

On the way out of the park I suddenly leave her and run
up to a <u>tree</u> and start to pretend to be bonking it . . . she
laughs . . . and the horseback policeman casts me a cold
eye but smiles nonetheless.
- Careful you don't get bark rub there mister.
- Yes Sergeant O'Connor.

<u>tree</u>
There is a band of cells no thicker than a film that
separates the bark from the wood. This is the
cambium. Only the cambium has the power to
make new wood. Fair play to you. Every year it
deposits new wood on its inner side . . . thickening
the trunk of the tree . . . and thus it has to grow itself
. . . it also adds phloem or inner bark to keep up with
the expanding circumference. This is clever. Within
this narrow zone of bark, cambium and ring of
wood the tree's whole circulation system works.
Sap rises in the new wood and comes down in the
phloem.
 Now, answer the following multiple choice
questions:

1 The band of cells separating bark from wood is known as:

   a) Cabra   b) carbon   c) cambium   d) Chicago

2 The inner bark in known as:.

   a) filler   b) phartzite   c) phloem

   d) Philadelphia

3 The cambium cells are no thicker than:

   a) a fax machine   b) a flute. c) a film   d) Fargo

8

that little brother of mine

I seem to be back inside the ambulance now . . . just after the shooting. This temporal too-ing and fro-ing is playing havoc with my head. An eight-year-old kid is sitting on the end of the ambulance trolley holding a Wendy's balloon in one hand and a melting ice cream in the other.

This is bad.

When you see an eight-year-old sitting on the end of the bed in the back of an ambulance hurtling through the streets of a faraway city with blood oozing out of you from three bullet wounds . . . you know things are not great.

- I'd say you was fucked Shem.
- Thanks Little Bro.

We say nothing for a while. There is a lot of commotion going on around and about us in the ambulance but nobody seems to pay him much attention. Santos is barking orders at Louie while trying to set up some sort of an IV drip..Louie keeps craning his thick neck around to see what is going on and I wish he'd keep his eyes on the road in case we crash. That would be fun actually . . . being in a car wreck and then having to explain which injuries belonged to which incident and the lawyers arguing this way and that, although I probably wouldn't give a flying fuck.

The needle is in my arm now but there is no pain. Little Bro winced but more out of mockery than genuine empathy. We settle down to watch the THE FEATHERED HAT. Little Bro snuggles in to me just like he used to do when we were allowed to stay up late of a Saturday to watch *Starsky & Hutch* and maybe *Match of the Day*. He feels warm and cosy and smells of liquorice and cheese & onion crisps. Santos is ignoring us both and seems happy to stick needles and tubes into me. If that's what gives him his kicks then who am I to stop him. It's all covered on the medical anyways.

❑ THE FEATHERED HAT
He is waving.

She is waving. Camera zooms in on her. She is beautiful.

Black and white film-star look with that hazy allure only the really good ones seem to possess. Fitted burgundy twinset. Feathered mushroom hat which could have been mistaken for a meringue that someone had accidentally sat on . . . well maybe on any run-of-the-mill normal person . . . but on her it is resplendent. Good call by the director. Bit of eccentricity always makes the characters more memorable.

Oh, she deliberated and wavered and fussed for weeks beforehand . . . it was too new at the time but she persevered and wore it despite the disapproving looks of her mother . . . stirring something over the stove and nodding her head rhythmically like a pendulum on its last few swings before Chaos Theory inexorably kicks in.

I have never seen this film.

Her hat is pinned to auburn hair. Not brown, not red, not russet . . . auburn. She was very particular about that. Auburn she insisted . . . subtle blend of Merlot and raw ginger. They threw away the recipe after they made her. No, in fact there never was a recipe . . . she was not for cloning, this one.

The rest of the ensemble . . . black patent shoes and handbag . . . elegant leather gloves. They are perfect. But best of all is the poise, right hand holding the filigree strap . . . the left held at a precise angle of 45 degrees to her body. The director shouting yes yes yes hold it right there that's it don't move a muscle.

Her husband is standing beside her waving. Presidential smile. No, in fact, Husband-of-the-President smile. Broad. Confetti remnants dandruffed on raven-black hair. Suit fitted like water in a ribbed vase. They are so impressive as a couple standing on the damp concrete. Turning back to wave before they board the plane. Other passengers have stopped as they are climbing the steps into the rear of the aircraft to gaze at this pair.

The caption in the corner of the screen flashes . . . 13th August 1958.

The flight is bound for Bristol. The plane is called the . . . *Éanna*. It is bedecked in the rather stolid Aer Lingus livery of the day. Straight upstanding no-nonsense lettering . . . not those streamlined italic shamrocks of today.

My parents are the last ones to board. Smile from the stewardess . . . later a small bottle of champagne compliments of the captain who wishes them all the best for the future.

Camera pans to some guy leaning against the wing in dirty overalls. Come on, come on, finish with the photo stuff and get on the bloody plane. He has no ear protectors and would definitely light a smoke if there weren't any bloody cameras around. He sees this every week . . . every plane . . . and they all look like they own the place. Always the same. Happy couple on the runway

His name is Martin Brennan and he has never been on a plane in his life and he never will be either. He always says dolefully that flying is for the birds . . . and he really means it. Went to Ballybunion for his honeymoon and it was good enough for him and his wife. Spends summer holidays in the west. Dying to light up the smoke when the plane eventually takes off.

Actually this bit of the movie makes me laugh . . . which hurts like hell . . . he is literally dying . . . the Martin Brennan guy. Cancer of the lungs diagnosed exactly six months to the day after my parents board *Éanna* on their wedding day forty-one years ago. Tough break for the guy. ❏

Little Bro with the Wendy's balloon on the end of my bed is looking pretty serious now.

- You don't think I'm going to make it Little Bro, do you?
- I wouldn't be here if you were going to walk.

He has a ridiculous grown-up accent that bothers me. Santos is sticking another tube into me but I don't feel a thing.

- You'd better eat that ice cream before it melts on you.
- I can get another.

But he eats it anyway. It is completely gone in three or four deft movements of his mouth. Way to go kid. I trained him well.

- So?
- So.
- That was a nice touch with the parents.
- Thought you might like it.
- And parts in colour as well ... I thought they only had black and white back then.
- Ah, you know ... they can do things now.
- Are you here to show me movie clips from my life and all that stuff?
- No. Unless . . . why, is there something you'd particularly like to see? You have the remote control.
- So I do.
- You really fucked-up out there tonight. What happened? Thought you had this sort of thing down to a fucking tee?

From such a young mouth the expletives throw me. I think about saying something but know that the role model speech is a little out of place at present.

- Yeah, well you know. I got sloppy.
- Sure did. I'd say your buddy Dub won't be too fucking pleased when he finds all his shit is now stuck in an ambulance somewhere. He'll probably kill you.

Our eyes meet and then spontaneously we both burst out laughing.

- Anyway, why didn't they take the bag of stuff, the guys who shot you?
- Yeah, I've been thinking about that. They mustn't have known I had it. This was a contract shooting. Someone paid them to bump me off. It was not related to the deal I was on that day.
- Curiouser and curiouser.

We pause for a moment.

- Am I going to die?
- It's not my call. Do you think I would leave you dying when there's room on my horse for two . . .

Our dad used to sing that to us when we were really young and him down on all fours and we clambering to be the first onto his back and he somehow always managed to fit us both on and then we would smack his bottom and try to get him to climb the stairs which sometimes he did and then Mother would call us for tea and we would run around him and beg him to let us stay up late to watch TV and he said we'd have to ask our mother.

- Thanks Little Bro.
- For what?
- For the memories.
- No problem. Would you like an ice cream as well? I know where we can get really good ones.
- Sure.

And as if by magic we are standing on top of Vinegar Hill, Enniscorthy, County Wexford . . . I say magic because I am no longer in the ambulance strapped into the trolley. The three wounds are still on me but they have stopped bleeding as if frozen in time or in the freezer or in the moment or whatever.

We have huge Neapolitan ice cream cones clasped in our hands. Big messy drippy ones. The low sun is at our backs and there are sporadic clouds . . . it is fresh and crisp. The hill is deserted except for us. A splodge of red cream lands on my left foot. Looks like my feet are bleeding. Damned stigmata.

- What age am I meant to be here . . . you know like . . . what age are you?
- Eight.

- Why here … this scene here … why all this?
- Thought you might like it. You do like it, don't you?
- Yes, I do … of course … it's great. This is exactly where I fell and cracked my wrist.
- Ah yeah, but we don't have to do that bit again … just soak up the atmosphere and relive the moment.

There is no single discernible sound wafting from the town of Enniscorthy below us … just a constant white noise. The unique frequency signature of the town … every town has its own one … like the 50 <u>Hertz</u> hum standing near a pylon.

- Dad bought us both crisps and coke on the way home I remember. And you held the bag open while I ate mine before you even opened yours coz of my wrist.
- Yeah. Real fucking goodie two shoes wasn't I? Mum gave me a medal that night.
- They're going to take this really hard, aren't they?
- Well, what do you think genius?

He hits me a deadener … it hurts.

Santos is sticking a big needle in my arm, which doesn't.

<u>Hertz</u>

Gustav Hertz (1887-1975), a German physicist, was born in Hamburg. He studied the effect of the impact of electrons on atoms. Badooooom. As a result of these experiments, Hertz and Franck were awarded the 1925 Nobel Prize for physics. This is one of the few instances where these two great names are used together. Another time when this might happen is if you wanted to rent a car in a French airport.

Hertz served as director of the Siemens Research

Laboratory in Berlin. In 1945 he went to the USSR
to continue his work in atomic research; he was
awarded the Stalin Prize in 1951 and his former
colleagues referred to him as the 'turncoat bastard'.
It is thanks to him that we now know how to tune
in our radio stations, as up until he arrived the little
Hz symbols on the dials made no sense whatsoever.

We eat our ice creams in silence. It seems like an entire
season passes. Clouds move overhead, the sun peeks out
meekly to see if anything is happening and little blotches
of rain dampen our hair. The sun sets and rises and sets
again in an instant. Strains of <u>Koyaanisqatsi</u> drift back to me
. . . it seems so bloody appropriate that I laugh. My younger
brother ignores me. He gives his third ice cream full
attention. He seems to be pulling them out of his pocket
but I dare not ask. He could equally be pulling them out of
his butt. He once stole fifty pence from my little red post
box money bank and we all searched high and low for it
and it was years later that he confided in me that he had
hidden it up his bum. I told him he could keep it and he
said it was long spent.

- What did you buy with it anyway?
- Preparation-H.

<u>Koyaanisqatsi</u>
From the Native American-Indian Hopi language
. . . meaning Crazy Life, Life in Turmoil or Life Out of
Balance. The Hopi prophecies predict that a container
of ashes might one day be thrown from the sky, which
would burn the land and boil the oceans. Remember
this was before the days of the atomic bomb, airplanes
and accurate meteor reporting.

Some people are of the opinion that this has happened already. Wham Bam Yucatan man. The composer Philip Glass wrote a haunting piece of music of the same name and that's the truth.

The Hopi will be proven not to be too far off the mark when the end finally comes. Especially the bit about the oceans boiling. – *Cadumphff*

We are disturbed by the sound of kegs being delivered to The Antique Tavern in the town below ... the echo of the metal barrels on the hay sacks like some muffled bell calling us back to double Latin on a Wednesday afternoon. This is a signal to the Little Bro.

- Right then ... I better be off.
- Is this it then?

He is irritated by my question.

- I'm not sure ... I don't know those sorts of things. I just know I have to go.
- Can we have a few more minutes?
- Sorry. But you can have another ice cream if you like.
- No thanks.
- Shem ... seriously ... I have to go now.

I take a huge breath. Fill every little sac and alveolus that hasn't tasted real air for yonks. Sorry Manhattan but I have to be honest and if you want me to say otherwise then you will have to pay me a lot of money and even then I might well appear on some chat show and tell the world that maybe New York is not all it's cracked up to be and the naff presenter of the chat show will laugh inanely and then I will show them my wounds and they will quickly cut to a commercial break and my career in TV will be at an abrupt end ... unless I appear in any more of these random programmes and movies that they keep showing on the TV at the end of my bed. I cough. Little Bro puts a hand on my shoulder.

– You haven't been looking after yourself properly.

Fraternal advice from the Little Bro can be disconcerting. There is almost a smile on his lips.

– Here ... this is for you ... I can't go back with you.

– But I thought ...

– No, I can't.

He is remarkably strong and in control and there is some ominous undertone in his voice that I know not to mess with. He hands me a photo in a tattered brown cardboard frame.

Santos has stopped whatever it was he was doing with me. He is on his cell phone now speaking to his wife I guess. I hope it's his wife as he keeps calling the other person 'honey'.

You know you are in serious shit in an ambulance when the paramedic is talking about what's for dinner.

I pathetically clutch the photo Little Bro gave me. I normally wouldn't be so sentimental but this is different. I can hardly make it out ... my eyes are watering ... blurring pretty badly now. Must be all that saline stuff they keep pumping into me. I don't give a flying fuck what the hell it is. The photo has that lovely sepia tint that only comes with age. The paramedic is laughing on the phone now.

– Yeah honey, we could do that. Maybe give Marcia and
  Pete a call later on ... yeah sure, that would be cool.

I sneak a look down at the bed sheets ... a large patch

of blood has formed ... from my viewpoint it looks like
Ireland but I know well that it's only the atoms and
molecules playing a spiteful joke on me in revenge for
ejecting them out of my body in the first place ... blood is
so important ... not to be trifled with.

But the photo is captivating. Two beautiful people
standing on a runway waving back towards the camera. I
love the way she holds her handbag ... in the background
there is a guy in overalls standing impatiently against the
wing, an unlit cigarette in his mouth.

I try to show it to Santos but he's not interested. I put
it under my pillow. I'll save it for later.

Santos is still on the phone. These guys are paid to look
after me. Come on. Although he was good earlier on ...
when he was getting me into the ambulance ... all busy
and attentive and caring ...

- You got medical insurance?
- Yeah ...
- Okay, better radio ahead Louie ... this one don't look
  too good ... come on move it. Make some room there
  please ... lady, excuse me ... will you make some
  room please? What's your name sir? What ... speak up
  I can't hear you. What? Hey, I think we need a
  translator ... this guy ain't speaking no English that's
  for damn sureness.
- *Shem is ainm dom*[4].
- What ... you'll have to speak up sir ... can you speak
  English? *Hablas inglés?*

I laugh. I think it's hilarious. His face all scrunched up near
me ... trying his best to understand. I can smell him. Coffee

4 Shem is my name. Do not memorise this to use unless your name is Shem.

from Dunkin's. Bitter and full of. Sweet 'n Low . . . but 79 cents . . . and that's what really counts. In America coffee is king. Cheap coffee is the heir apparent. Sometimes I think it will be the new currency. None of your e-money mullarky. Good cup of coffee and you're made. I said it to Bren and Seanie one night in The Orchard but they just <u>busted my chops</u> about it.

<u>busted my chops</u>
A quaint American expression for taking the piss out of someone or messing with them in general. Hence you may hear phrases such as . . . 'He said his SISTER would go out with me but he was just busting my chops.'

If you had a hammer and your own choice piece of lamb you could also, in theory, bust your chops. Please only try this at home with approval from the primary household earner.

It was then that I noticed the TV at the end of my bed in the ambulance. Santos flicked it on as he was working. He seemed to do it for my benefit, as he never looked at it once. The first thing on was a movie with me and my sister in it. As I said . . . when you opt for premium healthcare in this country you get personalised attention and personalised TV. God bless Hamayrika.

❑ SISTER
The crowd is sweaty. I am sweaty. Serious sweat. It is crazy sweat.

If some godly figure scooped us all up and squeezed us like a sponge over the Mojave Desert there would be green grass aplenty.

This does not happen.

The camera angles are so close that you can almost smell the sweat. This TV is excellent and well worth the extra few bucks on the insurance. I must tell the others about it. It is important when sick to be entertained as much as possible. If I was facing a firing squad like the Irish rebels of yesteryear I would insist upon a walkman with Clannad or something suitably soporific . . . they did not have walkmans back in 1916.

I think Clannad was around then though.

My sister and I are pushing our way to the front of the stage.

The band are giving it loads . . .

'I saw the crescent . . .'

We are at the front now . . . the camera ignoring all the extras surrounding us. We are transfixed by the face of Mike Scott doing his stuff . . . the other Waterboys are also doing their respective stuff as well . . .

'You saw the whole of the moon.'

Me and sister smile and sing our own words in tandem:

'I saw her crescent . . . but you saw the whole of her moon.'

I have to adjust the picture on the TV coz the screen is getting fogged up from all the crowd and stuff.

It is the Olympic Ballroom. Camera zooms back to pan over the seething mass of young people. There is a glitter ball hanging precariously over the centre of the room . . . each mirrored square of it shows a different TV channel . . . oh, this is clever . . . this is really good . . . this director has a good eye for the unusual.

One of the panels of the ball is showing security camera pictures in black and white from a street corner in

Manhattan. A young man is standing there holding a sports bag in one hand and a laptop computer in the other. He looks mighty suspicious if you ask me. A car speeds up beside him . . . a door opens up and there are three gunshots.

The camera zooms out quickly, pans around and settles on the contorted face of the lead singer . . . 'But you saw the whole of her moon.'

My sister beside me grabs my hand and waves it in the air.

- This is great isn't it?
- Yeah Sis . . . fantastic.
- Don't be looking at the glitter ball. Concentrate on the band. Do you remember this gig?
- I do . . . we even managed to get up on the stage.
- Right fucking gobshites the pair of us.
- And you hugged Mike Scott before the bouncers got to you.
- I nearly wet myself.
- It was a good night.
- It sure was.

As if to remind me she sings, 'and I saw her crescent'.

- But you saw the whole of her moon.

We hug like two sponges embracing and the water flies off in every direction. She twirls me around and around and I can't help sneaking a quick glance at the glitter ball and the panel with the security camera is now just showing an empty street with no one around. In a fit of lavish special effects the director turns the glitter ball into a full moon with a smiley face and the entire room sings together . . . 'You saw the whole of the moon'. ❑

9

the basketball incident

The streets are remarkably deserted. This is unusual for Manhattan. Maybe they're making a movie or something. I dunno. No yellow cabs or nothing ... no one on the streets ... well except those two guys playing hoops. One of them is Larry, the bartender from my fave bar down in the Village: DOA. Great name ... stands for De Olde Alehouse but most people think it means something different. It is yet another coincidence that I'm on a hospital trolley and someone may very well write the letters DOA on a tag and place it dispassionately over my big toe.

But Larry seems unperturbed by such maudlin thoughts.

- What's up Shem dude?
- How's it hanging Larry?

Larry is tall, over eleven feet I guess. He's now riding sidebar on the trolley like the FBI guys do in the movies and sometimes in reality too.

- Where you going in such a hurry?
- I'm on my way to hospital.

91

- Man what you want to do that for? ... come shoot a
  few hoops with my bro and me. Come on Shem man.
- Sorry Larry, I'd love to but ...

I point to the large smudge of blood that has used some
sneaky osmosis to seep through the sheets. The stain is
almost exactly the shape of <u>Paraguay</u>. Now what are the
chances of that happening? And lead us not into Asunción.

- Okay Shem, but you take care now.
- See ya round Larry.

<u>Paraguay</u>
An inland republic in South America, bounded on
the northwest and north by Bolivia, on the east by
Brazil, and on the south and southwest by
Argentina. Nice neighbours if you fancy a game of
football. Asunción is the country's capital and
largest city. The country is 95% Catholic and it has
a lot of armadillos. The armadillos are not known to
be Catholic but this has never been proven either
way. A recent survey by Tarnation Consulting has
shown that over 60% of people in the world do not
know what an armadillo looks like. Another survey
recently conducted showed that nearly 100% of
people in the world do not know of Tarnation
Consulting.

Progress. Progress.

Larry hops off my trolley and goes back and scores a
beautiful three-pointer from about a mile away from the

hoop. *Maith an fear*[5].Larry. If only he'd been born in Galway . . . you never know what could have happened. He's a good guy Larry.

Larry is a *fear dubh*[6]. That's the Irish phrase for Black man . . . well it is with all the streetwise Micks over here. In <u>Gaelic</u> the real phrase is *fear gorm*, which translates literally as Blue man. I think Larry preferred my version.

As yet there is no known race of Blue men on planet Earth.

There is on the planet Rongagen in the Paxo Quadrant – and they will eventually be the ones to destroy Earth. – *Cadumphff*

<u>Gaelic</u>
Native language of Ireland. A few Gaelic words and phrases that may be useful are:

> *doras* = door
> *fuinneog* = window
> *Cad is ainm duit?* = What is your name?
> *Tá me ag dul amach* = I am going out
> *Tá an traen ag teacht* = The train is coming
> *Póg mo thóin* = KISS my ass
> *Cá bhfuil an leithreas?* = Where is the toilet?

These are all very useful words and phrases in an emergency situation . . . although in no particular order of importance. The thing about emergency

---

[5] Good man; also: go on, you good thing you; you're a grand article of a class of a fella, and other such platitudes.

[6] This is a misuse of the Gaelic term for a Black man, which officially is *fear gorm*. *Fear gorm* actually translates as Blue man. So *fear dubh* translates as Black man but it is wrong in correct usage. There are a lot of colour-blind people in Ireland.

situations is that you just never know when one is going to arise. Unless you can tell the future.

It is amazing.

On the trolley. Hurtling through the streets. Saline drip doing its thing. The buildings and skyscrapers whizzing by. The odd pothole or two changing my direction . . . ensuring that the trajectory of my trolley . . . if traced using a thin line of white paint . . . like the machine the guys who do the lines on the road use . . . would demonstrate admirably a chaotic path.

All this and the TV as well. Now that's entertainment. I like having the TV on the end of the bed . . . I personally think it's a nice touch. An even nicer touch is that I can get TG4, the Irish language television station, on it as well. It relaxes me and makes me feel at home . . . although we only used Irish in our house when our uncle from England came over and we wanted to talk about him. Even then we were not very good and could only ask each other's name which we obviously knew or if we could go to the toilet which thankfully we could also do. But TG4 is good and the reception is excellent.

❑ KISS

Aisling is the pretty TV announcer. She looks fresh and intelligent and full of the joys. She is announcing the next programme.

There are subtitles for the 6 billion people on the planet that may not understand my native tongue. I fill with pride as I watch her but the pride seeps out though the few extra orifices I seem to have developed of late. There are no adages to tell you of this particular problem, so be careful.

She is talking about a new programme. Introducing it. All about how kids from the cities go to an Irish-language summer school – called a *Gaeltacht* – and the adventures they get up to and how it is all quite serious and it is really food for their young minds. She smiles broadly near the end of her little intro speech ... she beams as she says the name of the programme, *Baile Átha Bia*[7].

Surprisingly enough I am one of the stars again. My versatility is quite amazing ... and as I could also say when I look down at my gaping wounds ... I never knew I had it in me.

I am fourteen. Myself and Malachi are in a *Gaeltacht* called Leitir Mór in Connemara. We are speaking surprisingly good Irish but the subtitles are what I am watching from my bed. It is freaky to see yourself on telly talking a language that you never knew you were fluent in. The camera style is hand-held documentary and it is quite apt, if a little shaky at times, and lapses from colour to black and white at seemingly random moments. This could be due to interference from the high buildings all around me ... you just never know for sure. ❏

I think about doing a quick <u>Rayleigh Scattering</u> calculation to determine if the aperture between the buildings is comparable to the wavelength of the TV signal but decide that that is being far too clever and no one likes a swot.

<u>Rayleigh Scattering</u>
Sir John William Rayleigh (1842-1919), British mathematician, physicist, and Nobel laureate,

---

[7] Pun on the word *Baile Átha Cliath*, which is Gaelic for Dublin. This term used above does not mean anything as such but it could be translated as The Town Over the Food.

known for his research in wave phenomena. His scattering theories are a real blast. Sounds like a great name for a cheap sci-fi book ... and then all the sequels ... *The Time of the Scattering*, *Moon Scatter* and *The Scattering Part IV*. Maybe not.

Rayleigh engaged in research into physical optics, light, colour, electricity, the dynamics of resonance and vibrations of gas and elastic solids. Swot. Oh yes, and bicycles.

In 1894 he and the British chemist Sir William Ramsay discovered the inert element argon. You should be very proud of yourselves. Many an episode of *Star Trek* would have floundered if these men had not discovered argon.

❑ The picture on the TV seems familiar. Malachi and I are on a small pier with two girls. We are now speaking English because none of the teachers or *cúntóirs*[8] are around. It is a heinous crime to speak English in the *Gaeltacht* ... punishable by death ... but the director insists that we act naturally and that is what we do when we are alone ... otherwise we wouldn't be talking to the two girls ... unless it was to tell them when the next train is coming, ascertain what their names are, enquire if they know where the toilets are or delicately seek their opinion on the possibility of obtaining a kiss on the butt.

We are all virgins. This not immediately discernible by our youthful looks or innocent demeanour . . . it is discernible by the little flashing caption in the right hand corner of the screen ... 'All Virgins'.

The two girls are slightly older and we are trying to

[8] Grown-up kids who act like prefects

impress them … which is not easy as I am dressed in moss-coloured corduroy pants (my mother thought they would blend in with the landscape), with non-matching white runners, and a garish blue tee-shirt with a red band around the collar. I think I look fairly cool. Malachi is dressed even worse. I also have a nascent Charles Bronson moustache whereas Malachi has the first fledgling sproutings of a beard.

The girls are giggling. I do not think it is at our clothes. Believe it or not we are probably the coolest and trendiest people in the *Gaeltacht*. The rest of them stay indoors a lot of the time.

The camera pans from the girls' laughing faces to a boat in the pier. One of the girls … either in a fit of folly, as a test of our manhood or by a gross miscalculation of the aerodynamics of wool … has thrown one of her socks into the small boat moored to the pier. The camera pans around to our young fresh faces and it is obvious that it is up to us to retrieve the said item. She is not the girl that I fancy and so it befalls to Malachi the Bold to do the chivalrous thing. He smiles that beardy smile to the camera … no problemo.

The girls giggle.

Malachi jumps into the boat and retrieves the small sock. I applaud and cheer.

The girls giggle.

The camera pans from one smiling face to the next. Malachi raises his hand in victory. Champion.

I cringe at the sight as the camera zooms in on my malformed moustache. I wish they would concentrate on Mal's which is … well Mal-formed. You can count the individual hairs on mine. My older brother slagging me about the 'bum fluff around the bread bin'. Bastard. ❑

The trolley enters and exits another pothole. The TV wobbles on the end of the bed. I really think that it will fall off for a moment but it does not. Larry whizzes by on his air-powered trainers, stabilises the trolley and then tightens one of the holding nuts for me. A big wink and he is off again to shoot some hoops.

❏ The wobble of the TV has translated into the actual *Gaeltacht* scene and the boat is rocking from side to side. Malachi curses in Irish and realises that he'd better get out fast. So he clasps the mooring rope and goes to haul himself up. Newton's Third Law kicks in and he is unceremoniously dropped into the water.

We are all hysterical with laughter. The cameraman's hands are also shaking with laughter. Malachi clutches the rope and is as red as a tomato. He looks out of the TV screen and directly at me in the bed on the trolley, which is most disconcerting . . . and says that it is all my fault. I shrug my shoulders and he realises the folly of it all and then begins to laugh loudly himself.

He has won the heart of his fair maiden. The 'Virgin' caption disappears from the screen.

That long summer evening I get my first-ever kiss. The camera catches the tender, awkward, sloppy moment of our two sets of lips meeting . . . and manages to get the sun shining through right where we touch.

I wish I had shaved.

I wish she had shaved.

I wish. ❏

· ·10

DooOooppler Effects

I'm picking up speed now ... pale red haze around me and my trolley ... the <u>Doppler Effect</u> don't you know ... wish it was more towards the blue ... but at least I'm blending in with all the neon signs. Feels kinda warm. Nice. Funny that. It was snowing about an hour ago. Earlier. When I was ... well what did happen exactly? I was on the street ... and someone came up to me ... no that's not it at all. Damn it, what's in that saline? I can't remember too clearly.

- Daisy bring us some more of that coffee will ya ... and maybe one of those blueberry muffins on the side.
- Sure thing honey.

<u>Doppler Effect</u>
Christian Johan Doppler came up with this ingenious gem in 1842. He was an Austrian and first wrote about his theory in a monograph on the colour effect of double stars ... *Über das farbige Licht der Doppelsterne* ... basically the theory states

that the pitch of an object moving towards you as a stationary listener will increase while that of an object moving away from you will decrease. Rocket science.

This is demonstrated on a daily basis if you hear an ambulance or TRAIN approaching. The siren sounds louder in pitch as it approaches you, reaching a maximum as it passes and then lowering as it recedes into the distance. The same theory also holds true in the decidedly unlikely scenario whereby the ambulance is stationary and you are moving away from it at speed.

❑ TRAIN

It is a movie I have seen before … guy on a train … on the roof of the train to be more exact, hurtling through the Swiss Alps. The guy is Gene Hackman. He is shouting at another guy on the roof. This other guy is me.

My hair is very long and I have jeans and an amazingly horrible avocado-green leather jacket that used to be worn by Hungarian soldiers. My mates commented that the Hungarian soldiers must have used it as a formidable weapon because any approaching army would simply fall down laughing when they saw these guys in avocado-green leather jackets trying to look all butch and macho.

Gene Hackman is getting nearer although progress on the train's roof is slow and treacherous. Olga the German Virgin has popped her head out of the train window and I can just see her hair billowing over the rooftops. She is keen to see what is going on and is probably worried about me. In fact I can just hear what she is saying now above the din … 'Be careful.'

I had met her four days previously and we decided to travel together. She let me kiss her but wouldn't let me ride her. She kept saying that Irish guys were terrible for getting their way and then legging it. She didn't use the phrase 'legging it' but made a disappearing motion with her hands. I got the general idea. As if to try and single-handedly prove her wrong about Irishmen I doggedly stuck by her side across Europe even though there was no chance of a ride. Sometimes you have to make sacrifices for your country.

The camera work is excellent but the sound is shite.

Olga the German Virgin is now begging me to come down off the roof and stop making an eejit out of myself.

I'm having none of it. Up on the roof of a train with Gene Hackman . . . it doesn't get much better than this.

He takes a lunge at me and grapples me down.

- Where is it?
- Where's what Gene?

He pummels my face with a few carefully feigned blows which look real enough but they are not. What a professional this guy is.

- Don't fuck with me Shem. We know you have it.
- What?

Olga's shouting reaches me . . .

- Give it to him, give it to him.

The pitch and nuances of the phrase are lost on me and I don't know whether she means to thump him or to give him the 'thing' that he is so desperate to find.

Hackman saves me the decision and reaches in and takes out my wallet. He holds me down using his knees and rifles through it until he finds what he has been looking for.

It is an out-of-date <u>InterRail</u> card. The camera zooms in and momentarily highlights the date stamp on the card, mainly for the American audience.

<u>InterRail</u>
The InterRail system was the brainchild of the Union of International Railways devised to celebrate 50 years of international transport law. Yeah right. It was basically a ticket anyone under 26 and living in Europe could buy and then travel unlimited distances for a month on the rail networks of 21 European countries. The tickets were dead cheap. It does not exist anymore . . . someone copped on to all the backpackers.

There is one thing that should be cleared up here and now . . . the InterRail was not the precursor to the InterNet . . . can we get that straight right here and now? Good. While it did enable cheap communication across international boundaries and empower the less advantaged, it must be noted that sending an e-mail is not comparable to sitting in a smelly carriage in Turkey somewhere exchanging pen pal addresses with a load of German virgins.

- You see that punk . . . do you see that you little schmuck . . . thought you could get one over on me did you? Thought you could hitch a free ride on the InterRail, hah?
When he says the word InterRail the camera zooms in real close and there is a sparkle from his front tooth and he smiles momentarily. Then he resumes doing the

pummelling thing with the hands ... which looks great from where I am viewing all of this.

Gene is getting very animated now and this is surely Oscar stuff. Dramatic, stirring music wafts in over the noise of the train.

- We spend our days and nights looking for people like you. Little punks who think they can pull one over on us. Well let me tell you something, mister ... there is not one single hour of one single day or one second of that hour ... so long as I am able to draw breath ... that I will not track down little punks like you who are trying to freeload on the great tradition of the railways that have provided a means of transport for the common man from an Early Age and enabled him to go forward and sow his intellectual seeds across the continents ...

Camera zooms in on me and there is an obvious look of repentance which is caught quite nicely. The music is swelling up and Hackman is now towering over me, the pride cracking in his voice and the knowledge of a sure Oscar-winning performance firing him on.

There are tears welling up in Gene's eyes. Suddenly one of his eyeballs is shot straight out of his head as he is smacked against the low bridge that none of us saw approaching, so caught up in the speech were we ... not even the director saw it coming ... and as Hackman's headless torso bounces along the roof and his head bounces off the side of the track I can just hear him say ... 'Why didn't you warn me, you little punk?' ... with the last couple of words trailing away in a classic example of the Doppler Effect. ❑

11

the Empire State

Trolley is slowing down now. Just passed 33rd Street . . .
should be able to see the . . . yes . . . there she is . . . the
Empire State Building. Everything turning black and white
now . . . must be the smog . . . have to write a letter . . .

Dear Mayor
Can you please put the colour back into this city
. . . I am an Irish immigrant living here illegally but
nonetheless I feel it is my duty . . . fuck no, better be
careful about that . . . no seriously, the smog is very
bad and I won't vote for you next time unless I can
clearly see you from the top of Macy's on a busy
Friday afternoon.
Yours sincerely, etc.

Empire State Building
This used to be the tallest building in the world. Not
any more. It is 381m high and was completed in

1931 by the architects Shreve, Harmon and Lamb. One fourteen-and-a-half floor section was finished in a week. There was a bonus for the boys that Friday. People used to jump from it every now and then but now they know that there are now bigger places to propel one's self from. Prestige counts a lot when one is going to propel one's self from a building. This is true and there are survey results to prove it.

If you were outside the 80th floor of the Empire State Building and someone whistled past you on their way down it is very probable you would experience the Doppler Effect first hand. Do not try this with friends. Enemies yes, friends no.

Billy and I ran up 34th Street towards Macy's that day when Ireland beat Italy 1–0 in the Giants Stadium, during the 1994 World Cup Finals. I can remember it so clearly now ... and even though the streets are deserted I imagine I hear the shouting and the singing. They say nothing stops the traffic in New York ... but the hordes of delirious Irish fans stopped the traffic that day. U2 also stopped the traffic during the shooting of the video for 'Where the Streets Have No Name'. Irish people are infamous in New York for their traffic-stopping capabilities.

I have a great photo of the two of us with a cop. I scanned it and now have it as a screensaver on my laptop. It kicks in now ... and I can see the face of the cop who is smiling even though he looks Italian and his name tag says Farini ... and then we go into all the Italian restaurants and sing and shout and they shout back at us and then we do some more shouting. It was a veritable shouting match.

A guy we didn't know but who is just visible in the photo behind myself, Billy and the cop, is another Irish guy called Jimmy Rubber. He was a waiter up at a very famous restaurant on Second Avenue and he doesn't look too cool in the photo . . . he is Irish and we won . . . but he shoots himself up through the roof of his mouth about two hours later. Ireland's finest hour.

And here's to you·Jimmy Rubber, Jesus loves you more than you will know.

He owed money. A lot of money. He was a traitor though . . . as he had bet an enormous amount of dough on the match that Italy would win 4-0 . . . the Italians weren't taking bets on losing . . . he was in major debt to some of the not-so-nice Italians who were not policemen . . . and who would not pose for photos even though their side lost . . . anyway Jimmy was in major shit and he owed a ridiculous amount of money and he liked <u>cocaine</u> a lot and so he shot himself and that was that. Moresthepity. 1-0.

But that Macy's place. They say it's the biggest department store in the world. It only grossed $11.06 on its first day of business but that was back in 1857. There is an entire race of Macers that live in the store all year round and have never been outside its walls. Most of them stay around the perfume section, which has its own micro-climate. If you get lost don't worry about it. It may take a few years for you to get out but time does not move inside the building so nothing will have changed when you come out. Except the credit rating on your Visa card.

<u>cocaine</u>
This ·'substance occurs in the leaves of the Erythroxylon coca plant, a tree indigenous to Peru

and Bolivia. In 1884 Freud advocated the use of cocaine to treat depression and alleviate chronic fatigue . . . he would write you a prescription and everything . . . and he described its effects as inducing exhilaration and lasting EUPHORIA. This may be true.

Until 1903 Coca-Cola contained approximately 60 milligrams of cocaine per 8 ounce serving. In 1914 Harrison introduced his much-maligned Narcotic Act banning the incorporation of cocaine in patent medicines and beverages. He was known forever thereafter as Spoilsport Harrison.

The trolley is almost at a standstill now in front of the Empire State Building. It is eerie. High up way above my head is another eyrie. An eagle swoops down and almost takes my head off. One of its wings knocks against the TV and causes it to change channel. A sitcom is just starting.

❏ EUPHORIA
The TV announcer is very pretty.
- And now we have our ever popular sitcom, *The Dub Show*, so sit back and enjoy. And remember, you never know what the mad bastard will do next.

I settle myself as best I can in the bed and the wounds seem not to hurt as much. The TV starts with the theme tune. It is fun music, all happy, silly and yet serious at the same time . . . a cross between *Blind Date* and *Panorama*.

The scene is a fairly ordinary apartment. Upper West Side. In it Becky and myself are sitting at a table cutting up cocaine on a large glass table and then weighing it and putting it into bags. Every time I turn to put one of the bags into a suitcase Becky snorts a wee line for herself. The canned laughter from the audience breaks in every time she does this and I turn quickly only to see her wiggling her nose and pouting me a kiss. The audience thinks this is hilarious and I put on a stupid gawky face. The camera zooms in on me each time.

- Say Becky, you wouldn't be taking some of the merchandise for yourself there now honey, would you?
- Of course not sweetie, I just have a terrible itchy nose.

Canned laughter.

- That means we are going to have a row.

Canned laughter.

The door bursts open and there stands Dub . . . filling the doorway with his arms akimbo. The audience breaks out into wild applause and whistles. He looks ridiculous in a long white leather coat, covering a white linen suit, white shoes, a black silk shirt and a white silk tie. He wears the coat gangster style over his shoulders without his arms in the sleeves. He sports a pencil moustache and has a shamrock tattooed on his forehead, which he is very proud of.

- Hi Dub.
- And how is the beautiful Becky?
- Great Dub.
- And have you been looking after me merchandise, pumpkin?

She turns earnestly to camera and nods her head vigorously.

- Oh yeeaass Dub, of course.

Canned laughter.

- Now Shem, I hope the work is nearly finished. You know how my Colombian friends hate to be kept waiting.
- Sure Dub, we are going as fast as we can.

Just then Dub swirls around, his coat tails fanning out like some crazed peacock and takes a gun out from some inner pocket and presses it firmly against my temple. The audience go mad with excitement and there are shouts of 'Go on, Dub, do it.'

- Now Shem, you know that when I took you under my wing I expressly said that you were never to question my authority . . . isn't that right?

Camera pans in on my head which has beads of sweat breaking out on it.

- Yes . . . Dub.
- Good.

He just as quickly lets me go.

- Because I have a big job on next week that I want both of you to carry out for me.

Becky claps her hands and seems genuinely excited.

- Oh good, Dub . . . you know how I like to serve you.
- I know sweet button.

They rub noses and the audience go 'Awwhhh'.

- Don't you just love her little button nose Shem?
- Yes Dub.
- Now how about the accounts . . . are they all up to date? . . . let me see them.

Shem takes out a laptop computer and presses some keys on it.

- Everything is up to speed Dub.
- It's not the speed that I'm worried about . . . it's the cocaine.

The audience burst into laughter and Becky claps her hands and bounces up and down in her chair.

- Of course Dub ... that is fine as well.
- This shipment next week ... you will have to deliver it by hand ... and I want you to take Becky with you as a decoy.

Shem turns to camera.

- That's if it hasn't been snorted by her already.

Canned laughter.

- What's that Shem?
- Nothing Dub, ... I was just saying it would be nice to be escorted by her already.

Canned laughter.

- Hmmm ... sometimes I think you've been sampling too much of my merchandise on the side Shem.

Laughter as the camera zooms in to a spot of white powder under Becky's nose. She giggles nervously and shrugs her shoulders to the audience.

- Right.

A big sweep of his coat then rather poetically and dramatically:

- Well I will arise and go now, go to look after me.

The audience clap at his tag line.

- Goodbye Dub.
- Ah Dub why is it you're always just zapping in and out of my life? Hah, now why is that ... don't you care for your little Becky-wecky?
- You know I do sugar pumpkin. Don't you sweetness?
- I suppose so.

Dub makes a huge line for her on the table.

- Here you go sugar ... you have a little snorteroony for yourself.

Big innocent face on her . . . audience react.

- Oh but I couldn't Dub.
- You go right ahead . . . it's okay.
- Okay.

She plugs the whole line in one deft movement and lets out a big expletive.

- Yes, fucking magic!
- Dub . . . could I possibly . . .
- No. You know I don't like anyone messing with my stuff. And that goes for Becky too, if you get my drift.

Shem turns to camera.

- I get your drift. I am well and truly drifted Dub.

Some muted laughter.

- Time to go.

He sweeps one last time and waves to all. The audience go crazy and clap and cheer . . . the credits roll and the music blares. ❑

12

the truth about Dub

Dub is a nasty piece of work.

Every one says so.

Every one except Becky, that is.

She idolises him.

To look at him you'd be scared ... to look twice at him you'd be very scared ... he is not particularly big or broad or anything ... quite the opposite ... unstable and basically fucked-up in the head. He claims that his father beat his mother regularly and that one day when he was only sixteen his father came home and tried to beat the mother to death but Dub intervened and ran a garden shears through the guy's gut. He had to flee and came to New York and can never go back. No one knows his real name because he is convinced someone will rat on him or get him arrested and sent home. He never leaves New York. This is enough space for any man, he reckons.

The truth about Dub is that he was an electrical contractor with a firm in Dublin and he cheated the gaffer out of a load of copper wire and the gaffer said he would kill Dub if he didn't return the gear, but he had already sold it all to his brother-in-law and so rather than suffer the ignominy of a thrashing he absconded ... first to Liverpool, then Amsterdam and then to Boston. He was run out of Boston for double swiping credit cards in a restaurant and ended up in New York. Working on the building sites got him introduced to a number of shady characters and he worked his way into their good books and eventually he worked his way into their books. He has never killed anyone with a garden shears but would think about it if all the guns in the world suddenly stopped working.

He is still a mad fucker however and anytime someone does something to displease him there is no telling what he might do. Well you can tell ... but at your own peril. His rule is one of tyranny and uncertainty with the latter proving to be the more effective.

- Fuck them before they fuck you Shem.
- Aye Dub.
- That Becky one ... you should stick with her.
- Aye Dub.
- But if you fuck around on her I'll smash your balls with a hammer.
- Thanks Dub.

He said this casually to me, while eating breakfast over in The Greek Diner on Queens Boulevard. A bit of egg juice dribbled down his chin and it seemed to enforce the imagery of my balls and the hammer. Dub wiped it away as if the egg juice had insulted him ... Dub would ensure that the chicken and all its relatives would come to an untimely death and end up in KFC or somewhere like that ... whatever was hell for chickens he would find out what it was.

> - She's a special kid and I don't want anyone fucking with her head.
> - Sure Dub ... no problem there.
> - How long you been shacking up together?
> - A few months now.
> - Hmm ... that's good. I want the two of you to do some work for me. Not the shitty little jobs I've had you doing ... bigger stuff.

And I knew this was not the casual offer of a job and I knew that there was not an option to say no. Even now on the ambulance trolley hurtling through the streets I can still remember the feeling that day and I knew when he said it that this would alter the course of my life. There was a nauseating movement in my bowels and I had to adjust myself on the seat to stop from puking. The sensation made my skin crawl and I had a flash of being in the zoo many years ago as a child looking at a strange animal ... an armadillo I think it was ... I have no idea why that image came to me then.

> - You'll be making a lot more money as well.
> - I like the sound of that.
> - You and Becky should take a holiday somewhere.
> - We're thinking of going back to Ireland for a break.
> - Good, you can look up a few people for me when you are there.
> - Sure Dub.

Dub has three fears in life and they are probably all that he has ... death, being double-crossed and taxi drivers. Dub was once on the Yellow Cab Drivers' Most Wanted List. He would never pay for his ride and frequently accost the driver if there was any guff . . . and New York taxi drivers are generally not to be trifled with . . . but Dub would strike first from behind with the butt of a gun or whatever he had handy. He was never caught or arrested but I dare say his face is emblazoned indelibly on many a cabby's mind.

Many a cab driver's neck hairs stand on end when they hear an Irish accent. Dub used to rationalise it by telling about the Blacks and the Irish fighting for jobs during the turn of the century . . . he had read all about it . . . he just never quite explained where he had read about it. The fact that only a small percentage of cab drivers are Black does not matter to The Dub . . . he quite literally tars them all with the same brush.

- They're all Black *fear dubh* bastards one way or the other.
- Yes Dub.

13

Great-uncle Donal

The funny thing is that while I'm passing the Empire State Building on my trolley . . . it isn't even finished yet. There is some serious chronological messing going on here. I am sure this saline stuff is fucked up. I crane backwards to try to see up to the top. It's only half way there. Girders and cranes and concrete and raw steel . . . looks a little like my innards at the moment. Hurts now.

But they'll sort all that out . . . the guys in the ambulance . . . once they realise I've fallen out they'll come screeching around the corner any minute now . . . they know I have premium medical . . . or I used to have . . . or did I ever get it . . . well I certainly thought seriously about it for a while. Guy in Molly's one night said he could get dodgy social security numbers for illegal Micks. I bought an ID card off him . . . 100 bucks and three bottles of Coors . . . good bargain . . . said he'd post the paperwork to me and I so wet behind the ears that you could go swimming there.

Can't remember if he did and at the moment I couldn't give a flying fuck.

High up . . . I can see a group of eleven men all sitting nonchalantly in a row on a ridiculously high girder . . . eating their sandwiches . . . must be Irish or <u>Native American Indians</u> . . . inured to the vertigo apparently . . . something in the genes . . . and so high up there . . . so high up for all Ireland and for all the world to see. It would make a great photo so it would. One of them is playing the harmonica while the others chomp, chomp, chomp on their batch loaf and cheese.

One of them looks down as I'm passing. Fuck it but if it isn't my Great-uncle Donal, never met him but you could tell by the nose . . . they always said that about our clan . . . oh, there they go and you can always tell them by their noses. That's what they said.

- Howya Shem . . . bit of a cut you got there?
- Sure it's only a scratch Great-uncle Donal.
- You want to get something for that.

The others snigger into their cheese sandwiches . . . they know I'm completely fucked.

- Here, don't be going on empty-handed . . . you're probably starving with all that stuff falling out of you.

He throws me down a big hunk of a sandwich . . . sesame seed bread . . . but most of the seeds fall off on the way down. It's a long way down. The bread seems to hang in the air for an eternity. Terminal velocity. The seeds spray out like raindrops and then bounce on the ground and make an awful clatter . . . noisy things . . . that would be the roughage I suppose.

- Take care of yourself now son.
- Aye Great-uncle Donal, I will.

Again the others snigger. One of the men in dungarees splurts into the little milk bottle full of tea and Great-uncle Donal casts him a scowl. Obviously the main man around here is my great uncle. He gives a great roar.

– Right . . . everyone back to work.

And so the Empire State Building climbs another few inches into the sky.

– You best be off now Shem lad.

– Aye Great-uncle Donal.

Native American Indians

The Indian Removal Act was passed in May 1830; it empowered the President of the United States to move eastern Native Americans west of the Mississippi . . . to hell or to Okie . . . to what was then 'Indian Territory' . . . aka Oklahoma. Is that a raw deal or what? All this messing eventually ended with the slaughter of Sioux men, women and children as well as the soldiers of the US 7th Cavalry, at Wounded Knee, South Dakota, on 29th December 1890. And so close after Christmas and all. Someone at the battle did actually wound his knee but it wasn't the worst injury by a long way.

One tribe used to own what is today called Manhattan. They sold it for $24. Some of them would sell it again for $24 if they had the option. The others sit around in Daisy's diner all day waiting for the back rents they are owed to flow in . . . about 30 trillion dollars last time they reckoned . . . and eat pecan pie with toffee sauce.

There's a machine at the top of the Empire State Building that will squash a penny or a nickel out flat and put it on a necklace or a keyring for you. It only costs a dollar and it takes about three seconds. You then have a nickel or a penny on a string or keyring for yourself.

Great-uncle Donal would have liked to have one of those I'll bet. I should buy him one next time. Next time. Hah! Do you hear me with my next time? I am sure he would be very happy to know that the towering edifice he helped build now has a machine that squashes nickels for a dollar and puts them on a piece of string or keyring.

Progress.

- Always have a few pence on you son . . . you never know when you are going to run into trouble.
- I always know when I'm going to run into trouble Great-uncle Donal . . .
- I know son.
- It's a talent I seem to have picked up over the years.
- Your grandmother was much the same when she was young.
- In fact anyone can train themselves to do it if they really want.
- Is that a fact now Shem?
- It is easy Great-uncle Donal.
  Step 1: Always get yourself into a situation where there is going to be trouble.
- Sounds realistic.
- Step 2: Do not, under any circumstances, leave the place where the trouble is brewing.
- Good advice.
- Step 3: If possible, exacerbate the impending trouble with some seemingly innocent remark or gesture.
- That's clever Shem . . . that's mighty clever.
- Step 4: Try to make your palms sweat when you

know the trouble is only seconds away.
- Jasus Shem . . . your are an awful man.
- I call it my four-step plan . . . what do you think Great-
uncle Donal?
- I could have gotten you a job on the buildings instead
of that messing you ended up in.
- Aye, I suppose you could have Great-uncle Donal.
- But then again you can never tell the future son.

My trolley is back on track now . . . the colour slowly seeps
back into the city and it looks more like nowadays . . . a
scruffy guy with a huge pike is pushing me along. Without
even asking me he does a sharp right-hand turn and we
end up on a battlefield in Ireland. This is a surprise . . . but
not a massive one . . . things like this have been happening
ever since Santos wired me up to this drip. Surprised Dub
hasn't copped on to this and started selling the stuff to all
the Micks in Queens. Get the last of the saline drips now .
. . get your saline drips here . . . two for the price of one,
this week only.

We seem to be in the middle of a fierce battle. The man
with the pike and the ragged clothes jumps off and runs
up the side of a river. I think this is the Battle of the Boyne.
This fact is confirmed to me when I see a stately figure on
a white horse charging through the ranks. This is William
of Orange, though he looks more tangerine to me.

A kindly looking priest approaches and gives me the
once over.
- Dear child, you are not long for this world . . . let us
get you to safety across the river.
- I'm okay here Father, if you don't mind.

He pushes me nonetheless . . . weak-willed in front of

the religious. We could never really stand up to the Church back home. He gets there puffing and panting . . . he does not look too good himself. He blesses me and says some Latin and then rushes off to engage a group of soldiers in fearsome combat. This is what he says in Latin though his accent was a bit garbled: *Pax tuteor bellum est* 'Peace is safer than war.'

That is the best thing a priest has ever told me. And seeing as he said it in the middle of a battlefield I also thought it was the most relevant thing a priest ever said to me.

Good man Father. Give it loads. He sees off the few soldiers with some deft karate kicks . . . Mawashi Geri Chudan and Ushiro Mawashi Geri Jodan . . . and then comes back to me. He hands me a duty-free bag stuffed with Tayto crisps and Crunchies and asks if I would deliver it to his grand-niece Brenda who works in a bar on the corner of Third Avenue and 56th Street. He said a lot of 'great' words before the grand-niece but I can't remember how many. Then he runs off again. Jasus, he is an awful man for the running off.

The guy with the pike returns. He is also wounded.

He pushes me down the far side of an embankment, over a small field and around a corner and onto Fifth Avenue again. It's good to be back.

The place is still devoid of life . . . but you can't have everything and if you can I want ten per cent, because ten per cent of everything is still everything and that's good enough for me. It is an infinity thing.

Mr Callaghan my Leaving Certificate physics teacher is now standing on the sidebars of the trolley like Larry was earlier on . . . FBI style. He is not eleven feet tall. He is exactly half of that. Clever bloke Mr Callaghan. Bit weird to look at . . . he has·yellow hair, not blond, yellow on account of an incident with some potassium and water that he only ever briefly·alludes to. And he always wears the same clothes . . . even now on the side of the trolley he is wearing the green corduroy trousers and the plaid jacket with the leatherette patches on the elbows. That was always his style and it never really caught on but he persists with it anyway and you have to respect him for it.

Cookie Callaghan we used to call him on account of him looking so . . . well, so Cookie really . . . and then just Cookie when we got to know him better. Used to sit the exam every year with the students. Said the year he didn't get an 'A' he'd retire, though it was rumoured by the other teachers that he used to cog.

I have to ask him about Newton's Third Law and he prattles away . . . mostly to himself . . . as I have to pay attention to the streets we are hurtling along.

Anyway he's yapping on about infinity . . . he was always on about infinity . . . never gave it a break. Bored bubblegum-filled kids trying to discern new patterns in the flaking paint on the walls by looking at it intently (a science that would later become known as <u>flakology</u>). I used to listen to him however. I was his pet student. I once got 100% in one of his exams all about nuclear physics and he was so pleased he photocopied my exam script and passed around copies to all the class.

I was given several deadening thumps in my arms during the lunch break that day. The type that make your arm numb for days and when the feeling does return it hurts like crazy and you wish you were numb again. This is life.

I wish I had studied biology instead as I could probably have a go at stitching myself up now. Not much use knowing about the Wall Effect of the liquid in my feed tube. But there you go.

flakology

This is the science of being able to predict the future by reading the pattern of how paint flakes, tree bark or other materials fall away from their original structures over long periods of time. Supposedly the molecules of paint have a higher understanding of the Laws of Gravitation and peel away from the rest of the wall at precise, determined moments. The pattern of this peeling away could then be looked up in von Noimann's Flake Tables. Depending on this value a certain set of circumstances could be predicted with a high degree of probability.

The general equation used is

$$F = \frac{zM_1 M_2 T}{d^2}$$

Where:

F is the degree of flaking.

z is von Noimann's constant, measured in Jongles (Jo), dependent on the type of paint or material used.

M_1 is the mass of the wall or structure, measured in kilograms (kg).

M_2 is the mass of the piece of flake, which peeled away from structure M_1, also measured in kilograms.

T is the time that has elapsed between successive flakes falling from M_2, measured in seconds (sec.).

d is the distance the flake falls from the original structure it was a part of, measured in metres (m).

Most observations carried out in Cookie Callaghan's class, using a standard sized classroom wall, Temperature = 25 degrees, Crown Magnolia Paint (Matt), and a z value of 6.838 microJongles (μJo), yielded F values of approximately 0.994 ... which usually meant that nothing major was going to happen.

An F value approaching 1.0 is known as Absolute Boredom.

An F value of zero is known as the 'Certainty of Something Big About to Happen' value.

Flakology values of 0.001 were reputedly recorded around the time the Yucatan Crater occurred.

I digress. It's not my fault ... it is Cookie ... he just doesn't seem to be able to hold my attention like he used to do. Must be something to do with the blood oozing out of me or the speed of the trolley on which I am a passenger or the knowledge that all is not really well with me at the moment.

- Shem, I've come up with a great way of explaining all about infinity ... better than what I used to tell you guys. Do you want to hear it?
- Sure ... why not?
- Imagine that you are a bee and that you land on this huge piece of rock the size of the sun ... made of metal, the hardest one you can think of.
- Gold Mr Callaghan.
- Close. And this bee right? Are you listening?
- I am.

The pain is kicking in again.

- Well, this bee, lands on the clump of metal every one thousand years, right?

- Ouch . . . one thousand yeah, right with you Mr Callaghan.
- Now when the bee . . . this is important Shem . . . when the bee has worn away the metal planet . . . get that . . . when the bee has worn it away . . . by the attrition and friction of his feet . . . that is only the beginning of infinity . . . only the beginning!

He is ecstatic.

- That's a very powerful explanation Mr Callaghan.
- Thought you'd like it Shem.
- I do Mr Callaghan, I do.

He starts to tell me about some new theory he has been working on when something catches my eye. We are passing a little Thai restaurant and inside I can see a flake of paint just at the point of peeling away from the wall. It drifts down into a pot of some brightly coloured flowers. I do the sums quickly in my head . . . hmm . . . a flakology value of 0.013 . . . this is not at all good. I look down at my wounds again . . . of course how stupid of me. Zero means certain death so I guess there is still a small chance . . . pretty small though.

Cookie jumps off the trolley now. I can hear him talking to himself in the distance . . . fading away . . . his pitch lowering, thanks to the Doppler Effect. . . fading away . . . not vanishing . . . he sort of ripples away into the ether like a bored <u>sine wave</u> . . . never completely gone.

<u>sine wave</u>

$y = \sin (wt + k)$ is the mathematical description of a sinusoidal waveform and it is a periodic function. It is part of a branch of mathematics called TRIGONOMETRY. If Angle A = Angle B and along comes Angle C then what is the relationship between Angle A and Angle C? And does Angle B feel left out and isolated? And if not, why not?

If trigonometry had not been invented there would be no intercontinental ballistic missiles or TV. Honestly this is true.

Cookie was a good teacher though and so was the guy who taught me maths. I used to love those classes . . . he made us feel we were constantly pushing back the frontiers of mathematical knowledge and understanding each time we solved one of his problems. We were in truth only pushing back the desks onto two of their legs and rubbing our pens in our heads. The TV is showing the Open University now. Hmmm, mathematics.

❏ TRIGONOMETRY

The camera pans in on the spotty face of a fifteen-year-old kid. A bead of sweat is trickling down his forehead. The camera zooms in on this . . . it is like some Escher painting from which the shape of a classroom can be discerned, reflected in the bubble of liquid. A teacher is at the top of the class, two leatherette patches on the elbows of his jacket. The teacher has a wild mop of red hair.

The chalk screeches across the board and the students groan in unity. The teacher smiles and apologises.

Zoom in on the board. It is covered in Greek characters comprising complex trigonometric equations.

Teacher: Now, class . . . if anyone can solve this beauty before the end of the class there is a £1 prize.

Camera pans around to Jones, the messer at the back of the class. .

Jones: Is that cash or cheque, sir?

Teacher: You'll never know Jones that's for sure.

Camera pans back to the kid with the bubble of sweat on his forehead. He seems to be in some sort of frenzy and his copybook is already crammed with obtuse Coptic scribbles and complexities. He stops short and the camera zooms in extreme close-up to the bead of sweat ... within it there is a light shining. It is a street light and under the street light is a lone man standing ... he looks into the light and on a piece of paper he has scrawled the answer to the equation. A car is heard screeching up towards the man and three shots are fired. The man falls to the ground and the piece of paper wafts gently to the ground. The camera follows it as it lands in a mound of slush by the side of the road. The equation's solution is visible just for a moment before it is dissolved away.

The young boy grabs this moment of enlightenment.

Shem: Sir?

Teacher: Yes Shem?

Shem: I think I have it, sir.

Teacher: Have what Shem? (titters from the class)

Shem: The solution sir.

Teacher: Already?

Shem: Yes sir.

Teacher: Okay ... well let's have it then ... up you come.

Camera pans back to the apprehensive face of the kid. The bead of sweat, in a moment of indecision, cannot make up its mind which side of the nose to go. Straight down the ski slope and off into oblivion or what.

Shem: Sir, can't I just read it from here..(again titters from the class)

Teacher: Ah now ... come on up Shem, and don't
             be so shy.

Again the camera zooms in extreme close-up on the bead
of sweat dangling perilously from the end of the kid's
nose. The rest of the boys' faces in the classroom can be
seen in the absurd convexity of the water droplet. Their
voices become distorted in some nightmarish aberration
of Doppler's basic principles ... all of them melding into
one cacophonous drone. The camera freezes on the very
moment the droplet leaves his nose and crashes onto the
copybook just at the equals sign at the end of the solution.
It smashes into smithereens and the watery shards scatter
and rip into the boy's stomach.

The camera cuts to a street in Manhattan where the
piece of soggy paper with the solution is washed away
down the gutter. ❑

There is a crude and sudden commercial break in the
programme and along comes Daisy selling her homemade
pecan pie and toffee sauce mix.

    – Remember, you can't buy this in the shops.

A little caption flashes in the corner of the screen and
    this is what it says ... 'Liar, liar, pants on fire'.

    – Jasus Daisy, will you ever fuck off and leave a man
      alone?

She seems to be able to hear me through the screen
... this is interactive TV at its best.

    – Sure thing honey.

· 14

the truth about Guptha

Guptha is not from India. He is from San Francisco but he has relations back in India and he keeps in touch with them via e-mail. He loves e-mail. He loves the Internet. It will be the great leveller among races and nations. He firmly believes this. The Internet will empower all those who need empowering. This is what Guptha feels passionately.

By day Guptha drives a yellow cab around the most fucked-up city on the planet. By night he is King Guptha of the Internet. He participates in hundreds of newsgroups, sends copious e-mail ... a lot of spam ... and spends hours surfing aimlessly over the net. He also wears a turban and is very proud of it despite what some of his customers say and do. Some nights he comes home and finds cigarette butts, sweet wrappers and worse stuck into its folds.

He also runs a therapy site for yellow cab drivers who have been injured, abused, spat upon, urinated upon, cursed at or drivers who just can't take the hassle anymore. There are quite a lot of visitors. He calls himself

Fergal O'Byrne

King Kabbie at the site and answers all the e-mail queries or newsgroups' visitors himself. He calls the site www.yellowcabdriversunite.com and he is very proud of it. There is a section called Wanted which allows drivers to describe particularly bad customers and give brief descriptions or details. The picture of the mayor of the city is number one on the wanted list, on account of the flat fee he imposed from JFK airport into central Manhattan. Most drivers considered this a personal insult.

A character called Dub is firmly anchored in the second spot. He has been known to attack at least six drivers on separate occasions. He is considered to be a racist and a danger to all taxi drivers. Guptha has a photofit-type picture of this man and it is remarkably accurate.

Most of the visitors to his site just want somewhere to rant about customers or the mayor or the Department of Transport or Lousy Tippers or the Irish. Guptha has a section with a pull-down menu whereby you can vote for a nationality which in each driver's experience is the worst to take.

The voting always returns that the Irish are the worst. A similar voting pull-down menu for Best Tippers also places the Irish at number one. It also transpires that the vast majority of visitors to the site are Irish. This always annoys Guptha as he is really hoping that other ethnic minorities be better represented.

Someone sent him an e-mail saying that the Irish were an ethnic minority and Guptha wrote back saying that in his experience this was not true for New York ... especially among the police force.

The Irish also topped the online polls in the following categories:

Ethnic grouping most likely to call Indian drivers Apu and make Homer Simpson noises.

The most likely to be drunk.

The most likely to quibble about the fare.

The most likely to tip extravagantly.

This always fascinates Guptha and begrudgingly he has a respect . . . albeit skewed . . . for this illogical race. The bottom line is that Guptha likes tips and so by inference he can tolerate the Irish. But he can still have a damn good rant about them on his website, however.

A page from Guptha's website has just zapped up on my laptop. I think it is quite funny. Memories of childhood . . . two Chicken Find-the-Loos, one Pillow Rice and a Toilet Roll please. I remember Little Bro and me running out of the takeaway . . . and Mr Ali rushing out from behind the counter and chasing us down the road . . . and mother asking us if we had been annoying the nice gentleman who always came around at Christmas time with onion bhajis and samosas and other delicacies that mother would then hide . . . and they would have tea and all leave as great friends and Dad would give Mr Ali two warm bottles of Smithwicks that he had left over from last year and Mother would throw out all the food because our granny had told her that 'they' catch rats and cook them and that 'they' are not clean. And at the door Dad and Mr Ali would smile and wish each other a happy Christmas and shake hands.

A passing yellow cab snaps me back into reality. It is not Guptha.

- Hey, turn down the goddamned TV Mick. What you think you're doing coming into our neighbourhood and blaring your TV like that . . . don't you got no respect?

The yellow cab driver has not been watching where he is going because he is so intent on chastising me and his car disappears into a manhole that has no cover on it. Smoke rises from the manhole like the belch of a hungry city.

15

will the real Santos please stand up?

Temporal distortions. I seem to be inside the ambulance again. Come on guys what's going on here? They are fucking with my body clock. Not to worry, it is only a flashback. Phew!

- What happened to this one Santos?
- Got shot.
- Oh really? Tough break.
- Yeah . . . tough break Louie.
- What's in the bag?
- I haven't looked yet.

Louie sneaks a quick look and puts on his 'rabbit about to be run over by a Very Big Truck' face.

- What's wrong with you now?
- Eh, I think you better take a look at this Santos.

And Santos takes a reluctant look because he was thinking about ringing his wife and telling her all about the shit he is in. She would be real nice and comforting on the phone but she would probably beat him senseless with a sharp implement when he returned home. He often thought about not returning home.

Santos thought about staying away from home now ... in fact he was thinking about never going back home ever again. Never going back to work and never even coming back to New York. These thoughts flashed before him like the headlights on a Very Big Truck ... the one that is already about to run over Louie.

He looks at the bag then to Louie's questioning face, back to the bag again and then back to Louie. A few beads of <u>sweat</u> have appeared on Louie's face. Santos' mind is racing. Even with all the thoughts and permutations he still wished that Louie had taken a shower. He was always busting his chops about it but Louie insisted that one shower a week was sufficient. Santos often thought about raising this with his superiors ... it was simply not good enough when working around wounded people. Hygiene was important.

Louie was also a statistic of American weirdness in that he was an Aqualite. They are normal enough people except that they believe water is the all-powerful panacea for true happiness and life preservation. Because of this it is considered sinful to use water merely to clean or bathe oneself so it is used sparingly. Louie had very few guests around.

sweat

There are two types of sweat glands ... the eccrine and the apocrine. It is estimated that each person has about one million eccrine glands ... though this can double on a first date or when stuck in an elevator. They occur throughout the body but are more numerous on the palms and feet. Sweat is actually odourless and contains 98% water . . . the other 2% being made up of sodium chloride, fatty acids, urea, sulphates, albumin and skatole. Yum yum!

The odour is actually caused by the decomposition of the sweat by bacteria and this is why frequent bathing is advisable. No really . . . frequent bathing IS advisable. Write an essay in not less than 1,000 words about a fun time you and your friends had with sweat.

· 16

the thing about dragons

I fell down a mountain once. Some would call it a hill but
I fell down it which or whether. It was called *Tóin le
Gaoith*[9]. It is shaped like someone's bottom sticking up
against the wind. I laughed when my father said 'bottom'.
I was ten and he was a lot older. I was holding his hand
. . . he was telling me a story about how the <u>dragons</u> had
come along to help the Irish win a battle but on this
particular day one of the dragons got sick . . . so the brave
Irish soldiers were beaten and then we were plunged into
65 million years of oppression by the English.

He also said that the English were responsible for the
dinosaurs disappearing.

This is also true.

I was so engaged in what my father was saying that I
fell over a clump of rock and rolled all the way down to
the bottom . . . in much the same way as some of my
ancestors must have done.

[9] Ass to the wind. Similar to *póg mo thóin* which means 'kiss my ass'.

At the beginning of my roll down the hill I was actually enjoying it . . . it was like a roller coaster ride but then the pain kicked in . . . my wrist was shattered in a bazillion places and when my father caught up, or down, with me I suppose . . . well he was white as a ghost and for a moment I thought I had died and gone to heaven and that he'd rushed over to save me from damnation but instead he bought me a packet of original Tayto cheese & onion crisps and brought me to the hospital.

They had a helicopter landing pad there but I arrived in the father's beige Hillman Hunter . . . I think that hurt more. The arm was fucked and I would never be able to throw a hoop like my friend Larry.

<u>dragons</u>
These creatures have had a fairly ambiguous history. In the sacred writings of the Hebrews the dragon frequently represents death and evil, and in Christian art the dragon is a symbol of sin. However, the ancient Greeks and Romans believed that dragons had the ability to convey to mortals the secrets of the Earth. Among the Chinese people the dragon is traditionally regarded as a symbol of good luck. So if you see a dragon in Chinatown you are in for a treat.

That was the thing about my dad . . . he could convince me of anything. He could convince most people of most things. He convinced me about the dragons. Once me and Becky were in Chinatown doing a drop for Dub and it was the Chinese New Year and there were dragons. Me and

Becky had been doing far too much *sneachta*[10] around then and I saw the dragon chink its way towards me. I was rooted to the spot and Becky was trying to grab me along and all I saw was my father's head superimposed on the dragon's body and he was shaking it from side to side and there was one huge tear in the corner of his eye. Then the dragon turned and went up a side street and Becky thumped me in the arm and pushed me into a yellow cab driven by a guy with a turban on his head.

That day I fell … up on the mountain with Dad … the Tayto cheese & onion crisps tasted great. The little smiley potato man on the front of the packet with the red blazer on and the funny hat … wonder what marketing guru came up with that one. Like to shake his hand … the guru not the potato man. People from Iowa are called Potato Heads over here.

I'd love a packet of crisps now. Whenever anyone asks me what I really miss about Ireland I always say the crisps because they are so good. Only the real Tayto ones though … none of your fancy flavours for me. Crisps are called chips in America. Chips are called french fries. I don't know what crisps actually are over here.

I'm nearly in Chinatown now … the colour is back with a vengeance. Garish in fact. I fade it down with the small remote control panel on the left side of my bed. Looks better. Chinky guy comes over to my trolley and pokes his finger into my wound.

---

10 Gaelic word for snow. Also slang word for cocaine among the Irish community in America. It is a fine white powder that sometimes falls on your head and sometimes falls up your nose. And so is snow. If you were to throw a snowball made of cocaine at someone it would cost you about $2,000 and a court appearance. Do not do this.

- You need <u>ginseng</u> and frosa.
- I do? Would you have any on you?

He looks genuinely disappointed.

- No, all gone. All gone when Clinton took over. But maybe I can get you some frosa.
- What the hell is that?
- Frosa.

He has said it so matter of factly that I figure further enquiry is futile.

- Sure, let's have some of that then.
- You got major credit card?
- Well ... yes ... but the guys in the ambulance have my wallet and all my stuff. And I gave the last of my cash to Becky to buy smokes that time.
- No cash?

He is looking earnestly at my wounds.

- No I gave it to ...

But he is gone. There are other souls in more need of solace than me and in more possession of cash or plastic than this poor sinner.

ginseng

This is the common name for the family Araliaceae and for its genus *Panax*. Ginseng is classified as *Panax pseudoginseng*. Show off. Some races consider it an aphrodisiac but they would say that wouldn't they? Drug companies have made billions on this pretext ... it is possible that they are right ... so maybe don't be so sceptical.

Other reputed aphrodisiacs include ground rhinoceros horn, powered pterodactyl wing and alcohol. Brendan Behan, infamous Irish playwright, once said that the best make-up a woman can wear is fifteen pints of beer in a man's stomach. He was a bit of an alco and he reportedly went to Canada because he had seen an advert saying 'Drink Canada Dry'…and he said it sounded like an excellent idea. This is true.

.17

it all happened on Ellis Island

I'm nearly at the end of Manhattan. It's as if someone has taken the map and held it up so that I'm literally dripping to the end of it like some Dali clock. I can see it now. Battery Park ... used to be a fort ... I don't know how to stop this. I have no call bell ... damn what am I going to do?

Battery Park

This was named for a battery of guns the British stored there from 1683 to 1687 and is now a chaotic chunk of green on the very southernmost tip of Manhattan Island. It is known locally as Assault and Battery Park. You can see the Statue of Liberty from here. And on a good day you can see forever.

You can buy hotdogs and pretzels and drugs and other things too. Try not to talk to strangers here. No really ... do not talk to anyone ... especially the mad guy dressed in army fatigues who goes around shouting and reciting bad poetry and will drop his trousers and urinate at the slightest sign of interest from a tourist. He seems to be able to urinate on demand and in impressive quantities, unlike millions of people in doctors' clinics all over world each day who cannot.

Some say he drinks the water from the East River . . . others say it's the Hudson.

My trolley hits the end of Manhattan with such force that my whole body jolts forward . . . sailing out into the night sky . . . somersaulting all the way. The three judges sitting along the walls of Castle Clinton give their scores . . . 5.9 . . . 5.9 . . . 5.8 . . . I am disappointed with the last one and will have to practise more I think . . . though there may not be much time left for that sort of messing.

Cerchunk, clang, clang, clang . . . *Badumphff.*

I land on <u>Ellis Island</u> with a bang . . . or an assortment of sounds similar to the above.

I'm in a queue . . . a line . . . the place is crowded and people are coughing and spitting . . . some of them need showers or need to wipe their arses . . . the man in front of me has a big piece of poo sliding down his leg. Well he won't get in for starters. Louie is there giving out fliers to the dirtiest of them and shaking their muck-covered hands as if each one was the Messiah of the Aqualites. It is prophesied that one will come from among the great unwashed huddled masses and turn all of the land and the seas into the freshest drinking water imaginable. Kevin Costner is one of their high profile devotees. What exactly is meant to happen after 'The Great Watering' is not really expanded upon in any of their literature. But there are great rewards promised for those who practise the faith and can convert others to become Aqualites. Louie is very active in this area. Louie is in fact an Aqualitic Convertor.

Some of the crowd could make better use of the hospital bed than me but these things are beyond my control I'm afraid. I feel guilty but I also feel wounded so that sort of balances things somewhat.

<u>Ellis Island</u>
This small clump of land had over 15 million people pass through its gates between 1890 and 1920 and was where immigrants had to be processed, which according to most peas is not a pleasant experience. This place was known as the Island of Tears. Some cried because they were turned away … others cried because they were let in. Some were so fatigued and sick after weeks and weeks on a rattly, smelly ship that they faded away when they hit the Island. 'Thousands are sailing across that western ocean … to the land of opportunity.' Bring me your huddled masses and we will give them a Visa or a MasterCard.

Tap on the shoulder.

Two burly guards. This way please sir. They are always so polite over here just before they're about to beat the shite out of you. It's kinda cute in one way and not in another.

One is big … O'Malley name tag on. The other is Larsen … looks like good cop bad cop scenario with the exception that the good cop is off sick today and the bad cop from another team sided with this guy. I play the Irish angle.

- Sergeant O'Malley … you wouldn't be anything to the
  O'Malleys of Ballyvaughan be any chance?

O'Malley pokes me in my upper wound with a rubber baton. It hurts like crazy . . . in fact it is excruciating.

- None of your fucking paddy-whackery guff with me my lad. We are sick of you snivelling paddies coming over here and ruining it for the rest of us.

Larsen leans down and in one miasmic breath says . . .

- Yeah.

Larsen is the bigger one and just over his left shoulder I can see all the way back across to Ireland. The world is flat. It is true, thank God. And Becky is waving a hanky at me. Good luck Shem . . . she is on the runway at Shannon . . . Flight EI 0115 is taxiing along beside her and she's not even wearing ear protectors . . . oh there will be trouble . . . and she is waving a . . . oh no, it's not a hankie, it's a piece of paper . . . a list . . . things to get in Hamayrika . . . peanut butter cupcakes, beef jerky and <u>Hershey</u> bars (the white ones if they have them) . . .

- Don't worry Becky, I won't forget.

But the two guards are taking me down a corridor. O'Malley frowns at the noise from the dicky wheel of my trolley.

- Can't you oil that bloody thing? You are a disgrace to the Old Country.

Larsen nods emphatically . . . Yeah.

I have seen enough movies and I know not to reply . . . this is an opening for him to browbeat me with his superior superiority and I'll be damned if I'll be giving him the satisfaction. Why, if I wasn't in this bed with all these gunshot wounds . . .

There are screams and shouts from every room we pass. My arse leaks a little bit. I can feel it. Larsen wriggles his nose in disdain.

- Sorry about that . . . you know yourself . . . when you

get scared and half of your intestines are missing anyway ...

He does not smile ...

- Please refrain from conversation while in our company sir.
- Yes sir Sergeant O'Malley.

<u>Hershey</u>

Lewis Blain Hershey was an American army general who for three decades was director of the Selective Service System. Alfred Day Hershey was an American geneticist who won the 1969 Nobel Prize (with Luria and Delbrück) for their discoveries concerning the replication mechanism of VIRUSES and their genetic structure. Barbara 'Seagull' Hershey is an American actress who won an Emmy among other awards.

Hershey is also a very popular brand of chocolate. The Hershey Almond Bar showed up as America's favourite in a recent survey by Tarnation Consulting.

They bring me into a room and O'Malley nods to Larsen and exits. Larsen goes to the corner of the room and stands arms akimbo. A movie starts on my TV.

- Would it be all right if I watch this movie Sergeant Larsen, sir?

He does not respond and I actually think he is sleeping as he stands. I did think he was a horse of a man but this is pushing it somewhat.

❑ VIRUSES

The TV shows the inside of a computer up close – very close. The microchips and PCB tracks look like massive ceramic-clad tower blocks and shining copper, conformal-coated motorways.

Zoom in on Commander Broderick played by Samuel L. Jackson. He is strong and fierce-looking and has the sort of chin you could land a helicopter on. A blast of code comes over his inlaid earpiece.

Jackson:	Go on . . . yes . . . affirmative. Understood. Over. Hey you . . . Irish? (Pan to a geeky looking nerd with thin glasses, unkempt hair and an ill-formed moustache.)
Irish:	Who me sir?
Jackson:	What's your name?
Irish:	*Shem is ainm dom.*
Jackson:	(Zoom in close on Jackson's head. The nano-technology internal circuitry of his head shows a billion billion lines of code scrambling past the sockets where his eyes should be. The software momentarily stops and highlights a program called Babel and accesses a subsection called Gaelic Language and translates this into English. This takes approximately fifteen femto-seconds.) Okay Shem, have you ever tackled a Melissa before?
Shem:	No sir . . . but I am ready to try.
Jackson:	(Zoom in on the faint smile creeping across his titanium lips.) I'll bet you are Shem.

(another crackle on his earpiece) We have to move fast. We have to get to the CPU immediately.

(he barks an order to the others) You men get to the ALU and await a further instruction set.

(Jackson and Shem move their feet slightly to be on one of the shiny copper motorways and they are almost instantaneously zapped to their destination, in a blurry haze of movement.)

We may be too late.

(Camera pans around to the massive gold-plated foundation pillars that anchor the ceramic colossus into the green substrate below. Between these giant pillars small cracks are just about discernible in the almost reflectionless black surface. Out of these microscopic fissures a trickle of 1's and 0's are oozing out. They do not appear to be in any particular order and seem purely random.)

She's leaking data already.

Shem:	Is there nothing we can do sir?
Jackson:	Nothing . . .
	(dramatic pause, close-up on his face) . . . unless.
Shem:	What sir?

151

Jackson: Unless I can distract the virus with
             some heavy-duty downloads while
             you get to the BIOS and disrupt
             secondary and tertiary level
             programs. You may then be able to
             delete the virus at source.

Shem: (close-up)
             I can do it sir.
             (What follows is a thrills and spills
             action sequence that results in me
             . . . Irish as he calls me . . . being
             mortally wounded with the exact
             wounds as in real life, except that
             he . . . the me on the TV . . . is
             haemorrhaging 1's and 0's instead.
             Mandear.)

Jackson: We'll never forget you son. What's
             this your name is again?

Shem: *Shem is ainm dom.*
             (At that a large explosion is heard
             and Jackson looks adoringly at me.)

Jackson: We'll never forget you Shem iss
             anum dumb. ❑

O'Malley comes back in smoking a pipe and clicks his
fingers. Larsen snaps to attention and turns my trolley out
into the corridor . . . except that it is not a corridor but it
appears to be some sort of an alleyway. I have seen too
many movies to know that they are not taking me for ice
cream but, if on the slim chance they are, I am going to
order the hazelnut praline with extra chocolate scoop.

A spanner hits O'Malley on the back of the head from

above. It is Great-uncle Donal and his ten cloth-capped friends. They rush Larsen and batter him with dry bread. Great-uncle Donal shoves a few nickels into my hand as if in some grand gesture of self-sacrifice, the mean bastard ... here Shem, you'll be needing these ... now go quickly ... you're illegal and they'll be looking for you.

Great-uncle Donal looks to the water that separates us from Manhattan and gently pushes me and my Klinowitz chariot into the lolloping water. I am about to remonstrate that it is back to Ireland I want to go but it is too late.

Halfway across I can feel my palms sweat. This means something is up of course ... what else? The trolley is bobbing nicely up and down on the gentle confluence of the Hudson and East Rivers ... there is a scraping noise and I feel something clang against the underside of the trolley. I am raised up ten metres in as many seconds.

Me and my trolley are resting atop the *Red October*. The hatch opens and a rather pissed-off Sean Connery emerges. The moonlight glints over and off his head as only moonlight can. The man is statuesque ... and bear in mind that there is stiff competition around here.

- Hmm ... thought it was you all right Shem.
- Mr Connery ... Sean ... how are you?
- Better than you by the looks of it.
- Yeah, I had a bit of an accident. Well ... actually I was shot.
- Best city for it ... if you are planning to be shot then this is the place.
- Couldn't agree more Sean. Eh ... you wouldn't be going near Ireland by any chance? It's just that I was hoping to go back and see Becky, my girlfriend.

- Sorry Shem, we are on a top secret mission and we are going to have to get you off this submarine I'm afraid. Sorry can't be of more help.
- I know . . . I understand. Listen though . . . I just wanted you to know that I thought you were excellent in *Darby O'Gill and the Little People*.

He casts me a look of disdain and lowers the hatch brusquely. The siren sounds, the sub descends and I am left bobbing in the water again, Manhattan bound.

<u>Sean Connery</u>
British motion picture actor, best known for his portrayal of James Bond, secret agent 007. He played his first leading role in the film *Another Time Another Place* in 1958. Connery gained wide popularity as a result of his performance in the role of James Bond in *Doctor No* (1963). In 1987 Connery won an Academy Award for best supporting actor in *The Untouchables* (1987) . . . here endeth the lesson . . . he also starred in the popular films *Entrapment* (1999), *King of Scotland* (2002), *The Man Who Should Be King* (2005) and *A Farewell to Charms* (2010).

For an old guy he still appears on the 'sexiest men in the world' lists. It is probably the Scottish accent . . . 'thiish should not preshent any shigniphicaant probleemsss' . . . or maybe the rugged good looks. Who knows?

Back on the mainland now . . . the *Red October* pulled a sharp turn to starboard and slingshot me up the East River. It was nice floating along on the trolley . . . under Brooklyn

Bridge ... then under the Manhattan Bridge, then ducked my head under the Williamsburg Bridge and I slip quietly across Franklin D Roosevelt Drive and come out on East 14th Street ... feeling a bit cold and wet now. My trusted trolley seems to sense the degree of despair I feel and we head straight down towards Union Square Park ... but take a sharp left on Fourth Avenue ... heading into The Bowery where I trundle through the doors of that all-night café on the corner ... like the one from that famous <u>Edward Hopper</u> picture.

<u>Edward Hopper</u>
American painter (1882–1967), whose highly individualistic works are landmarks of American realism. His paintings embody in art a particular American 20th-century sensibility that is characterized by isolation, melancholy, and loneliness. One of his best-known works, *Nighthawks* (1942, Art Institute of Chicago), shows an all-night café, its few uncommunicative customers illuminated in the pitiless glare of electric lights. There was actually no pecan pie left in the café the night the picture was painted hence the long faces. Isolation, loneliness and melancholy my arse ... good dollop of Daisy's pie would sort them out.

There are four guys playing cards in booth number three ... Daisy is the waitress. I stop momentarily at the table. One of the guys shows me his hand ...'all hearts ... he has the king, the queen, the jack, the ten and ... the nine is pulsing and beating in time with my own ... the little droplets of blood dripping into his coffee . . . Daisy is there to top it up every time it gets one degree colder. Good girl Daisy.

Pump pump pump goes the heart . . . drip drip drip goes mine.

I really should see a doctor. Daisy gives me a quarter and shows me the phone out back . . . I have to squeeze through a little corridor out to the alley . . . it is cold, it is very cold. An ambulance siren sounds in the distance. Like the last train whistle. Alarums. Alarums.

There is a bright light in the corridor that momentarily blinds me. You expect that on <u>Broadway</u> but not when I took the other fork of the two fingered salute and went down The Bowery.

<u>Broadway</u>

This is one of the principal business thoroughfares of NYC, extending in a generally north-south direction. It extends 27 km to the city's northern boundary in the Bronx. In lower Manhattan, where it passes through the financial district, Broadway is the traditional route over which national heroes and distinguished guests are escorted. Ambulance trolleys are generally barred from the route. There are exceptions made, however.

18

we are all in the gutter

Rhue rhue roooel.

An empty can rolls past on the sidewalk. I can read the ingredients clearly, the word <u>aspartame</u> aspartame aspartame rolling over and over ... spinning away from me ... and away from the sun tilted at an angle of $23^{1}/_{2}$ degrees.

This is a flashback. I am sure of it. It is due to some temporal distortion or whatever it is Captain Kirk would say. He would ham it up a lot more though.

<u>aspartame</u>
Consists of two amino acids, aspartic acid and phenylalanine. Foods containing this substance must be labelled to notify individuals with phenylketonuria, a rare disease that requires control of dietary phenylalanine. A lot of soft drinks contain this ... whereas very few hard drinks do ... the conclusions are yours for the making. ·

Spinning bodies on bigger spinning bodies on even bigger bodies . . . and the wheels of the train . . . the Universal Clock ticks on another <u>second</u> exploding us out further into the Unknown . . . they say the galaxy is still exploding outwards because it is showing a shift to the red end of the spectrum which means it is still moving away from us . . . thanks to that nice Mr Doppler. Where would we be without him?

My laptop has bounced on the ground and is now lying open in front of me. The CD-ROM drive is whirring and making an awful racket. It keeps pumping up pages from a CD encyclopaedia that I had in it . . . and spewing random pages from the Internet. I really wish I had not dropped it.

I really wish I was not lying on the ground.

I really wish I had listened to my mother and not gotten in with the corner boys.

My laptop computer is an AST Ascentia M-Series with 80 Mb of RAM. Aficionados would be impressed.

It is all 1's and 0's to me.

<u>second</u>

The Earth is turning too slowly. This is true. Be afraid, be very afraid. One leap second is sometimes added at midnight GMT to allow atomic clocks to be re-synchronized with astronomical time. Friction from winds and tides and changes in the Earth's core all contribute to slowing the Earth's rotation, which is measured astronomically by reference to the position of the stars. The Earth takes longer by one or two milliseconds to rotate on its axis in February than in August. This change affects everything that is synchronized by satellites . . .

air traffic, TV, laptop computers etc ... scientists must account for the discrepancy because the cumulative effect would mean that over a century a clock would gain several minutes. And who gives a flying fuck?

I suppose I need to explain things at this point. You see I was waiting on the street corner when the shots rang out ... three in all but you can never be sure ... I know how Kennedy must have felt. Becky was in the shop getting smokes. I used to call her my angel from St Paul ... that's twee but she liked it.

We met in Molly Blooms over on Third Avenue. Nice place ... but full of Micks. She got me into the coke scene ... or at least introduced me to Dub who got me into the coke scene. Dub thinks he is the Irish Mafia ... actually he is the Irish Mafia.

With my college background ... electronics ... sums and wires ... he thought I was the man for the job. Oh, I never delivered bags of shit for him or cut the crap up ... no, no, that was for the Seans and Brendans of this world ... well, actually that's the way it was at the start but eventually you end up doing whatever Dub wants you to do. He has this way of persuading people.

I thought I was destined for greater things ... Dub gave me the laptop and all his accounts and transactions and shit were on it ... he never wrote anything down and that was his way ... he was totally fucked up in the head but that was his way and he had a gun and lots of people at his disposal who would break bones in your body so he more or less had his way and that was that.

This is the background ... bear with me ... I was lying on the ground and the freezing cold sidewalk was only being warmed up by my blood trickling down the side of the road so forgive me if it doesn't make much sense. A lot of it doesn't make much sense to me either.

It had been snowing earlier and I always got excited by that coz it usually meant no school the next day back home. Ireland closes for the day when it snows.

The laptop was only inches from my face and it kept churning out useless shite from the encyclopaedia CD and the Internet pages cached or maybe it was online over the cell phone link . . . I don't know.

Dub used to think I was his clever man . . . not the muscle like the others which is just as well because I had no muscles like the others and wouldn't know what to do with them if I had. He would ask me questions out of the blue in the bar or in his apartment while I was doing his accounts like what is the capital of Paraguay and he would be fascinated by how I would be able to answer him . . . oblivious to the whirring of the CD-ROM drive or me nonchalantly surfing the net for the answer. Gobshite . . . God bless him.

I don't know where the shots came from exactly . . . someone someday with a little cine camera might prove what really happened but for now it's a joyful and sorrowful mystery. And they will show the grainy movie again and again and come to the conclusion that I was not shot but that I was hit by a bizarre sequence of tiny meteors that just happened to be shaped like bullets . . . some physics ·professor from Yale will explain the mathematics of this and then they will get Ed the Drunk as a witness to say he was on the street corner and he saw everything . . . burp . . . and burp . . . if they paid him he would see it all again . . . burp.

A car pulled up, the door opened and then I saw three feet ... four of them in fact ... two in sneakers with bubbles of pumped-up air ... expensive. The others in boots ... brown leather with a faded bull ... two clouds of snort emanate from its nostrils. Scary stuff. Glad I have no red on me ... except the blood but that came later and bulls are colour-blind anyways ... a trickle from the corner of my mouth rolled toward my left eye ... glad it was not the right one ... much prefer my right eye ... everyone says it ... you've a nicer right eye than a left one Shem.

Down there ... there was a siren. The four feet make a move ... jump back in the car and screech away. They do not take the bag of drugs which leads me to suspect they didn't know about them. This was a hired killing, not a robbery.

I was alone.

The siren was getting nearer. I wished that a <u>yellow cab</u> would appear out of nowhere ... just like in the movies. The driver would open the door for me ... royal treatment.

- Queens. Is it all right to take the laptop?
- You'll have to pay extra.
- No problem. Just get me the hell out of here.

His name would be Guptha ... something like that ... whatever. Moustache like one of those seagulls you'd draw as a kid ... with black crayons and yellow for the sun. Spinning sun. 23$\frac{1}{2}$ degrees.

<u>yellow cab</u>
Yellow cab drivers are a well-recognised sub-species and David Attenborough would have made a documentary about them if it was not for the extreme danger involved in approaching these

people. They have their own language, customs, politics and culture . . . the culture bit is somewhat misleading . . . it is more like a yoghurt culture that grows under the hand rails in the back of most cabs. It is not inherently dangerous but if the proper tip or gratuity is not given the driver can trigger a bio-mechanism, which will cause the culture to activate and become potent . . . this develops into what is commonly known as Yellow Cab Fever.

The number to ring for information about lost luggage, complaints on fare rates or symptoms of Yellow Cab Fever is 800–NYC–TAXI.

Forgive me, this is all in flashback and it is a mite confusing but I seem to think I was in that yellow cab when perhaps I was not.

I roll sideways . . . Guptha thinks I'm going to be sick . . . tirade of Indian . . . maybe a prayer . . . Shiva Shiva Ima believa anda Illa believa youa ifa Ia cana. Micky Dolenz was it? . . . where is he now? . . . and the other guy with the stupid hat . . . never remember his name. The Monkees. I laugh.

Over Queensboro Bridge now . . . lights twinkling behind me double up in the glass. Rear window heater is a grid guiding me home to Rongagen IV in the Paxo Quadrant. My real home. Lieutenant Worf looking sternly at me from over his row of buttons and flashing LEDs . . . half of the Wicklow Mountains on his forehead.

- Captain Picard . . . Ensign Shem looks decidedly unwell . . . perhaps he is unfit to be carrying out important duties on the bridge?

Queensboro Bridge Worf you fool . . . tell the Captain the truth goddammit.

- Very good Worf, take him down to Holodeck Two. Program in some suitable scenario for him and return at once. I would suggest New York City . . . United States of America . . . Earth circa 2001 . . . without the music . . . oh and make sure he has some of the local currency with him. He'll need it.
- Aye Captain.

Guptha hasn't heard a word of this . . . or else he chooses not to. Home man and don't spare the horses. Chicken Vindaloo and hold the chips. I laugh . . . it's absolutely fucking hilarious. Brendan Grace . . . two number thuurty three's and hold the rice . . . crowd in the Burlington Hotel, Dublin breaking their shite laughing and I a waiter . . . I a waiter . . . I waiter . . . I robot . . . four pints of warm Heineken with the bar staff after the maddening crowd has gone home. I used to clean up the streamers and corks and flaccid party hats. Happy hour in the happy house. Three umbrellas, two scarves and a wallet. The detritus. Share the spoils among us.

- *Cá bhfuil oifig an phoist?*[11]

Guptha looks askance.

- Do you know where the post office is? . . . Jasus, don't you know any Irish . . . what did they teach you back in Bombay High or wherever you went . . . where's your fucking green card man?

Another barrage of abuse . . . lost on me . . . Noam Chomsky give me a call . . . must check out www.indian-language.com . . . not now though . . . too incoherent and the laptop's battery will probably die soon anyways . . . see if the guy is calling me a bollix or not . . . got his license number memorised . . . 8128 . . . a perfect number . . .

[11] Where is the post office?

<u>Fermat's Last Theorem</u> thingimebòb/ . . . follow Guptha around for weeks and then blow his brains out one rainy night in the city. Dub would do it for nothing . . . a pleasure . . . all part of the service. All sing along now . . . and another cabby died tonight, oh dear.

<u>Fermat's Last Theorem</u>

This famous theorem which has led to important discoveries in algebra and analysis. It was proposed by the French mathematician Pierre de Fermat (1601–65) that when the Pythagorean theorem is altered to read $a^n + b^n = c^n$, the new equation cannot be solved in integers for any value of n greater than 2. That is, no set of positive integers a, b, and c can be found to satisfy, for example, the equation $a^3 + b^3 = c^3$ or $a^4 + b^4 = c^4$. Try this for yourselves, as homework, with various values of a, b and c.

Fermat said he wrote the solution in the back of the book but no one ever found it. In 1994 Andrew Wiles solved the theorem using really hard sums that Fermat could not have known about at the time, the spoofing bastard.

Fermat had originally said he had a proof but there wasn't room in the margins and it was never found anywhere else. I tried that once in a chemistry exam and then later burst a pen all over the pages of my script and wrote a note explaining the accident and beseeching the examiner to be lenient and understanding. I failed and hated anything to do with chemistry ever since . . . except maybe the chemistry between Becky and myself, which is a separate thing altogether.

Queens Boulevard now ... in Guptha's taxi ... dreaming of White Castles' mini-burgers and fries ... you really don't know unless you have tried them ... twenty miniature burgers served by miniature people ... and picture yourself in a boat on a river with tangerine trees ... lost that album at a party once in Ranelagh ... some biker heads turned up and robbed a load of my stuff. Always hated bikers until I got a bike of my own, then it was cool.

An urgent e-mail zaps onto the laptop screen ... it's from the planet Rongagen, in the Paxo Quadrant.

To: shem@nyc.earth
From: rongagen@paxo.iv
Subject: NOT SAFE
Shem
Do not enter burger place called White Castles ... not safe, repeat ... NOT SAFE ... return home and drink lots of water and take a dissolvable <u>vitamin C</u> tablet IMMEDIATELY ... we need you to infiltrate the Empire State Building tomorrow and you will need a clear head.
Reply ASAP
Regards
Billy

I delete it ... sorry I know it's rude but they don't know how hungry I actually am ... and that's not a word of a lie. Must be something to do with all my insides slipping out like that. Plenty of room left for burgers and things.

Guptha keeps looking nervously in the mirror to check I'm not leaking onto his upholstery. He'll be ranting about the bloody Irish on his website later.

<u>vitamin C</u>

This well-known vitamin, ascorbic acid, is important in the formation and maintenance of collagen, the protein that supports many body structures and plays a major role in the formation of bones and teeth. It also enhances the absorption of iron from foods of vegetable origin. And here's another thing . . . it tastes good.

Scurvy is the classic manifestation of severe ascorbic acid deficiency. Assertions that massive doses of ascorbic acid prevent colds and influenza have not been borne out by carefully controlled experiments. In other experiments, however, ascorbic acid has been shown to prevent the formation of nitrosamines . . . compounds found to produce tumours in laboratory animals and possibly also in humans. The body cannot store the vitamin so any surplus is merely peed out of the system. So you have to run into the draughty toilets in the subway station and then you catch a cold and you take more vitamin C and then you have to . . . the cycle goes on.

Vitamin C is worshipped by a tribe of Native American Indians in Idaho, in their song, 'I danced and had oranges'.

The Queensboro bridge starts to buckle . . . Guptha seems unperturbed by this. I panic. Scenes from a physics class many moons ago . . . some bridge in <u>Tacoma</u> . . . hit its resonance one day . . . steady winds and the whole thing oscillated like an accordion . . . and he who pays the piper . . . collapses after about five hours . . . concrete folding like crepe paper. Triumph of elements over man.

Stop the fucking cab Guptha . . . I want to get out here
. . . he just laughs like something out of an early Bond
movie . . . oh, oh he must be a baddie so . . . shrouds of black
cloud stream in through the window caressing and
touching me . . . Guptha is laughing . . . teeth of rhinoceros
ivory . . . worth a fortune to hunters. Must tell Dub.

Tacoma

Okay now listen to this . . . in 1940 the Tacoma
Narrows Bridge in Washington, a particularly
narrow and flexible suspension bridge 850 m long
was destroyed by a steady wind blowing at forty-
two miles per hour for about seventy minutes. Up
and down oscillations of the bridge, travelling like a
sine wave along the length of the roadway, had been
noticed since its construction . . . so much so that
the bridge had been nicknamed 'Galloping Gertie'.
This is true.

These oscillations were caused by winds blowing
at right angles to the bridge which, as the flexible
roadway moved up and down, hit the bridge
alternatively from below and from above, naturally
in resonance with the period of the bridge
oscillations.

The name Tacoma is derived from the Native
American term for Mount Rainier, which is visible
from the city. Some Native American Indians
probably sold this mountain for $24 and a slice of
pecan pie.

Little Bro Little Bro . . . where the fuck are you? My little
brother running to my aid as I dangle from a frail branch

over the sewer of a river down at the back of our house.
Clasps my hand just before the bough breaks. Oh Little Bro
mo chroí[12] where are you now?

The clouds get thicker . . . can't breathe . . . GUPTHA
raps the Plexiglas shield between us . . . laughing . . . so
that's the plan eh? . . . trying to suffocate me and there was
me secure in the knowledge that the Irish were meant to
drown come That Day . . . I thought that was our destiny
. . . obviously Shiva has other ideas . . . she would do,
wouldn't she.

The smoke is so thick that I pass out but I wake up
again hearing Guptha tapping on the glass.

– Six dollars twenty.

– After all the abuse? Are you serious?

I throw the money through the front window. It's a ten.
I have no change . . . he speeds off before I can think . . .
8128 . . . I got your number you bastard.

I can see him later at Dunkin's drinking 79 cents take-
out coffee . . . bragging to the other cabbies and flashing
those pearly whites . . . four dollar tip and make no mistake.

❑ GUPTHA

The TV at the end of the bed is showing *The Simpsons*
. . . well sort of. The cab driver is now Apu and I am
Homer. The drawing is quite good. I am in the process of
stealing some doughnuts from a shop that looks
remarkably like one in Camden Street, Dublin near where
I used to go to school . . . where we used to steal the Swiss
Rolls. But these are minor details. Guptha catches me.

– Oh Mister Shem, this is not good. You Irish people are
    always taking things from the poorer and more

12 My heart. Used as a term of endearment.

ethnically challenged Indian community. Please refrain from doing so:

Chief Wiggam bursts in the door and shoots me three times and I fall to the ground. Instead of blood coming out it is mint-flavoured slurpy but Guptha is unimpressed.

- Oh Chief Wiggam . . . who is going to pay for the cleaning and sterilising of my shop floor?
- Eh, we'll sort it Guptha . . . now if no one is going to be using that slurpy I wouldn't mind taking it.
- Please be my guest Chief . . . any man who can protect me from those Irish persons is a true patriot and worthy of the free things.
- Great Guptha . . . does that include doughnuts?
- No, they are three for a dollar plus taxes. ❑

19

midnight, silence and memories

Lying on the sidewalk the night starts to drift back to me like a dripping tap.

Drip drip drip.

A club . . . the music pushing into my ribs . . . drum and bass . . . drum and bass . . . drum and bass . . . and me out there dancing like I was a voodoo doll in a pin factory . . . you'd like that one Emerald Eddie . . . a comedian who used to do the Irish circuit in New York . . . but maybe not . . . voodoo doll in a . . . pinprick . . . pinprick, pinprick . . . ehh ahh iiiii oooohhh you you you.

Memories slip back . . . summers in green fields . . . the smell of old battles . . . and they died for us . . . with their pikes and their bombs and their bombs and their bombs . . . Little Bro is explaining something to me . . . something he's just learned in history class . . . and their pikes and their bombs and their bombs and their bombs and their bombs . . . Snarl at the jukebox . . . suddenly flashbacked to Bloom's . . . corner of 33rd and Third . . . that's tuurty turd and turd . . . good old Brendan. Grace . . . my best Dublin accent not forsaking me now . . . kick the damned juke twice . . . come on, I put in a dollar . . . face from a CD cover smiling back at me . . . looks like Guptha the yellow cab driver with those pearly whites.

Eamonn the bar owner scowling at me . . .

- You wouldn't do that in your own place you little fucker . . . take it easy there now, Shem. Stop acting the fucker. Here have one on me and then go home and sleep it off.

He pours me a large one . . . fuck that hurts . . . the heat at the back of my throat . . . blade swallower . . . must introduce myself to the crowd . . . do my Riverdance and fall into a group of businessmen out scoring some *sneachta*.

Pardon me, gentlemen, but I was dancing my way to the men's room and you just had your feet all over the place . . . Eamonn casting a watchful eye over me as I try to do my best to keep upright . . . more threatening that way . . . Desmond Morris . . . Chapter Three . . . body language . . . say something Desmond . . . say something that will get me out of this mess.

I'm nervous. I have a meeting, a drop, a rendezvous, a fucking deal that could blow up in my face. If it goes wrong, bye bye Shem, leave your money on the bar and we'll raise one to you. Play your favourite song on the juke . . . all sing along as your cortege passes by . . .

- And the boys in the NYPD choir were singing Galway Bay . . .

Guptha has left me off at the wrong place however . . . this isn't Molly's . . . hey, what's going on here? . . . I wanted to burst through the doors heave myself up on the bar . . .

do my party piece from Riverdance and watch them all clap and applaud.

- Go on, Shem, you mad thing.
- Jesus, your man Shem's an awful fucker, look at the cut of him.
- Hey Shem, you've sprung a leak, did you know that?
- Get down off my bar now Shem . . . ah look, there's bits of your guts falling into people's drink . . . I can't be having that.
- Jesus, Eamonn, chill out man.

I'm now at a very desolate place . . . a street corner. A dog barks. I can understand it . . . funny I could never speak dog before . . . fringe benefit of being near death I suppose. The dog is saying . . . 'There's Shem . . . you know the guy from Ireland . . . he's a mad fucker with a few on him . . . you wouldn't have a bag of *sneachta* on you by any chance . . . its just me and some of the bitches were thinking of having an all-night barking session.'

There is a door slightly ajar. An intense light seeps out. I am drawn inexorably towards it. I step through it and find myself back on Dun Laoghaire Pier holding my father's hand again. He is promising me a packet of sweets if I'm a good boy. The wind is quite impressive . . . whipping up white horses in a gallop across Dublin Bay . . . he brings me to a thing that looks like a sundial where you can squint up against the metal and stone and see where the two church spires actually blend into one . . . parallax and religion mixing it a bit.

A bee buzzes by and momentarily catches my attention. Rimsky-Korsakov at neg 60 dBs . . . I try to refocus on the spires but I'm now sitting on the edge of the Grand Canyon, a bottle of Coors Lite resting perilously on the precipice. I can't speak . . . I'm absolutely overwhelmed by the view. I wish my father was with me . . . but he is not.

Purples and browns cascade across the rock face. It's like in one of those time-lapse movies . . . *Koyaanisqatsi* . . . the clouds racing overhead, then night, then daybreak, then noon . . . the colours in sympathy. Then night again and I'm back in New York . . . it is New Year's Eve and we are all in Molly's . . . the entire place is frozen still, motionless . . . except me . . . I'm at the juke with a grimy George Washington that I somehow manage to feed into the slot . . . I think of one of Emerald Eddie's jokes about the gynaecologist that could wallpaper your hallway through the letter box.

I hit F7 and the whole place springs to life and starts to sing . . .

It was Christmas Eve babe,
In the drunk tank
An old man says to me . . .

All the faces flush with Eamonn's hot whiskey. We all sing along . . . embracing and smiling . . . the desperate longing of collective wanting to be back home.

Exiles in ecstasy. Some were on coke but most of them were on ecstasy.

Rimsky-Korsakov

Nikolai Andreyevich Rimsky-Korsakov (1844-1908), Russian composer and musical theorist, one of the greatest composers of the Russian nationalist school, a great master of orchestration and without a doubt one of the coolest names in classical music.

Born on 18th March 1844, in Tikhvin, near Novgorod. He studied piano as a child as opposed to nuclear physics. In 1856 he was enrolled at the Naval Academy at St Petersburg but continued his musical studies. He was the dominant figure of a group of young, nationally conscious Russian composers including Modest Mussorgsky and Aleksandr Borodin, who probably have the second and third coolest names ever. No contest.

I'm flashbacked into the back of a yellow cab with Becky. She's cutting up a bag of *sneachta* with a credit card. I'm tapping the roof loudly. It's hot and sticky. She smiles as I kick the rhythm up a notch ... it is the theme music from *The Late Late Show* ... she cops it ... she has never actually seen it but I've told her all about it.

　　- Ladies and Gentlemen ... to whom it may concern this is *The Late Late Show*.

Guptha driving ... tilts his turban slightly at 23$\frac{1}{2}$ degrees. I am annoying him I think.

　　- And here is your host ... Turban Byrne.

Becky bursts out laughing. There is no reply from Guptha. We get out at 32nd and Third. We're to meet the others close by. Do the deal and then off again. Becky goes into a shop to buy some smokes. I hear the car pulling up behind me.

The three shots surprise me. Shit, someone must have been shot ... another drive-by shooting. I think about Becky in the shop ... is it a robbery? It's nearly a minute before I feel a tingling sensation in my stomach. It's like I have just run for miles and miles and I'm sweating like a bastard. The blood looks so stupid. It's purple not red ...

all those ridiculous movies. I'm on the ground. Amazingly alert ... like I've taken a shitload of speed ... and out of the corner of my eye, exactly 90 degrees away, I see Becky ... running towards me ... but she's five or six miles away ... in silhouette down a tunnel.

The blood on the ground has traced out a perfect 3-D map of Italy. I can pick out the cities and the mountains so clearly. There's Rome ... Rimini ... <u>San Marino</u>. Becky is holding me now ... God, what a fast runner she is ... I must make a note of that ... good thing to know ... here Becky, deliver this package to Boston for me ... you've got an hour ... bring me back a Hero on the way. Paul Revere is a fag.

She runs off again ... she is screaming ... Jesus Becky, I only asked for a Hero.

Inside the ambulance they have me wired up ... my chest looks like an explosion in a hi-fi store. I hand the paramedic an oxygen mask. It's the least I can do.

– Thanks ... but who let you in here?

– No one.

– Okay but you gotta be quiet.

– I promise.

– This guy is in pretty bad shape.

– Is he going to make it?

– Don't know yet ... lost a lot of blood.

– It actually looks red in the artificial light inside.

– Everyone says that.

– Oh, I see.

<u>San Marino</u>

This tiny republic should not really exist. Hod was musing over a 3-D map of Europe, trying to decide what to put where ... rivers, mountains and such. He was trying to think what he could do to make

Italy look even more ludicrous. He was mulling over
the map when a small piece of beetroot fell from
the sandwich he was chomping. Two angels
swooped and immediately removed the vegetable
debris. But the damage was done and no one, not
even the Mighty Hod, can remove beetroot stains.
So the small blob stayed and he decided to call it
San Marino, which happened to be the brand name
of his favourite beetroot.

This is true.

Becky is crying . . . holding my hand. Her mascara is
running . . . she has looked better.

She is cradling my laptop in her lap, which justifies its
name. A little tear drops onto the lid. It runs off
immediately. I hope it doesn't get into the circuitry
because I know someone who ruined their laptop by
crying on it because the salty water caused awful hassle.

I wish Becky wouldn't cry.

I wish I wasn't bleeding.

I wish it had all been different.

I wish I . . .

- Sorry Shem, but your three wishes are up.

- Oh, and who are you?

- I am the Keeper of Wishes.

The title sounds very grand but there's that Old Black
Man standing beside me on the pavement. I thought it
would be some sort of a genie or whatever. He looks
genuinely concerned which troubles me somewhat.

- I see . . . well is it possible to change one of them?

- Sorry . . . no changes are allowed after the fact.

- Okay . . . well do they have to be carried out now
then?

He is frowning and I know this is not good.

- Maybe if I just . . .
- Okay Shem, that's it . . . we don't have to put up with this . . . why don't we just cancel the whole thing and leave everything as it is.
- Okay . . . sorry . . . but can Becky have a wish at least?
- Yes . . . I don't see why not.

And Becky in that instant of looking at me on the ground, and wishing she was somewhere else sees the web page from Kylemore Abbey on the laptop screen and she makes a wish and the Old Black Man nods and that is that.

20

funny guy Emerald Eddie

It is troubling me that all these people are coming up
alongside the trolley. I wish they would just fuck off and
leave me to enjoy the saline and drift off for a bit of a kip
but not a bit of it. And just when you least expect to be
cheered up along comes Emerald Eddie. Eddie is about
fifty-five and he's been here since The Famine . . . that's
usually his opening line. He does weddings, funerals but
not Bar Mitzvahs and also a regular Thursday night slot in
Ashton's down off Second Avenue . . . he is a chain smoker,
probably drinks too much and wears a green jacket all the
time. He was told two years ago that he only had a year to
live and he took this very seriously so he lived to the hilt
. . . even cultivating a heavy cocaine habit fed by Dub . . .
which probably helped him to live longer or at least feel
like he did . . .

He is alongside me now and he sits up on the end of
the bed.

- Shem' . . . would you like a quick snort?

179

- No thanks Eddie ... it's that stuff has me like this in the first place.
- You look like three of your ex-girlfriends all found out about Becky at the same time.
- That is true Eddie.
- I heard Becky hasn't touched a drop since she had that blackout ... and I hear she's going out with him again next week!
- Jesus, that's a funny one Eddie.
- You heard the one about the *fear dubh* who went to the doctor and when he went home to his wife he had bought a new suit and shoes and a cane and gloves and his wife was all worried and she was also surprised to see him dressed up so because he worked in KFC and he earned fucking nothing and the wife asked him why he was dressed up so well and he says that the doctor told him he was impoootent and if he was impoootent then he better dress impoootent. That's a good one Shem, do you like that one? Wha?

And he knocks me in the arm to reaffirm the question ... do you like that one? ... and he lights a smoke and with his other hand manages to shovel a key full of coke up his flaring nostrils. He has been doing so much coke that one of his nostrils has actually collapsed and he now looks like one of the witches from *Macbeth* and he smells like one of them as well. He should not smoke next to me but he knows I'm fucked anyways and if you're going to go then you are going to go.

- Come 'ere Shem, I have another one for you ... what do you call a Black woman after seven abortions? ...

A crime prevention officer ... do you like that one, Shem? Wha?

Eddie thinks racist jokes are hilarious and he has hundreds of them stored away in the various ethnic compartments of his brain. There is not a race or nationality which he has not got some vulgar joke about. Except maybe some of the newer nations. He doesn't keep up with current affairs so some of the Eastern European countries are safe for a while longer.

I have managed to wiggle my bum slightly and the Klinowitz trolley has reacted favourably ... Emerald Eddie falls off and seems to disappear into a pothole but as I crane around I can see him extricating himself and shouting after me ...

- But I have the whole Jewish set to do as well ...
  come back Shem ... they're great, you're gonna love
  'em ... come back.

But he is Dopplered.

First night I met Eddie I was with Dub. Funny Guy Eddie was telling Dub how he was dying and Dub gave him some coke in a gesture that was bordering on evangelical. Then a few days later Funny Guy Eddie again in Ashton's cadging Dub for more and this time there was money involved. Dub had another little fool in his pocket and me there grinning and smiling like I was his right-hand man.

And Eddie setting me up in front of Dub and the whole lot of them conspiring with his Nixon joke ... this was the Nixon conspiracy first hand.

So when Nixon was in office and his wife ... eh ... now what was her name again? ...

... And the others all keeping stum around the table and me, like the fool that I was, jumping in and saying ...

- Eh I think it was Pat ...
- Pat, Pat ... Pat Nixon ... that's it Shem ... Jasus Dub he's a clever one, you'd want to keep an eye on him ... and anyway Pat Nixon was so bored with ... Jasus what's her husband's name again? ...
- Richard Milhous ...
- Jasus Dub, this guy is sharp ... and anyway she was so bored with Nixon that she ended up spread-eagled on the White House carpet with Nixon's Foreign Minister ... Henry ... Henry ... eh ... Henry ...
- Kissinger ...
- Oh, no ... he was fucking her all right.

And the others guffaw and it takes me a second to get it and there is nothing to do but laugh along with them and Eddie is ecstatic and I feel like dying.

Here is a little advice from a guy on a trolley with three gunshots in his belly ... this is it ... are you writing this down? ... Never wish you were dead ... take it from me ... it may just come true.

Eddie had another joke which he liked to tell at every given moment.

- Did you hear this one Shem? ... A Canadian, a Yank and an Irishman were in a bar and they were having their pints of beer and three flies come in and land in each one of them and the Yank kicks up a big fuss with the barman and demands a new drink and the Canadian just gently brushes the fly away and continues drinking without saying anything and the Irish guy picks up the fly, grabs it by the throat and shouts, 'Spit it out you little bastard, spit it out' ... funny that one wha? Did you get that one Shem, wha?

Then the cough and the cocaine snort and he nearly on death's door.

Emerald Eddie will die on Christmas Day in the year 2002 while telling a very funny joke. The joke starts like this . . . 'There were these three Irish guys who run for President of the United States and the first one says to the TV interviewer . . . ', but unfortunately he never gets to tell the punch line.
  – *Cadumpbff*

It would be very nice if someone came along and changed the sheets sometime. You tend to leak a lot and I don't just mean blood. I have tried the call bell many times but the wrong people keep showing up and that is not good so it isn't. If Santos was around I could ask him but he is not and so I cannot. But then again if he was around I wouldn't need new sheets in the first place.

Altogether now . . . bawdin eyelomee dimi go moran bawdin eyelomee dimi go day . . . Dub singing the only bit of half Irish that he only half knew and everyone singing along like the national anthem at football matches and the camera closes up on the English players with the Irish grandparents and they're mouthing 'Knees up Mother Brown'. Hour On Da Veen as Dub calls the national anthem and he told this to Emerald Eddie who nearly died laughing . . . and then he claps Dub on the back and asks him if he has any *sneachta*.

Hour On Da Veen.

21

on the subway

Garish.

The colours on the poster.

DR ZINKMOR WILL CLEAN UP YOUR SKIN
OPEN 7 DAYS
WE NEVER CLOSE OUR DOORS –
WE ONLY CLOSE YOUR PORES
CALL US NOW!
800–SKIN-CARE

This process may, in certain non-specified cases, actually worsen as well as improve your skin. Dr Zinkmor or any of his employees accept no blame or claims of litigation against themselves for any services provided or quoted for. Except in the state of Nebraska where claimants may file suit for malpractice or harassment charges. All calls to the above number are recorded and you may receive unsolicited calls, mail, e-mail or other such offers as are deemed of interest to you. You may opt out of these lists if you provide three signed copies of a letter requesting your wish to be removed from same and these letters must be signed by a senator, state governor or President of the United States of America. Reading this notice constitutes an eyeball agreement between the two parties.

The subway carriage rocks me gently. Rhythmic. Pulsing. Iron tracks with soiled cages darting all over the sprawling city . . . New York City . . . NYC . . . that's what they call it . . . that's what's embroidered badly on my hat. $5 from the guy on the corner . . . near the guy selling the hot pecans . . . over from the guy selling the umbrellas . . . $4 . . . you got change.

I look at Dr Zinkmor. Clear, pallid, surgical skin. Looks like a right prick. Sort of guy would appear on Oprah, tell us about the hidden pustules of puss in the fleshy bits of our ear lobes . . . waiting to explode. Waiting, mind you. And Oprah nodding.

– Hmmm, yes . . . hmmm . . . very interesting Doctor.

I nod off. Wake. Nod off. Wake. A rhythm. A sine wave. Sinusoids.

– Can you help me Doc? . . . I'm having terrible trouble with my sinusoids.

Then awake for good. It's so fucking cold. Foggy breath inside the train. At least when I get to Pallenski's the kitchen will be warm. That's why all the Chinks become cooks . . . clever people.

I have the remnants of a $40 bag in my pocket. Keep it for the break. Later. Halfway through the shift. Pick-me-up. Never get through the shift otherwise.

Carter, longest serving bartender in the city . . . always greets me in the same way. 'Hey Shame you're late.' Thinks this is hilarious. Always laughing his fat head off . . . Hey Shame do this and Hey Shame do that.

Big Polish prick. Used to be called Cartenski but thought Carter was better. Car nearly ran him over on his first day in America and him staring up at the Empire State Building.

We call him Can't Cook Carter . . . not to his face though . . . bit of a reputation . . . four gold caps for a smile and fists that could pummel metal.

The subway carriage shudders and jolts. I fall into the tramp beside me. She is holding a large bag of onions. Shit. The smell will be in my jacket for weeks. Onions. You have to learn this early on over here. Especially on the subway. Tramps = Onions, Winos = Cabbage, Druggies = Marlboros, the real ones not those poxy Light ones. Her smell is permeating the fibre of my sleeve, through the denim shirt and settling like dew on the hairs of my forearm. Fuck. Better scrub hard in the kitchen.

I finger the small cellophane bag in my pocket. Last night's detritus. My powder . . . all mine. Maybe enough for two regular lines . . . or one big one. That's the way I prefer it. Not the back-of-the-key rubbish like some of the others. One big J Edgar Hoover and get it into you. Good man.

A guy gets on at Penn Station . . . a snake wrapped around his neck. Nobody looks. I'm wearing my shades. November. A little trick Jimmy Rubber taught me.

    – All the fucking *fear dubhs* stare at you . . . wear a pair
      of shades and you can ogle at who you like.

    – Yes Jimmy.

    – Are you listening to me?

- Yes I am Jimmy.
- That's the trouble with some of you young fellas that come over here . . . you don't listen to us that have spent lifetimes here.
- Yes Jimmy.
- And don't get involved in any of that nose candy stuff either . . . there's too many of your compatriots who have gone down into the snowy valley and never come up, if you get my drift.
- I do Jimmy.

Jimmy pulling on the ubiquitous smoke hanging out of the left-hand side of his mouth . . . bobbing up and down like a magic wand. He has been here for thirty years and he says he is going back home. When you ask him where in Ireland he is from he always laughs and says that you should never expect a man to remember such a thing.

- Never look anyone in the face on the subway. That's the rule Shem, that's the rule.
- Cheers Jimmy, you washed-up no hope fucking drunk.
- Not cool Shem, not kosher, not good, not advisable.
- Yeah sure Jimmy. Give him a Jemmie there Sean.

The snake moves. It scares the shite out of me . . . but thank God it's not real . . . it's a tattoo, all around his neck and throat. Undulates with each swallow. Hiss. Looks Germanic . . . Herman Hiss. I can feel a bead of sweat on my forehead. I know it's there. It's probably going to wait there forever . . . little capillary pressures holding it against reason to a wrinkle . . . <u>surface tension</u> . . . zoom in real close . . . little model of Santa on his sleigh and the snow all around . . . had one just like that as a kid . . . shake it up and watch it

snow ... then the drop rolls down the left side of my face
... hangs on to my chin for dear life ... then plonk ... gone
... it makes an almighty crash on the floor of the carriage
but no one notices ... no one looks around ... bastards
... here I am leaking away and not one of them takes any
heed.

surface tension

A condition existing at the free surface of a liquid,
resembling the properties of an elastic skin under
tension. The tension is the result of intermolecular
forces exerting an unbalanced inward pull on the
individual surface molecules; this is reflected in the
considerable curvature at those edges where the
liquid is in contact with the wall of a vessel.

Now close your eyes and repeat all that.

I blink behind the black glasses. Must stop taking those Es
Becky keeps getting for me. Think she gets them from Dub
but where the fuck does he get them? Some Turkish guy
with a big melting pot of ingredients in a basement
somewhere ... a little bit of this and a little bit of that.

- Stop taking the drugs young man.
- Thanks for the advice Jimmy ... why the fuck did you
  stay anyway?
- Built the railroads over here you know.
- Really Jimmy? Sean, give him a beer as well, will you?
- Everyone flies now of course .... don't want an old
  workhorse like me.
- Sure Jimmy, here go play a tune or something.

Train moves smoothly now. Forward a lot. And side to side
a little. Perfect side to side, in fact. My body responds ... it

is calming. Simple harmonic ·motion. Tracing out sine waves across the barren Manhattan scrub rock . . . seen from above . . . $y = \sin (wt + k)$ . . . order among all that chaos.

I try to do a quick calculation . . . train rocks me side to side in two seconds . . . that's half a hertz . . . wow . . . half a hertz . . . this city really rocks baby.

The woman tramp beside me spits . . . it lands just beside my sweat drop and I panic that they might mix together and form some hideous primordial soup . . . how would I explain to Mother? . . . she's not Catholic but well you know about bodily fluids that pass in the night . . . and she's a really nice person . . . and wait till you meet her family.

My grandmother always told her daughters never to have more than three kids because she had heard that every fourth child born in the world was Chinese. Emerald Eddie.

I fix my hat . . . my woollen hat . . . warm . . . very warm . . . head like a piece of toast. And tighten my scarf . . . Guinness badly embroidered on it . . . present from the sister when she came over last time for a visit. Scarf, gloves and tee-shirt with logo. Crunchies, crisps and Bewley's chocolates. Krochnick's Store on Queens and 47th Street sells all that shit. I didn't have the heart to tell her.

Her boyfriend produced a bottle of Jameson like it was the lifeblood of Ireland. But I was suitably ohhing and ahhing. Sister introducing her new beau. Wear the sibling smile. And the whiskey was good. Empty bottle used as a doorstop now, three-quarters full of dimes . . . phone bill for a rainy day . . . well, I won't be calling anyone when the sun is splitting the stones.

Onion beside me shuffles in her seat. Thigh touches

mine. Fuck sake. In the bath for an hour tonight. These
fucking subways. Shudder again. Carriage rocks . . . over
tracks that have cambered due to the cold . . . two metals
at slightly different temperatures . . . <u>piezoelectric effect</u>
. . . sparks . . . yippie . . . Thanksgiving again . . . extra tips.
Light in the carriage flickers . . . then again . . . then another,
slower shudder.

Then suddenly nothing . . . blackness . . . powerless.
Voice over the PA . . . crackling . . . 'hit . . . something . . .
delay.' Shit. Onion starts to rock beside me . . . humming a
mantra . . . check my wallet. Safe. Inside pocket.

<u>piezoelectric effect</u>
This is the appearance of an electric potential across
certain faces of a crystal when it is subjected to
mechanical pressure. Conversely, when an electric
field is applied on certain faces of the crystal, the
crystal undergoes mechanical distortion. Pierre
Curie and his brother Jacques discovered the
phenomenon in quartz and Rochelle salt in 1880
and named the effect piezoelectricity. They could
have called it pix and made it a lot easier for school
kids all over the world to pass physics exams, but
they didn't and the kids keep suffering.

Dr Zinkmor now in the dark . . . poster is luminous, green
skin, white wall, orange letters . . . 800-SKIN CARE. Come
on, come on. What's the problem?

We're like ants stopped in our tracks . . . pausing,
confused . . . mandibles rubbing . . . formic acid at the ready
. . . I know that smell. It's freezing but I sweat . . . an iceberg
melting. Jesus Becky, what are you feeding me?

Pheromones in the carriage . . . why are we stopped?

... why are we stopped? ... infinite nested loop in a subroutine ... does not compute. Exterminate. Ex-termite.

Half expecting a huge Monty Python cartoon foot to come crashing down on us. Oops. Sorry.

Small flicker ... then nothing. Sure I saw that snake on the floor. Driver in the cabin teasing. Bastard.

Tension grows again. Thoughts of spending the night, days, weeks ... who would be eaten first? Alive. Cabbage, Onion ... such choice. Marlboro after the meal. Another jolt. Driver with a yo-yo up front. Come on, come on.

- Hey Shame, what's your excuse this time? You're two fucking hours late. Take a hike pal.

Fuck, Carter would be in his element.

- Hey Shame, you banging those tramps on the subway again?

Four by twos was his slang for Jews and he thought it was hilarious in his own fucked-up little way. And then the laugh and the cackle ... too many Winstons before lunch, Carter my man.

Another shudder. This time we move. You can sense the relief. Not overtly of course ... that would be uncool ... don't let on you're afraid ... one sure way to get killed in the jungle ... the other animals can smell it.

- Don't stare at the animals and you won't get into trouble.
- Jesus Sean, can't you send him home?
- I'm only saying that's all.
- Yeah Jimmy, whatever.

Jimmy Rubber ... think his real name is Casey or something ... everyone calls him Jimmy Rubber coz ... well he's always rubber ... liver like asphalt ... Preparation-H

from sitting on a bar stool all day. Came over in the forties
... think it was the 1840s.

- Oh, those ships ... Jasus, I'll never forget the smell on
those ships.
- Yeah Jimmy, go annoy someone else will you.
- Ah Shem ... have you no heart at all?

Think before I reply ... sometimes you do have to
check over here.

Thank fuck the train is moving again. Only be a few
minutes late for work.

- Jesus Shame, what's wrong ... you're nearly on time?
- You know the way it is Carter.

We stop at Queensboro Plaza.

This big guy gets on wearing a leather vest and jeans
... used to call them waistcoats but you have to speak the
language here ... you say tomayto and I'll say tomato ...
map of Ireland on his tee-shirt ... the green fading from too
many washes ... he turns to look out the window and half
of Cork disappears under his vest.

I imagine some innocent Mary driving down Oliver
Plunkett Street minding her own business ... ends up on
the floor of the 7A to Brooklyn ... has to ring home and
say she won't make dinner ... maybe later whenever she
can catch a flight home ... but I wouldn't hold my breath.
And Mary's got a new job working in the bar ... making
lots of money ... and giving it to Lar ... Lar's the married
boyfriend ... been that way for a year ... slapped her in the
face once and says he loves her ... Oh Mary.

More people cram in and the tee-shirt is right up close
to my face. I can see Galway Bay like a little mouth waiting
to be fed. I want to touch it but I don't ... look Dr Zinkmor
that's where I used to go as a kid ... to the *Gaeltacht* ... *cá*

bhfuil an traen ag dul?[13] . . . *níl fhios agam*[14] . . . that would clear your skin up . . . standing out on Salthill on a winter's day . . . none of your 800 rubbish.

We reach Grand Central. And the ants are in the anthill making lots of money . . . and the queen is in the counting house. A busker tells me all about Jesus. He looks like Séamus Phelan from 3B . . . never had his homework done and was always late yet he lived the nearest. Seemed impervious to the leather. Brother Budderly panting after each wallop . . . that will teach you to be late . . . swoosh . . . and that will teach you not to do your homework . . . swoosh . . . and that will teach you to be singing on the subway and making a holy show of the education we are after beating into you. Never knew Séamus Phelan could sing though. He has a bowl with about 78 cents in it. Coffee in Starbucks is 79. Few more bars yet, Séamus.

It's not raining . . . it's not snowing . . . it's that horrible inbetweeny shite . . . glad sister bought me the scarf after all. Tramp woman got off at the same stop . . . she is ahead of me on the escalator . . . she turns left . . . I turn right . . . phew . . . close one that. Eight million people and less than 1% worth knowing.

- You never really make friends over here you know.
- Is that so Jimmy?
- I've been here years and I don't think I've made any lifelong friends. All the good ones went back home eventually.
- You never thought about going back yourself then Jimmy?
- Ah sure you know yourself . . . you get the feel for a place . . . you know the way.
- Sure Jimmy. Give him a Coors there Sean.

[13] Where is the train going?
[14] I don't know

I take a long drag out of my smoke. One thing I really love over here. The white filters on the smokes. Makes it all seem so clean and surgical somehow. And they're in soft packs. Less of an impact on the lungs.

I can still feel the motion from the subway . . . side to side . . . side to side . . . bump into some guy . . . shouts abuse. Don't answer . . . don't even look around. Nearly there now . . . and the kitchens will be warm. Have a <u>coffee</u> . . . put on the apron . . . serve the tables . . . good tips today . . . feel it in my bones. Fucking cold though . . . feel that in my bones too. I finger the little cellophane bag again. Yes. The wind whips up Second Avenue.

I shudder.

<u>coffee</u>
Coffee contains a complex mixture of chemical components of the bean, some of which are not affected by roasting. Chemicals extracted by hot water are classified as nonvolatile taste components and volatile aroma components. Important nonvolatiles are caffeine, trigonelline, chlorogenic acid, phenolic acids, amino acids, carbohydrates and minerals. Important volatiles are organic acids, aldehydes, ketones, esters, amines and mercaptans. And you thought it was just a drink.

Caffeine can be removed from coffee by treating the green beans with chlorinated hydrocarbon solvents. The beans are roasted by ordinary procedures after removal of the solvents. Decaffeinated coffee is used by people hypersensitive to the caffeine present in regular coffee . . . these people are collectively known as wimps.

+22

Louie on the phone

Louie is on the phone and he is saying, 'Yeah, yeah' all the
time and not saying anything else. He hangs up. He is in the
back of the ambulance with Santos. They have parked over
by Riverside Park. Santos has lit up a cigarette, which Louie
has only seen him do in moments of stress. Louie also
knows better than to mention that he shouldn't be
smoking in the ambulance.

- So Louie ... is it sorted?
- Yeah ... it's sorted. The cousin knows a guy who
  knows another guy who will take it off our hands.
  Subject to purity and all that.
- When?
- Tomorrow night. Santos, are you sure? ... we could
  get in serious shit. I mean if we hand it over to the
  police there may be some reward or something.
- You want out Louie, you just let me know. I am going
  for this. What ... you think that guy is going to lodge
  a complaint or file it with stolen property or

197

something? God knows where he is now . . . we lost our patient remember. How do you think that is going to look? We'll both be out of jobs at the very least. This way we get looked after just in case.

Santos taps the Guinness hold-all bag just to reassure himself.

- Suppose so Santos. You know best.
- Even if we did find the guy and the trolley . . . you think he's going to make a big song and dance about his bag of coke . . . we can just say 'What bag? There wasn't no bag when we picked you up.' Anyways you saw the guy, he wasn't going very far with those wounds.
- You know best Santos.
- And stop saying I know best, you have to start thinking for yourself Louie. It's a crazy world out there.

Louie looks out the window as if Santos is pointing to some particular area of the world, and in particular New York, that is crazy. Santos sees the deep frown of stupidity on Louie's face and wishes he was not stuck with this cretin. Just outside the ambulance a man with a large snake wrapped around his torso walks by. The man is tattooed like the snake's skin and so it is difficult to see where the man's skin ends and the snake's starts. Santos is concentrating too hard on exacting the four hundred known carcinogens out of his cigarette to notice. The snake turns to Louie and spits some venom, which lands like noxious bird droppings on the window.

- Yeah Santos I see what you mean . . . it's a crazy world out there.

But Santos ignores him. He is smiling a smile that he has

never smiled before. All those beatings from the wife, all the shame, all the pretence ... this is payback time ... this is how he will avenge the pain and suffering ... this is an Act of God. He holds the black bag to him as if it is a child rescued from an earthquake building.

- Okay Louie, here's the plan. Now I want you to listen very carefully. We have to have our stories completely straight. If we differ one iota they will smell something is wrong.
- Sure Santos. You know—

Louie manages to stifle the end of the sentence so as not to annoy Santos.

- The guy we picked up ... he discharged himself ... from the ambulance! He was only faking the shooting to cover up some other business and we were his decoy. You got that? And halfway to the hospital the guy arose like Lazarus and made us stop the ambulance and drive out here and then he jumped out and ran away. Okay, you got that?
- Yeah, but ... well what about the missing trolley and the bed? Did he use them as a getaway?

Santos wanted to pulverise the frowning face before him. He really wanted to stab his cigarette butt into those questioning eyes. However, much as he hated to admit it, the kid had a valid point, probably the first ever in his entire life. It was important to celebrate this moment with an ingenious answer.

- The guy pushed the trolley out of the back doors before he jumped out himself to make it look like he had fallen out so that if his drug-lord friends ever came looking for him, as they will no doubt do, he can claim that he fell out of the ambulance and that

he really was injured and that the trolley was then hit
by a car and he has amnesia!

Santos is delighted with this answer but he sees that
there were perhaps too many words in it for Louie.

- And then if the hoods come interviewing us, which
they might do, we can simply say that he ran off with
the bag, which is believable because he is not going
to fake all this and then leave without the bag of
drugs.

Santos is saying all this aloud more for his own benefit.
He knows that Louie is now staring out the window
wondering where the guy with the snake has gone to.

- Can we get some burgers now Santos? I'm getting
hungry.

23

incoming e-mail

The screen blips to life again and I momentarily take my eyes off the fascinating nature programme all about trees and plants and things. Soporific-voiced narrator telling us they have feelings. And I have feelings too. Just not around my stomach area at the minute. An e-mail zaps in.

To: Shem
From: Aido
Subject: Kylemore Abbey
Hi Shem
Are yourself and Becky still going to da auld country for a vacation? I have an aunt working in the gift shop in Kylemore Abbey and she can show you around. She also has a B&B in Clifden if you're interested.
TTFN
Aido

I think about responding but don't really feel there is much point to it. I don't seem to give a flying fuck about anything anymore. All I want to do is get back to Becky.

The Old Black Man is on the end of the trolley again.

- I can get you to see Becky if you really want.
- Yes I do. I really do.
- You know where she is and all, right?
- I do. So what do I have to do?

Fly says he.

Fly says I.

- I'll push you and when you get to the end of Manhattan again brace yourself. It will be bumpy but we should be able to do it.
- Well ... I suppose.
- There is no supposing. And this time there will be no landing on Ellis Island.

He gives me that smile that he used on the Southern Comfort advert and it is very reassuring.

24

the subway incident

The TV is showing one of those scary movies now. All dark lights, shadows and deep bass music. I feel uneasy. The trolley slows down and some of the street lights flicker on and off. A dog barks in the distance. I am glad it is in the distance because dogs seem to enjoy biting me and even from the relative vantage of my trolley I do not feel safe. The reason I find the movie particularly disturbing is that it is a real life documentary about me. All about one of my scariest moments. The documentary style allows my INNER THOUGHTS be known. Now that's a cheap trick and I curse the director inwardly, though he probably knows that.

❑ INNER THOUGHTS
Screech. Sound FX.

The train surfaces like a leviathan. I cast a cautious look left and right ... shouldn't be too long now. A small bead of sweat forms ... camera zooms in on it. I seem edgy and paranoid and the director latches on to this.

The lights outside blink, disappear, back underground now, count the seconds. Under the belly of the city ... ants under the anthill.

I wish I was back in Queens ... Bloom's, Molly's, The Jaunting Cart ... Dub would see me right ... he'd out-stare all these bastards. Dub would sort out these wasters. Say what you like about him but Dub would be the man to sort them out.

A big Black guy nestles a bottle in big fat hands ... he stares at me.

- What the fuck you looking at honkie?

His voice echoes off the walls and lands like right hooks on my reddening cheeks. I haven't heard the word 'honkie' in so long, I almost laugh ... but I don't.

- Nothing.

I try to curb the last falling cadence of the 'ing', spread out the 'o' ... but phonetics are fading fast.

- Where you from White ass ... you ain't no NYC?

Think, think, think.

What would Dub do? Think. Poke him right between those crimson eyes. No questions asked ... Dub, Dub where the fuck are you now? The swish of the white coat.

- Queens.

I put a hard drawl on the word.

- You a fucking Mick? Man, we sure scared of you fucks.

He scrapes a laugh from somewhere deep in his Marlboro throat.

- I'm not looking for any trouble, right?
- Maybe you just found it.

He takes a deep swig from the bottle. A small piece of moist brown paper clings to his lower lip. It is annoying . . . I wish he'd remove it. He fixes his eyes on my forehead.

Dub, Jesus where are you?

The carriage jolts to a stop.

– Jamaica. This stop Jamaica.

The voice over the PA bored and Black. You learn how to tell after a while. It's a survival mechanism. It's important. Thanks Jimmy Rubber . . . put him on a pint there Sean www.jimmyrubberadvice.com . . . no messing, real stuff here . . . no cyber-tyre-kickers need visit.

– Belmont next . . . next stop Belmont.

– Where you getting off Mick?

The sound of the liquid moving down his throat is empty, hollow . . . this guy is big . . . wide neck, cavernous throat . . . emptiness.

A pretty Black girl sits down three rows in front. Big Fat Fucker is distracted. His head reels about . . . new fruit in the vegetable zoo.

– Well hello there sister . . . and what's your pretty little name?

– Don't hit on me man . . . I've had a hard day.

She is beautiful. Large, swimming-pool eyes. She stares him out. He gulps more whiskey.

– I'm only playing girl. You got such pretty eyes. No honky girl got eyes like them. Know what I'm saying, sister?

She turns away. I wish she'd turn back again. Keep him occupied.

– And what you staring at Mick? Don't you got your own babes back in Iraland?

It may as well be Iran or somewhere else the way he

pronounces it. Dub would have gone for him after that, no mistake about that . . . he hates it when people slag off the homeland. He busted a guy once for sitting during Hour On Da Veen.

– Bet they don't put out . . . right?

The girl looks around. Neutral. I am White after all . . . a menace. But he is Black . . . menacing me.

– Why don't you have some Mick?

The bottle is no peace pipe. To refuse an insult. To accept . . . greed. And the state of his mouth . . .

– Leave him be.

Her voice, angelic.

– Hey baby, don't tell me you fancy a bit of the Irish . . . you Notre Fucking Dame or somehan?

– I don't fancy no one.

– Hey Kali, the sister here fancies a bit of the Irish. What about that?

Shit, there's another one of them, slumped down in the seat. I arch up slightly but all I can see is the peak of a baseball cap. The voice is slurred. Drunk maybe. Hopefully.

– Fuck her.

– Hey Kali man . . . here have some of this.

– Next stop Merrick, Merrick next stop.

Big Fat Fucker mimics the voice.

– Merrick, Merrick . . . next stop fuck-you Merrick.

He laughs too loud and too long, the words trailing off in coda.

The remaining couple of people upfront disembark. Now there are only four of us in the carriage. Jesus Dub, why didn't you come with me? It's always the same . . . into Manhattan on a Saturday night, then the long ride back out to Wantauk on the Long Island Rail. Hour and a fucking half stuck in these stinking cages . . . no better than the coffin ships our ancestors came over on.

Progress.

The clickety-clack of the train reminds me of the clickety-clack of my mother's knitting needles. Sitting in front of the fire with the gold gauze spark guard prisming the light from the fire into hundreds of flickers and shadows. I squint to try to make my eyes the same size as the slits in the guard and then I can see all the colours in a magical array. Little Bro beside me running his Dinky car across the marble fireplace and Mother saying to him, 'Stop that now and be a good boy . . . Daddy will be home soon' . . . but she doesn't really mean it and he plays on with the Dinky car regardless. And I am warm. There is the promise of dinner and the bread and butter pudding afterwards because we have been good today. Mother stops and counts the lines on the needles and then she is off again. Clickety-clack.

Clickety-clack.

Fade to scene outside the subway station where myself, Dub and Clodagh . . . Dub's latest flame . . . are standing shivering. They'd been doing a lot of *sneachta* and were fairly high. Eight-ball in the side pocket. Good man Dub.

– You go ahead of me Shem. I'll be back in the morning. Don't wait up for me.

Then the big wink . . . leaning in close . . .

– You'll be all right going back out on your own, won't you? I'll come out with you if you like?

I scoffed at him. I can handle myself. And if I was with Clodagh I wouldn't want to be baby-sitting anyone. Especially after a few lines of *sneachta* and a dozen Jagermeisters.

- Good man Shem. You see him Clodagh . . . he's the finest man that ever came out of Ireland and helped build America.

In a rare moment of personal contact he slapped me on the back and gave me the surreptitious wink again. Then they melted off into the Manhattan lights.

Fade back to subway carriage interior. Beads of sweat gather on my forehead . . . I can feel them . . . an image from *Total Recall* flashbacks onto the screen. The part where a holographic shrink tries to convince Arnie that he is hallucinating and that if he just takes the small pill being offered to him everything will be okay. He is just about to swallow it when the camera zooms in on a lone bead of sweat on the shrink's forehead . . . Arnie blows him away. Holograms shouldn't sweat, I guess.

Fade back to Dub scene.

- Do you want me to go back with you Shem?

Leaning in close . . . the big wink. Yes, yes, yes Dub . . . I want you to come back with me . . . Clodagh's eyes mocking me, her pupils still buzzing from the *sneachta*. And then Dub reluctantly saying goodbye. He wouldn't have complained . . . it's not his style. He would have just shrugged his shoulders and laughed. And he'd have protected me from these wankers, that's for sure.

Fade back to subway carriage interior.

- What's wrong Mick? . . . you gone kinda whiter than white. Take a look at this guy Kali. He looks like a snowball, and make no mistake.
- Fuck him.
- No Kali, you should see him . . . sweating like he was a fish or something.

Big Fat Fucker starts singing, cacophonous, low and menacing . . . 'He's a whiter shade of pale . . .'

- Leave him be man, he ain't doing you no harm.

Her voice pulls me back from the brink.

- Ah, the little sister speaks again. What's that you saying sister? That the White boy has a nice ass and you'd like to jump his bones . . . is that what you saying, sister? . . . coz me and Kali here . . . we're good with that . . . ain't that so Kali?
- Fuck yeah.

A hand is held up and Big Fat Fucker slaps it playfully.

- Just leave him be.
- Well whatta you think of that Mick? She wants to jump your little White bones. Ain't that a thing?

In a second flat Big Fat Fucker covers the distance between him and the girl. He grabs her.

- What you at, leave me alone you dumb motherfucker.
- Now, now, little sister, language like that ain't polite with us niggers . . . isn't that right Irish?

He has muffled her with his hand.

- Leave her be asshole.

There, I'd said it. Dub would be proud of me and he would undoubtedly say so at my funeral. No turning back now. Big Fat Fucker is delighted . . . a primed bull waiting for a red flag.

Kali stirs from his lair. He stands up. He is slender, tall. Clothes hang loosely about his lanky frame. The word 'Yankees' is frayed across his baseball cap. Bloodshot eyes peer out from under the peak. His nose is broken . . . like a boxer's . . . or a basketball player who plays rough. His cheeks are pock-marked as well, just like Santos . . . Jesus, what were they doing to these kids? . . . *rian na bolgaí* . . . I can remember a Leaving Certificate Irish class . . . *rian na bolgaí* . . . the mark of the pox . . . and we all

pre-pubescent in our sniggering . . . so long ago it seems
. . . back in the warm classroom . . . it was raining outside
. . . Brother Campbell standing arms crossed, an air of bored
authority, reciting passages from *Caisleán Óir*[15].

Kali stares at me.

- Don't fuck with the brother's Irish.
- I ain't looking for trouble . . . just leave the lady be.
- She ain't your concern White boy. We look after our
  own. We don't need no advice.

Imperceptibly, the train is slowing. The time between
each halogen light lengthens . . . a slight shift to the blue
end of the spectrum . . . the Doppler Effect . . . and I think
of blue skies . . . summers spent in Kilmuckeridge, County
Wexford . . . my first trip away with Malachi and Ray. Staying
in a mobile home and drinking and smoking. At night we
were the toast of Boggin's Pub. Malachi played guitar and
Ray brought out his bagpipes one night and nearly
brought the house down, literally. And then firmly
clasping Susan's hand . . . out in Moran's field, behind the
pub . . . hot fecund smells . . . new sensations . . . couldn't
wait to tell everyone . . . me and Susan . . . up above in
Moran's field. The big wink from Malachi . . . slap on the
back . . . that's my boy, that's my boy.

All this, these thoughts . . . in the flash of a second . . .
it's true . . . life does flash before you. It's just not the bits
you'd expect. I thought it would be more high-speed . . .
a roller coaster ride through my memories . . . birth, love,
pain, hate, family, death, girls, drink, drugs, .clips from
obscure movies, smells, tastes, wet dreams, sex, joy . . . all
convoluted into one moment of video . . . a blip . . . a
montage . . . a collage.

[15] *The Golden Castle*. A book that is not as boring as *Peig*.

Certainly not those nights in Boggin's Pub. That was like slow motion. All of us surrounded by Readybrek radiation shields, glowing with momentary fame. All so vivid.

- You tell him Kali. You show the motherfucker what's what.

I'm wrenched out of my reverie.

Kali struts over to the woman and pulls her blouse open. Four buttons race away down the carriage floor ... travelling at some velocity, the train at another, added vectorally, Cookie Callaghan again . . . teaching the intricacies of Einstein ... I can hear each button come to stop, spin like a coin would on a bar counter on a lazy summer's afternoon, then fall over. <u>Entropy</u>. The law of ever-increasing chaos. I never did understand that in school.

Entropy

The second law of thermodynamics gives a precise definition of a property called entropy. Entropy can be thought of as a measure of how close a system is to equilibrium . . . it can also be thought of as a measure of the disorder in the system. The law states that entropy ... the disorder ... of an isolated system can never decrease.

Disorder is here to stay, in other words. Don't bother brushing your teeth and clean the kitchen only when you really, really have to.

The buttons on the subway carriage have reached equilibrium but the train is still moving.

- Yeah Kali, go man go.

He whoops. Barely, above her screams, a bottle is smashed. Before I can react Big Fat Fucker has me in a stranglehold. I forget everything Jimmy Rubber tried to teach me. 'Never let the bastards get the better of you. Kick first and then run.'

I flail about. He has a firm grip. Out of the corner I see a flash . . . a tiny, starry gleam of glass. Not all that glitters . . .

- Don't want me to mess up that pretty face, now do we?

His breath is so close, miasmic, overwhelming. Her screams are smothered . . . Kali has rammed his cap into her mouth. His jeans are halfway down. I can see his brown thighs.

- Go Kali go . . .

I struggle. Pinprick of glass enters my skin . . . warm blood . . . a trickle. Her screams are now a whisper.

- Merrick, Merrick . . . last stop Merrick.

- Come on Kali, man . . . hurry up . . . we're nearly there.

My heart is beating . . . never before so fast . . . like it's not beating at all . . . just a series of rapid beats joined together. White noise. Kali is disturbed by someone coming into the carriage and he quickly pulls up his jeans. She is safe. The train slows down. I can just see her legs moving, jutting out from the seats. I strain to look further. Kali strides over to me.

- If we had time I'd have had your ass.

The blow comes from behind.

- All exit Merrick . . . Merrick last stop.

- Kali man, we better split . . . scram time.

The train jolts to a stop . . . doors open . . . I try to focus. Two smudged figures running away. Darkness.

Fade to later that night. It is early morning in fact. Daylight is creeping over the city.

A guard's boot wakes me.

- Come on mister. You can't sleep here. Train going back to Grand Central in ten minutes.

- But the girl . . . there was a girl.

I can hardly talk. My head is throbbing. The carriage is empty . . . swimming pool eyes is gone.

He laughs.

- There's always a girl, my friend, always.

He looks like that genial old guy in the Southern Comfort advert.

I gather myself together and step out onto the platform. The night air slaps my face. It is bitterly cold. I feel very hungry. There is a spilled tinfoil tray on the platform. A Chinese takeaway spilt for the parasites in the air. A lone piece of cauliflower has fallen away from the rest. Zooming in real close I can see the fractal patterns of the flower. ❑

The screen fades to black and the music rolls. I feel like I have lived through the whole thing again and the sheets are stuck to me with sweat.

25

the thing about masturbation

You should try and masturbate when you are on an ambulance trolley hurtling through the slippery streets of New York, with three gunshot wounds in the gut, a saline drip pumping something into you and various flashback people coming up alongside you and what not . . . it does not lend itself easily to concentrating on the job in hand.

It's the potholes that get me really . . . can't get any sort of a rhythm going and then *Badumphff* and it's back to square one again. Well, the potholes and the saline drip thingy . . . I'm sure they put bromide or something in it to stop the urges, if you know what I mean . . . can't have the last precious drops of blood inside me rushing off to where they are not meant to be rushing off to and we all know what that private little place is called. And then the TV isn't exactly tantalising either . . . poor old <u>Tantalus</u> and the nice word he gave us.

Tantalus

In Greek mythology Tantalus was King of Lydia and son of Zeus, ruler of the gods. Tantalus was honoured above all other mortals by the gods. He ate at their table on Olympus ... and once they even came to dine at his palace. He made a smoked salmon roulade for the starter that night.

To test their omniscience, Tantalus killed his only son, Pelops, boiled him in a cauldron and served him at the banquet ... after the smoked salmon roulade. The gods, however, realised the nature of the food. They restored Pelops to life and devised a terrible punishment for Tantalus. He was hung forever from a tree and afflicted with tormenting thirst and hunger. Under him was a pool of water, but when he stooped to drink, the pool would sink from sight. The tree above him was laden with pears, apples, figs, ripe olives and pomegranates, but when he reached for them the wind blew the laden branches away. The word 'tantalise' is derived from this story.

But to be perfectly honest it's the state of the streets that really gets me.

Badumphff.

And she danced like Marlene Dietrich and her shoes were all made from somewhere ... and your music lives on and on, yes it does, ha ha ha ha ... your man Sarsfield or whatever his name was. He was the guy that took over the siege at Limerick or was that Sarsted ... one fought for the glory and freedom of Ireland and the other was on my first ever *Top of the Pops* LP. Used to run up to the toilet for a

long undisturbed wank, looking at the busty girl on the
cover of the album who was always bending over to pick
up something or reaching at some impossible angle to
adjust the volume knob on the gramophone with her
blouse open and her moon units there for all to see
. . . so where do you go to my lovely when you're alone in
your bed . . . ha ha ha ha ha ha . . .

Once my older brother caught me coming down the
stairs sheepishly . . . though sheep are not known for using
the stairs . . . and he asked me curiously . . . for humans are
known to be curious . . . what I was doing with the album
cover and I told him it was a project for music in school
and then he told everyone at the dinner table and my dad
was fierce interested and I told him we were doing a piece
about songs relevant to Ireland in *Top of the Pops* and then
I said that your man Patrick Sarsted was the guy from the
siege of Limerick and I think Dad copped it because he
never said anything about it again. And my mother went
to pour the tea.

26

the pink boob tube

A girl in a pink boob tube on in-line rollerblades comes alongside the trolley. Charumm ... charumm ... caaaaarrrrr ... it is quite soothing in an irrational sort of way. They are in-line rollerblades but the girl does not use them in-sequence ... there is a slight beat frequency between them and I know if Cookie was here he would be able to calculate her velocity from this. I do not know and I do not care. Her pink top is nice.

She has a wooden tray carrying it aloft in one hand quite dexterously. She places this on the side bar of the trolley and it fits in snug as a bug in a rug ... and she lines up four glasses and pours in a row of whiskey shots ... straight without a pause, moving deftly from one glass to the other and she does not spill a drop.

Well actually she spills a little bit but nothing worth talking about. So we won't.

- Four shots for a dollar.
- Pardon me?

- Four shots ... for a dollar ... tonight's special.
- Really?
- It's a special for tonight only.
- It is? Wow!
- Tonight only. Real special whiskey ... your friends said you looked like you could use it ... needed some cheering up.
- I do?
- I'll say.
- Well ... you see it's not me really ... this guy Santos ... do you know Santos by any chance? (She is already looking around distractedly sizing where the next tip might lay) ... Well Santos ... you see he is the paramedic and he lost me out the back of his ambulance which is kind of a bit awkward at the moment.

She looks back to me having only half listened.

- You need a paramedic.
- Exactly! ... that's what I'm trying to tell you ... and Santos ... the guy ... well he has my wallet and so I can't really give you a tip.
- Listen mister, I'm real sorry about your predicament and all that but I'm trying to get through Med School which means I gotta wear this stupid boob tube and parade around on rollerblades to serve a crowd of drunks just so I can cure cancer you know ... so if you'll just drink the shagging drinks I can get sorted and get out of here tout suite. Get my drift?
- Yes.
- I may only be in second year of college but let me tell you mister that you are well and truly fucked and I'd say finding this Santos paramedic character should be your number one priority so I would suggest you

drink that frigging Mick whiskey and worry about
how the frig you're going to make it to morning . . .
you know what I'm saying?

There is a pause.

- And a dollar you say?

She is gone. She leaves the drink. So I do the four shots
straight one after the other . . . which is always a good way
to approach these situations in fairness. I grimace and
wince . . . some of the whiskey spills on the wound and
does not hurt at all unlike in those cowboy movies where
they would always pour whiskey on the guy with the
arrow sticking out of him and he would scream in pain.

The trolley whizzes by the girl in the pink top as she
is trying to sell her wares to a group of becapped and
rather anachronistic Micks who look like they work on a
building site. They are exchanging banter with her.

- A dollar . . . are you fuckhan mad girl? Sure I could get
  bottles of that for a shilling.

I see Great-uncle Donal but it is too late and I have
passed by. I crane around in time to see him being taught
how to rollerblade by the girl but then he was always a
crafty mover that uncle of mine.

- A dollar you say . . . sure that's daylight robbery . . .
  would there be anything extra going along with the
  whiskey now?

Many years from now a distant descendant of Great-
uncle Donal will perform the highest unaided free-fall
jump ever recorded from what will then be the tallest
building in the world, The Temple of Berners–Lee, in
a successful attempt to draw attention to how reliant
mankind has become on technology. He will not be
the last to do this. – *Cadumphff*

27

the Christy Moore event

The saline drip is half empty … or half full as Cookie used
to always tell us. So he did. Christy Moore is sitting on the
side of my bed. He looks very relaxed. His guitar neck
keeps tapping off the saline drip and I am perturbed by it
but I decide not to say anything because he is known to be
a bit cantankerous and might just head off without singing
an auld song.

   - Bit of a mess you're in there Shem.

   - Aye Christy, sure you know yourself.

   - Messing with them dirty narcotics were you?

   - Aye Christy, now that would be telling.

   - Sorry for your trouble …

   - And don't forget my shovel …

He does not seem impressed so I decide to shut up.

   - Will I sing you a wee song Shem?

   - Aye Christy, do. Do you know that one 'Nancy Spain'?

I laugh nervously but it doesn't matter because he has already closed his eyes and is concentrating very hard strumming the guitar already.

We happen to pass by the Nancy Spain bar . . . outside there are a group of lads the worse for drink. They spot Christy on the end of the bed.

– Go on Christy, ya wild thing ya . . . don't forget your shovel, wha? Hey . . . have you any auld autographs or tapes, wha?

His mind is already wandering and he has stopped playing and is sulking and muttering some Gaelic to himself. This could be trouble.

> – Sorry Christy, I know you hate being interrupted but it was those boyos and sure they don't know what they're saying half the time . . . sorry Christy, I didn't mean it like that but I'm not thinking straight at the minute and you know yourself. I think they're putting something in my drip.

But he is gone. I try to call after him but the TV is blaring now and I can't find the damned remote. My trolley passes a burger joint and I can just see a piece of paint peel off the wall and fall into one of the trays of French fries. Flakology values aside this could be a serious lawsuit but I am possibly the only witness and unless cryogenic suspension technology advances twenty years in the next few hours I'd say litigation is unlikely.

I haven't the energy to do any flakology calculations anyways. An e-mail zaps up on the laptop screen. It is from Aido . . . I am on his joke messing mailing list so I am and he's always sending me little nuggets of human thought and existence.

To: Shem
From: Aido
Subject: Y2K
Message: Hamsters
Hi Shem,
Any plans for New Year's Eve? BTW you gotta see the dancing hamster . . . I have attached the file (only 290 K) so give it a go, it's a blast.
TTFN
Aido.

I probably won't make it to the next morning let alone New Year's Eve so I don't think I am too concerned about the whole thing. What is it that that Black guy once said in Starsky & Hutch . . . oh yeah . . . 'And then you die, brother.'

At the moment all I give a flying fuck about is fucking flying . . . flying home to see Becky.

I wish the Old Black Man would come back and sort everything out for me.

28

Santos being hen-pecked

Life is strange.

Santos is now somewhere scratching his beard . . . and the pockmarks that will never go away . . . wondering where the hell I am and what major trouble he's going to get into when they realise I am not around . . . and that I have slipped out of the ambulance and maybe he should not have been talking to his wife on the phone and all that jazz.

And then Santos and Louie arguing about who was meant to be doing what at the time of the incident and who should take the blame. They are very big on blame over here and you can get quite a lot of money if you can blame someone for something and get them to accept blame for something and that sort of thing.

Where could he have gone?

And Santos on the phone again to his wife and trying to explain to her what happened.

- Yeah honey, something's after cropping up here and

I might not be home for dinner . . . .yeah I know I
promised but this is serious. We've lost the guy.

Yeah . . . no I know that . . . happens all the time but I
mean the guy ain't dead sugar he's lost! You know we
went around a corner too fast and now he's off
around the city somewhere on his trolley . . . and he's
got one of those TV beds. . . . yeah I told you honey
they're new . . . 50 channels . . . yeah with remote . . .
and the guy even had his laptop computer with him
and . . . wha? An AST or something I think . . . 80 megs
. . . yeah . . . well I never checked . . . there were three
serious gunshot wounds so I didn't really have the
time to check . . . well if I knew that honey I wouldn't
be out looking for him would I? . . . well how the hell
should I know . . . Louie should have checked the
doors were locked.

Louie remonstrates . . . quietly.

– I did too.

He does not really care now. They have the bag of
drugs and he knows where they can shift them too. Louie
really hates it when he isn't more assertive. His palms are
drenched with sweat, which means something bad is
going to happen. His shrink had been working on his
motivational priorities and had been honest and told him
that the assertiveness stuff would not start until early next
year. At least he was honest. What was Louie going to do?
Tell him no . . . say that he goddamned wanted to start the
frigging assertiveness stuff today?

– Yeah honey, gotta go. Well, put it in the frigging oven
then.

Louie looked around to try to see if Santos' demeanour
had changed some but he could only see the back of his

head. A small flake of paint from the roof dislodged itself and fell straight into his dark gelled black hair. Louie was not an expert on flakology but if he had been he would have easily calculated even by a rough rule of thumb that something unusual was about to happen.

And it was then that Santos turned around and looked at Louie with a very weird gaze.

- We will get another trolley from stores section this afternoon and say that some drunk stole the other one when we were attending to a patient. Have you got that?

Louie had most definitely not got that and he reminded himself of something his shrink said . . . when in a situation where you are lost in a conversation or a conflict . . . simply adopt the expression or characteristic of some actor you have seen on TV in a similar position. Louie looked back at Santos with a look that James Garner had perfected in *The Rockford Files* when there was something he was not 100% sure about.

There was the bag of drugs, which meant some serious money and some serious freedom to do what he liked, when he liked it.

29

the guy with the cell phone

Let me tell you about the guy with the cell phone. This is important. Only for him I'd still be on the spongy sidewalk that was inexorably soaking up my life force. He had a cell phone or a mobile or whatever the hell you want to call it. There was enough juice left in it for two calls and one of them was 911. This guy had heart.

But the guy ... his name is Robert O'Sullivan. He had just learnt that his Internet company, of which he was one of the co-founders, had been given 1.2 million dollars from some Venture Capital people. These VC people were big hitters and the investment meant that they could expand and build the business without having the banks on their backs.

Robert was understandably feeling good.

Here is a brief précis of background.

Came over from Ireland six years ago and worked the bar and restaurant scene. Good tips and lots of cash then blew half of it in one night, on a bender with some of the lads each impressing the other with bigger and bigger rounds and more generous tips. Money under the mattress ... no IRS number, no bank account ... post it or send it home wrapped in tinfoil and get the brother to save it ... then you hope the plane doesn't go down due to some fucked-up pilot or dodgy Kapton wiring and you can't claim that on the insurance. What could you do? ... Green card in the post but the delivery takes forever. As Robert always said himself ... you take your chances.

Only passing through here anyway and he will return home to the old country sooner or later and make no mistake about it ... home in a blaze of glory and buying rounds left right and centre and above and below and clapping him on the back and offering him a job and the way she might look at you.

And then a chance conversation in a suits bar down near Wall Street where Robert was doing a shift for a friend who had to get a flight home due to a sudden death in the family. All the suits out quaffing cocktails on a busy Friday after work. Robert was always tuned in to about six different conversations at once ... sign of a good barman and he knew about baseball and hockey and football and that was a sure tip-winner ... why don't you have one yourself which he wouldn't but pocket the cash and put it under the mattress and sure you never know when you might need it yourself.

The conversation he overheard ... three suits talking about their Internet company and how they couldn't get decent people who knew a bit about coding and a bit about a lot of other things ... blah blah blah they went on and on ... blah blah blah ... poking holes in the cigar smoke ... and Robert knowing all the things they mentioned after his four year electronic degree from Trinity and he only came over to work for a wee while and then the wee while got longer and that is the way it goes.

So there's Robert on the wrong side of the bar and he's listening to this and he waits and he waits and he's making sure they have their drinks and the peanuts are fully available and he waits and then at an opportune moment he interjects.

— Couldn't help overhearing you gentlemen but did you say you wanted someone with C++ and <u>HTML</u> skills?

And the suits look him up and down but he has been friendly and courteous and served them well and maybe he's got a nerve talking to them like that but maybe that is the type of nerve they are looking for . . . and isn't that what made America great? . . . this kid's got balls.

<u>HTML</u>
The team who first came up with this language were poor students and their parents would regularly ring and enquire how their finances were faring. The group were asked this so much that they originally thought of calling the language HTML as an acronym for How's The Money Lasting. Eventually under advisement from their lawyers and parents they opted for the more scientific-sounding HyperText Mark-up Language. This computer language is now behind the vast majority of websites.

A business card is passed across the pristinely kept bar top and the promise of a call and then a round of drinks on the house and more laughing and then one of them brings him aside and gets the lowdown.

- You're illegal right?
- I may be.
- And you want to be sponsored?
- That may or may not be true.
Never tell too much to anyone.
- Cautious aren't you?
- You have to be.
- I like that.

And then over the bar there is a ten-minute technical interview. Questions on all sorts of Internet topics. And the other punters are impatiently tapping their empty glasses and wondering where all the peanuts have gone and maybe they should go to another bar or forget the tip they were going to give. They can see Robert who is usually their friend and he looks like he's giving baseball betting tips to some suit and isn't it terrible the way a suit gets you more respect in this city. And the guy in the suit looks like some rich four by two and what can you do?

This is true.

Five months later Robert is drinking with the same boys of a Friday night and he looks good in the suit and his wallet is bursting and the boss thinks he's great and it is all going so well and isn't life weird all the same.

And now he's a heavy hitter with the tips and always a kind word for the barman and with enough drink he'll give them the speech about how he got out of the rat race of bartending and. got into the 'real' world and how good it feels and the respect and the money and the clout. And the barman will listen intently and hate him forever and vow never to end up like him ... unless the opportunity presents itself of course.

Robert gives them his getting out, getting on, getting up and getting, getting, getting speech and they listen and they hate the ten bucks he leaves when most would leave five and some of them blow it on a bet or give it to some bum. And before he leaves, Robert winks and shakes hands and exchanges some unspoken shibboleth and says you never know what's around the next corner. And all the Brendan Behans in the world couldn't say enough fucks about all the begrudging going on. Fuck them . . . you takes your chances . . . and you never know what is around the next corner . . . that's what Robert O'Sullivan thinks.

This particular night on 32nd and Second Robert did not know what was around the next corner. He heard shots but this is NYC so keep walking. Then he turned the corner and a car nearly takes his legs from under him screaming away from the sidewalk. He was on the phone to his fiancée at the time talking about going to see *The Marriage of Figaro* at the Met and how he had been given the tickets and all that. Progress.

Robert loves the food here but especially likes the way in the top restaurants they give you doggie bags and leaving some posh joint with half a cow wrapped in tinfoil under your arm and the other half swishing around in your gut being bombarded with enzymes and acids. Years of going back to college in Dublin and half a chicken wrapped in tinfoil with the clean socks and the pressed jocks and a crease down the middle and maybe eat the chicken on Monday and have a soup with it on Tuesday and Wednesday and then out drinking Thursday night and back home Friday with the dirty laundry and the empty neatly folded tinfoil.

There is no steak inside my tummy at the moment. I am glad about that. Maybe if I don't finish the saline drip they will wrap it for me to go.

> – Aw honey . . . can't you finish the drip? I'll wrap it for you to go.
> – Thanks Daisy.

And she carefully wrapping the plastic container and putting it in a carton and wedging it under my arm. Better leave a tip for the paramedics . . . 10% or double the tax. Although to be honest the service was crap.

But Robert.

Tall, handsome, bit overweight. Nothing to worry about for tuurty years or more and premium medical plan and they can replace everything now anyway and kicked the smokes two years ago. Full head of hair. Nearly tuurty. Hasn't lost the Navan accent even though in the bar trade you have to pretend and make sure not to say Tomaato or Patayto or anything like that.

Robert doing real well in the company and they make him a partner with tuurty tree and a turd per cent. Good man Robert and the other partners call him Bob and he jokes with them that they know him well enough they can spell it backwards and the American guys go 'Oh Really.' Bob de PALINDROME . . . and Robert thinks that's hilarious. And the guys reply 'Oh Really.'

❑ PALINDROME

The TV is showing an investigative journalism documentary type thing from back home. It is all based in the town of Navan in County Meath and how it has just been officially announced that Navan is to become Ireland's biggest Palindrome.

The reporter is on the scene, out and about in the town to gauge public reaction. Outraged locals already up in arms at the news and an interview with the local chairman of the Chamber of Commerce, who is steadfastly opposing the decision. The reporter does a tour around the town where there are already posters up ... 'No Palindrome Here' ... 'Navan says NO to the Palindrome' ...

And then the local politician trying to assuage the anger of the populace ... 'We should be able to ensure EU funding for the Palindrome. And sure wouldn't it be great to get all the facilities and resources and think of the tourism opportunities ... 'Visit Navan, Home of Ireland's biggest Palindrome' or 'Navan . . . Home of the Palindrome'.

And a rumour goes around the town that it is to be situated in a field about two miles west of the town and some locals start a 24-hour vigil. The local publican comes down to the field laden down with sandwiches and soup and he is being interviewed, the good Samaritan that he is, and they are asking him what he makes of it all.

– Sure aren't these people my customers and my bread and butter.

And secretly he is hoping for the Palindrome because he knows the extra business it will bring in.

Another of the protesters is seething with anger. She is adamant that as long as she draws breath that there will be no Palindrome built in Navan.

– I don't care if it's a Superdrome or a Hyperdrome or a Palindrome or whatever the hell they choose to call it ... it will not go up here. Why can't they have the thing up in Dublin, ha? Why do we have to have it here? It's blatant discrimination so it is.

Then the closing caption of the reporter standing earnestly with his microphone, trying to talk into the camera with a backdrop chorus of protesters chanting ...

'Navan is our home ... we don't need no Palindrome
Navan is our home ... we don't want no Palindrome.' ❑

But Robert is happy, walking along 32nd talking to his girlfriend. He turns onto Second and is nearly run over by a lunatic driver. A young man is lying on the sidewalk and his laptop computer crashed open near his head.

– Gotta go honey, someone's just been shot.

Incidentally, this very phrase uttered by Robert is not the most surprising thing you can say to someone on the phone in New York. The top three most surprising things you could say to someone are:

1 The cab driver got out of the cab and helped the cyclist off the ground.
2 The waiter came after me and said I had left too big a tip.
3 Gotta go honey, no one's just been shot.

And then Robert dialling 911 and telling them to come quickly ... like they're gonna come slowly right? And then putting his good Armani coat under the guy's head and looking at the blood which surprisingly is not red but more a type of purple. Then that Old Black Man arriving ... out of nowhere it seems ... and just standing there shaking his head ... and the woman running out of the shop and she was screaming his name ... Sean or Shem or Sham or something like that. Robert's cell phone ringing then ... it has a 'Danny Boy' ring tone ... and it was his fiancée again, all worried about the last call and was he all right. He assures her he is fine and that he can't really talk at the moment as he is waiting for the paramedics to arrive and he's trying to help the guy and make sure no one runs off with the guy's <u>laptop</u> which bizarrely seems to be churning out images from some castle or abbey or something like that in Ireland and Robert cops that the guy is possibly Irish. He asks the whimpering woman beside him but she is incoherent so he assumes it anyway.

laptop
The laptop computer is an AST Ascentia M series computer with 80 Mb of RAM, a Pentium II processor and 6.3 Gb of hard disk space. It was dropped once in Shannon Airport when only three weeks old and had to have a new screen fitted and some internal repairs. There is a saying about dropping babies on their heads when young. They will never be right, apparently.

30

the failed jumper

John Drexler is on top of a building contemplating his jump. He has been working it out for months. The actual jump was not a problem as such . . . that was pure physics. You jump and gravity takes care of the rest. The real niggly thing was the suicide note. He jokingly called it his Letter of Resignation. He was resigning from life after all. He had written eleven drafts of it and the twelfth was an amalgam of all the previous efforts. He was happy with it now. In fact it was the only thing in his life he was happy with . . . his Letter of Resignation.

He usually worked on the drafts of it while in various diners around the city. This was another part of his research. The point of the jump had to be right. Somewhere on an intersection was important to him. John had always liked the hustle and bustle of an intersection and he thought if he was going to splatter himself on the sidewalk then it must be a decent intersection.

While working on the penultimate draft he was sitting in a friendly diner eating pecan pie and drinking the house brew, which was strong and aromatic. The waitress was one of those 'long-suffering but content with her lot' types. She kept refilling his cup and eventually asked him if he was writing a poem.

- It's my Letter of Resignation actually.
- Good on you kid. I'd quit this job myself if it wasn't for all the fringe benefits.

And then when he was leaving she wished him luck with his new job. She said she hoped it went well for him. That's when John Drexler decided that this was the intersection for him. There was a huge billboard advert with the smiling face of a genial-looking old Black man and he thought that would be a nice last face to see.

In his research John had read about a tribe of Native American Indians who believed that the last sight you saw before you died would be the version of paradise awaiting you in the next life. Dying Indians would be dragged miles by their relatives just to reach some preferred destination and then they would contentedly drift off into their paradise. John surveyed the intersection and decided that this would be it. He had his note, the location and the means.

Here was John's rationale.

He believed that he was the loneliest person on planet Earth and that he was only taking up space and that the world would be better off if there was not this waste of space sucking on the precious resources like air and water and food. Drexler believed this ... that he was a waste of space. The coming to this conclusion was not based on any logic or reason but on the fact that John had been dropped on his head as a baby and was never quite right.

His parents died in a plane crash when he was three ... after the dropping incident ... and he grew up in foster homes and orphanages. There was no other family which he knew of and so he determined over a number of years that he was the loneliest person on the planet. It was that simple.

So now he was on the roof of the chosen building overlooking Manhattan just opposite the advert of the old Black man smiling and holding the saxophone ... looking like he was having a good time ... and Drexler guessed that he was a very good saxophone player. He would have liked to learn to play an instrument but had never got around to it.

Getting up on the roof had been no problem. Bribed the caretaker of the apartment block with $100 ... said he was a photographer and that he wanted some night shots. The caretaker never second-guessed him and never even looked twice when he saw Drexler had no cameras with him. Hey, it's not his job, right?

On the roof now. It had been snowing earlier and there were still pockets of melting snow on the roof. Drexler loved snow so it was like an added benefit to the whole ceremony. He checked he had the Letter of Resignation. It was still there ... wrapped in clingfilm and inserted into a strong plastic see-through envelope. This was important. He knew there would probably be lots of blood and guts and stuff and he wanted to make sure it could be read by whoever found him. He also had it strapped to his leg using special surgical twine ... the last thing he wanted was for it to fall off during the descent ... and watch it waft off into the night as he plummeted to the ground. That would not be cool ... and there would be very little he could do about it then anyways.

A chill wind sent a shiver up and down his spine ... a last little caress from Mother Nature ... pat on the back and wishing him well on his journey. Safe trip son. He stepped on the edge of the building. He was surprised at how little adrenaline was rushing around inside him. He had planned it so meticulously and gone over it so many times in his head that this was just like a prized athlete going through the motions of a pole vault jump. Except of course that there was no soft landing, rubber cushions or airbags.

John Drexler was just at the point of launching himself into his paradise when he heard three gunshots ring out from below on the opposite street corner. He nearly stumbled off the ledge with the fright. He had not expected this ... this was not in the plan. He did not like the surprise element and was actually annoyed. He looked down ... the long way down and saw a man lying on the street corner with blood oozing from him. His head was half on the sidewalk and half on the road so that his eyes appeared to be gazing up at Drexler and even at this distance he could discern the pain in those eyes. There was a moment of silence like the entire city had taken a sharp intake of breath and then the pause button was pressed the second time and there was a woman screaming and running to the man and then an old Black man appeared out of somewhere and then there was a guy coming round the corner talking into his cell phone.

None of this was anticipated ... it was most upsetting. Drexler leaned on the ledge carefully and looked at the tragic scene. How could he possibly jump now ... no one would take the slightest bit of notice and he would quite possibly ruin the other guy's chance of survival and cause all sorts of traffic problems for the ambulance and that maybe it wasn't such a good idea after all and that maybe this was a sign from some Omnipotent Being ... whoever that may be ... and that maybe he should just abandon the whole idea and go back to that diner across the street and have some nice warm coffee and that delicious pecan pie and wasn't that a great idea and wasn't it things like that ... the simple pleasures of life ... that really counted and maybe he could talk to that nice waitress and maybe she would become his friend and maybe they could talk for hours and drink the nice strong warm coffee.

Drexler noticed the biting cold for the first time and was consumed with craving for coffee. Yes, coffee would be nice. And then it struck him that maybe on his way down to the diner he could actually stop and help the guy on the street ... while planning for his suicide he had read up extensively on first aid because he was allowing for the possibility that he may not die on the jump and only be hideously wounded and that he should know the basics of how to treat himself because he was so alone that nobody would stop on the street to help him and maybe this was his chance to help someone else ... and at that moment John Drexler became a person again and any thoughts of suicide were erased from his head and he decided that no matter how lonely he was he would dedicate the rest of his life to helping people and that they didn't have to like him or even talk to him but he would help them anyways.

He stood up and emitted a long loud cry of affirmation and redemption and a few other things as well thrown in. He must go and help that man and then the rest of humanity.

Here on top of this roof on his twenty-fifth birthday ... for which he got no cards or congratulations or phone calls ... he knew that he would spend the rest of his days being a good and useful person. A humanitarian. He could tolerate the loneliness. Life suddenly felt good. He now did not want to know when he would die.

The tragic truth is that John Drexler dies exactly twenty-five seconds after making that momentous decision. Racing down the stairs to aid the wounded man on the street corner opposite he slips on some snow that has collected on his shoes and falls fifteen flights of stairs . . . hard metal ones with no covering . . . and is dead by the time the momentum of his body has surrendered its energy. He is found by the caretaker who will be in a great mood, having just bought a bag of cocaine with the $100. He intended to go out after his shift and blow the whole thing in one night of debauchery . . . and now he will have to call the cops and make statements and explain what the guy was doing on the roof in the first place.

And the police will find the Letter of Resignation and Sergeant O'Malley will scratch his head and wonder why the kid didn't jump as he said he would in his letter and maybe he was pushed and that maybe they had a fight over the bag of cocaine that they discover on the caretaker.

Sergeant O'Malley will sigh deeply and have to ring his long-suffering wife, Helen, and tell her that he will be working late all that night and well into the next day and she should arrange to go to the opera on her own. This is also tragic because she will be mugged on the way home from the opera and go into a coma from which she never recovers and the last words that O'Malley ever says to her is . . . 'Jesus Helen, lay off it will you . . . some crazy kid has just been pushed down fifteen flights of stairs and looks like Humpty Dumpty here and you're giving me static about going to see some fat Italian chick busting her lungs . . . I'll call you later when I see how this pans out.' – *Cadumphff*

31

never ever watch porno movies

It is getting late. Very late at night or early in the morning.
Half full or half empty.

I know this. And how do I know this? It's simple . . .
they are now showing porno movies on the TV set.
Normally this would not upset me one way or the other
. . . in fact Catholic guilt would ensure I'd sneak a peek just
to see what we'd been missing out all those years. It
troubles me now however. The movie is actually one I
have seen before . . . many years ago with six other
fourteen-year-olds all too embarrassed to leave the room
and Sean Dorgan fainted when the guy in the movie
eventually shoots his load and then Joey Maguire went to
the bathroom and returns ten minutes later and he is
forever known thereafter as Joey the Creamer . . . we are so
unforgiving . . . I tap in www.joeythecreamer.com into the
laptop but get a server not available which sort of
reassures me that there is hope and redemption in
cyberspace.

Love to know what Joey the Creamer is up to now. Sort of feel guilty because I was the one who came up with the moniker and it probably caused him major psychological problems into his late teens and beyond.

Remorse. Bleeding . . . hurtling through the streets of New York and the remorse for bad things done creeps its inexorable finger round the coil of my psyche. This is too maudlin by far and I should stop it so I will . . .

But the porno movie . . .

The one I have seen before . . . the first one I had ever seen . . . and the TV on the end of my bed is beaming the pictures to me as it has been doing with all the other clips from movies and TV programmes with the one subtle but important difference this time . . . I am not featured in this one. Typical.

Moresthepity.

Daisy . . . thankfully . . . is not in it either. The actors are so bored-looking. First time I had sex I tried to look as bored as they did in the movie and it had the opposite effect . . . and anyway I ended up wedging my willy between her bum and the brown velvet couch and the stain never came off the sofa cushion and it still bemuses my mother as to what it is.

The movie ends in a crescendo of ohhing and ahhing and I am glad it is over. There is not enough blood left inside me to induce a state of tumescence or maybe there is enough for a partial effort but I have no wish to do so. The movie is over and there is now a National Geographic Channel special on about sperm whales.

I have seen this also.

32

those nice Christian Brothers

The saline drip has miraculously replenished itself. I have no idea how this happened but then again there are a lot of things lately that I cannot understand let alone try to explain.

A guy from UPS drives up along beside me. He asks me my name and then delivers a huge hamper to me ... there is barely room for it on the bed. It obscures the TV set as well which is not necessarily a tragic thing as it is bad for the eyesight and all that and so is smoking and so are three bullet wounds in the stomach so don't do any of these things or at least not without parental advice.

But the hamper ... there is cheese from Denmark and a bottle of Fleurie. This is what it says on the label ...

'*Fleurie ... appellation fleurie contrôlée ... mis en bouteilles par ...*'

The UPS guy scraped away the rest of the label as he was sitting in traffic because he has recently given up smoking and he finds this therapeutic so he does. His van is still alongside the trolley and he is looking expectantly at me and I look back at him expectantly waiting for maybe another parcel but he is waiting for a tip.

I think about giving him the whole story about Santos and my wallet and the fact that all my valuables are now in an ambulance along with two pissed-off and irate paramedics and that maybe I don't got no cash on me right now so I give him the cheese back and he almost rams me in disgust as he had his eye on the wine . . . especially as he had read the label and it sounded nice. Hmm . . . it does sound nice but I can't eat the cheese and it will just come straight back out again and at least the wine is the same colour more or less as my blood and so no one will really notice that I'm leaking.

He pulls away with such force that he burns some rubber and there is an aerodynamic backlash that is not quite as uncomfortable as it could be and certainly nothing like some of the turbulence I have experienced on planes before.

When his van was alongside me his stereo was playing Tom Waits . . . 'Waltzing Matilda' . . . 'And it's a battered old suitcase in a hotel someplace' . . . and this reminds me of the Christian Brothers and school and all that. Well actually Tom Waits reminds me specifically of a Brother Budderly who used to teach us in fourth class and he looked very like Tom Waits although none of use were too clued in to this fact at the time which was just as well for all parties concerned . . . particularly Tom Waits.

Tom Waits featured regularly in our Tit Club meetings after school on Fridays. Each member had to bring in the album cover of one of their older brothers' or sisters' record collection, that featured tits on them. I used to bring in the cover of *Small Change* by Tom Waits. But one of the other lads knocked us all for six when he brought in the cover of one of the early Roxy Music albums that featured two naked women on it.

Most of the time the rest of us only managed those crappy *Top of the Pops* covers with the fake songs and even faker-looking tits. These were moments of reprieve away from Brother Budderly.

But we copped it later . . . don't know if it was some sort of a Borg-esque collective realisation or whether it was some random revelation. This is not important. One thing that we copped on to later was that he used to keep his leather strap down the front of his trousers . . . which were creased to perfection and which he seemed mighty proud of and then he would ask what the capital of Belize was and I knew it was Belmopen but he would not ask me because he knew I was good at capitals and so he asked Brian Burke who was not and when he did not know it gave him a ready excuse to take Big Bertha out . . . for that is what he used to call his leather strap . . . Big Bertha, and if any of us were naughty he would drag it slowly from within the nether regions of his black trousers and ask, 'Who wants some of Big Bertha?'

Again I don't know if this was a sudden collective realisation but it was a revelation and some of my classmates probably went back to the school and gave him a good kick in the bollocks.

Brother Budderly was defrocked and thrown out of the Brothers after he delivered the Last Rites to a fellow brother. This was not a defrocking incident in itself but they were both in the sauna at a well-known gay hostelry at the time. Brother Budderly will eventually find a job working as a barman in

Pocatello, Idaho. He marries and has two sons, twins in fact, who by a huge fluke of genetics will both turn out to be gay and announce this at their 21st birthday celebrations. Mr Budderly has a heart attack that night and never recovers. – *Cadumphff*

They were good to me and sure didn't I get a great education says Dad as I'm lying on this trolley suffering the ill effects of getting mixed up in the drug business 3,000 miles from home. But the A in honours maths was dead useful ... I could calculate the number of grains in a given sample of cocaine and compute this to 1% accuracy which always amazed Dub and then convert this into any other measurement he wished.

Another dodgy character was Brother Froggy who ran the in-school sweet shop. Am I rambling? ... More saline goddammit ... I've paid for this saline and I want my cut.

But Froggy ...

He sold sweets and crisps and things like that and we all got to work there one week in a year when we were in fourth or fifth class ... oh, how we dreamed of those days ... and we were paid in sweets and stuff ... hmmmmm ... it was truly a proud moment and something that only the most trusted boys got to do. I think I even wet the bed in anticipation and then dried the sheets with my sister's hair dryer before anyone got home although the smell of burnt piss was everywhere and we blamed the cat ... the one next door as we didn't have one ourselves.

So we worked lunch times and then we were allowed to go back to class late because we would have to help clean up and also eat our own lunch which was invariably tons of crisps and as many Loop the Loop ice pops as our teeth could manage. Then we would have to endure

Froggy's octogenarian lecture about morals and probity and how to behave as a young man in society and we'd sit there with our Loop the Loops and listen intently to words we did not understand ...: trying to eat all the chocolate off without having to get into the green lime part and then work on the yellow lemon bit ... it was hard work.

Froggy was eighty but smelt older. He looked like Grandpa Simpson in a penguin suit.

The lecture:

He would first make us sit on top of one of those storage heater things, which were busy sweating their own heat in the middle of a mild May. And there you would have to stay for the twenty minutes of the lecture on pain of forfeiting the crisps and Loop the Loops. And eventually there would be steam rising off our bums and he would pat them cool for us. Then he would tell us about the dangers ... mortal dangers mind you ... of ever, ever touching our own genitalia ... he could not have been clearer on this point. To touch one's own genitalia was a Straight-To-Hell Offence and make no mistake about it. To go to the toilet was fine . . . that was unavoidable but if we had an itch or wanted to touch them for any other reason we were to do as he was about to show us and then he would deftly put his hand down the front of our wee shorts and proceed to fondle and scratch our genitals for us.

And we would eat our Loop the Loops and giggle. It is only now, approaching the end of Manhattan and perhaps the end of my time around here, that I think about this. If he were alive I would like to punch him in the genitals. Scratch that Froggy.

There is snow on the TV . . . nothing on. No one runs beside the trolley. There is no one on the streets of Manhattan. No one heard my confession.

- Forgive me Father, for they know not what they do.
- And have you any sins to confess my son?
- Well, one of your crowd used to interfere with me when I was a wee nipper.
- Ah, yes, well that's not really the sort of thing we cater for here. And anyways we put an ad in the national papers to say we were sorry. So have you anything to confess . . . anything real that is?
- Well, there was this bag full of cocaine I was carrying when I was shot.
- Oh yes now, tell me all about that. Was it for personal use or for distribution?
- Distribution Father.
- Say three Hail Marys and an Our Father and we'll say no more.
- Thanks Father.
- Eh . . . you wouldn't by any chance have any of the cocaine to spare . . . just for the roof fund, don't you know.
- Sorry Father.

And he whisks off to save some other more deserving soul.

'Now the dogs they are barking . . . and the taxis are parking.'

33

poetry on TV

The TV is now showing a programme with people sitting around drinking coffee and discussing poetry and stuff. It is real shite. But one of the poems they discuss is one of my early works called 'No Time to Play'. They analyse it and astutely surmise that the poet is someone who is going to get into an awful lot of trouble and the interviewer looks straight into the camera and looks earnestly at me and tells me I am a very naughty boy. This is the poem they are discussing:

Poem #1
Darkness smothers the city once more
Into the Liffey the sewers they pour
Night's shining halo brightens the way
For the poor dismal wino begging our stay.
With his enchanted fiddle that plays on and on
To the unheard praise of the bustling throng
Rush-hour victims try to play dumb
Their thoughts far away from the deafening hum.

In an hour or more the traffic is gone
But the lonely old man stands on the bridge
And the now-muted fiddle lies dejected by his side
He fumbles through the coppers that will pay his
    meagre way
Another hour and yet another, to hasten forth
    another day.

I am so mortally embarrassed by the poem that I try to turn off the TV. I cannot and I feel as if my cheeks are gone rosy red . . . which they are not as this requires far too much blood and that would not do really. I turn my face away from the screen and actively ignore what they are saying. The channel changes after a few moments.

    - Don't worry Shem, it wasn't that bad.

It is <u>Dave Fanning</u> on a satellite link from the studios back in Dublin. I can hear the small motor of the saline drip whir as it turns and accurately alters the geometric shape of the plastic pouch into a concave receptacle for the signals zapping to and fro. I am impressed. Progress.

Dave is on the TV sitting on a leather couch and adjusting his earpiece and he is not startled at all when he realises he is live. This man is a pro. Him and Gene Hackman . . . they are good at what they do.

    - Ooopss. Hello there New York.

    - Hi Dave.

    - Howya Shem.

Dave Fanning

Dave is this really cool DJ and VJ and he is sort of credited with discovering U2 or at least giving them their first break and in gratitude for this he is the very first DJ in the world to get access to each new

U2 album as it comes on stream. This is very fortunate for Dave as it saves him queuing outside HMV in Grafton Street, Dublin, in the rain overnight.

- So Dave. How are you?
- I'm fine Shem, but you don't look too well.
- You know yourself.
- I do indeed ... now what's it to be ... I don't think we have this link for too long ... do we? ... (to sound engineer) ... how long has he got?
- They don't reckon you have too long Shem so we better get moving.

My wounds are worse than I thought.

- Okay Dave ... well I know it sounds silly and me being here and wounded and all that and it's more like a hospital request show that you perhaps used to do as a very young man but I was hoping you'd play my five favourites of all time and introduce the videos and you know yourself.

So here goes Dave:

1	Adagio for Strings	-	Barber
2	Rainy Night in Soho	-	The Pogues
3	True Companion	-	Marc Cohen
4	Running to Stand Still	-	U2
5	The River	-	Bruce Springstein

I actually e-mail Dave the choice and he is reading them from a screen nearby and he is all very nice about the whole thing.

- Eh, yeah Shem, we have all those on video except the first one as video wasn't around when he released it, however it was played for Kennedy when he died so we can use a clip of that ... quite appropriate really, yeah?

- What ever you think is best Dave.
- It sure is a nice mix . . . you got a bit of everything in there except maybe jazz and some post-modern stuff but it's cute.
- What would your own top five be Dave?

He laughs this off, knowing that this list could be worth a lot of money and possibly boost sales of whatever records he selects . . . but seeming to miss the point that what with the three gunshot wounds and everything, I am unlikely to profit from the knowledge. Still you can never be too careful these days what with the Internet and cyber crime.

- Come on Dave . . . you've seen the wounds . . . and you said I haven't long . . .
- No, I meant the satellite link . . . that we haven't long with the link . . .

He looks to the camera again and sees that I am telling the truth.

- Listen Shem, it may be too late but if there's anything I can do . . .

I think about asking if he can bell Bono and the boys and get them to organise a gig for the victims of Irish-American drug-related shooting incidents specific to the NYC area sort of kind of benefit thing . . . but let's be honest, the networks over here wouldn't touch it with a barge.

- Thanks Dave, but I think we both know I'm beyond that stage . . . maybe if we could just play the videos and that sort of thing . . .

Dave does so, with an excellent intro to each.

- Thanks Dave.
- Pleasure Shem. See you the same time next week.

He realises his faux pas . . .

- Well, you know what I mean . . .

And the TV turns to snow screen as the satellite link closes down.

34

there was a rooster

Cock.

Cock a doodle do.

'There was this rooster came into our yard and he caught them chickens right offa their guard.'

A line from a song years ago and I remember hearing it in some pub and it was a ballad group and they all looked like <u>Luke Kelly</u> and they all drank Guinness and they were all complete lunatics. There was a pall of invisible ultra-sinus vapour around them all the time ... brought on by the massive amount of Guinness they consumed. And if you could take a photo of them using ultra-sinus sensitive film there would be a lovely aura about them proving that they were extra-terrestrials and a lot of the media always suspected them of being anyways.

But I digress. This character that always hung around Dub ... he was actually Dub's shadow ... well he was called Rooster by all and sundry. He loved the name. Thought it was great. He also thought he was great and he was a big smash with the girls. And the problem was that he was. He always managed to get very good-looking women but they never hung around for long. He used to shrug his shoulders and say that they were boring him senseless.

Luke Kelly
Hugely respected folk and traditional Irish singer famed for his part in the group The Dubliners. He died early due to a brain tumour but is remembered for his unique and definitive rendition of 'Raglan Road', among other great songs. He was known to be fond of a pint and had this great beard that would have a little halo of Guinness stuck to it after he'd take a big gulp.

I am saying all this about Rooster only because I can see him approaching my trolley, slightly stumbling from side to side.

- Howya Shem.

It is practically the only time he does not follow the greeting up with a mighty and painful slap on the back. This seems to confuse him and he slaps the metal sidebars of the trolley a number of times to compensate. The sound rings hollow and bounces off the buildings like some call to arms.

- So Shem, not looking too good hah?

- No Rooster, I am not.

- Well, are you not going to ask me?

The trick with Rooster was to ignore him as much as possible and under no circumstances ask him a direct question about what he was doing with such and such a girl or on such and such a night.

- What am I meant to ask you Rooster?

- About these.

He motions to the rollerblades on his feet.

- Oh right ... aren't they great yokes?
- Well, there was this bird going around on them selling shots of whiskey ... you should have seen her ... big tits squashed into this pink boob tube ... mandear I tell ya. Anyways didn't I only score with her and get a rake of free shots into the bargain.
- And where is she now Rooster?
- Ah, I got bored with her.

Rooster has no penis. This is not a derogatory statement intended to belittle his manhood ... it is simply true. Or nearly true. He has a very tiny penis. He was born with this condition and so he does not really know what he is missing. It would be a lot worse if he had lost it in a mill accident or whatever. Even in my current state of dying I manage to cringe at the thought and try to cross my legs.

He is saving up for <u>phalloplasty</u> after he saw an advert on the subway. He nearly has enough for the operation.

phalloplasty

Laser phalloplasty, the newest procedure in cosmetic surgery for men. Phalloplasty is a penile shaft enhancement procedure that is simple, safe and designed to increase both the length and circumference of the penile shaft. Now done with the latest laser technique, healing is rapid and the patient is up and about the next day.

No foreign material or implant is used. This procedure does not interfere with sensation or function and is done on an outpatient basis in the confidential setting of our accredited state of the art surgical facility. Well, at least that's what the advert on the subway said.

- What's wrong there Shem . . . you don't look well all of a sudden?

This makes him laugh . . .

- Do you hear me with the 'You don't look well and half of you missing already' look? Mandear.
- So what's the story Rooster?

I know there is a purpose to his visit, as he does not have the intellectual capability to ever venture out on a random involuntary fact-finding mission . . . also known as a walk.

- Eh, I know it's a bad time and all . . . but Dub was wondering like . . . is there any sign of the bag of stuff? He was just wondering like.

Rooster was a linguistic phenomenon because none of the Irish people could ever tell what part of the homeland he hailed from. He had adopted and plagiarised phrases from all the main dialects . . . but this was not affected in any way it was just the way he was . . . Rooster, the man of a thousand voices . . . and no penis. He could certainly talk a good game though if nothing else and that was his secret with the girls . . . because once the girls found out his 'little problem' they tended not to hang around too long. They got bored.

- To tell you the truth Rooster my man, I think the bag of shit is now in the hands of a team of paramedics who are probably out looking for me right now. So I suggest you go and tell Dub that he should try to find himself an ambulance but he better be quick because as soon as those boys open that bag . . . kiss that shit goodbye.

- Oh, right, well I'll tell Dub what you said.
- You do that Rooster. And you better watch that truck parked by the side of the . . .

But it was too late . . . he thumped into the side of the parked truck and that was the end of him. I laugh . . . it is not funny and I do not wish him any harm. But if someone dials 911 now and he gets the same ambulance as I did, well we could both end up hurtling around the streets of Manhattan and normally I would not mind the company but I honestly think that Rooster would drive me around the bend after a wee while. If I could drive myself around the bend I would do so and try to head for a hospital . . . but I cannot seem to do this, which is actually a design flaw with this particular model of the Klinowitz trolley.

Me and Rooster and our trolleys and the night in Manhattan. I laugh again to myself . . . me and Rooster out on the town getting totally trolleyed. Me and Rooster out of our trolleys. Must check etymology of the trolley when I get a chance. Too busy right here, right now.

35

the last time I came

Here's a thought.

Pothole.

Safe now.

Sorry. Here's the thought.

Imagine you know when the last time you will ever have sex is ... the last orgasm you will ever have. Imagine you knew that.

Becky is astride me.

It is 4.17 pm of a Tuesday.

I know this because I looked at the clock beside the bed because I had to meet Dub to collect the stuff from him. Becky wants me to stay and nibbles at my ear. I never had the heart to tell her that this really annoys me and that it does not turn me on but the first time we were together she did it and I pretended to be aroused by it but I am not anymore and now she won't stop.

It is 4.18 pm. She has also had a fairly nondescript orgasm and that's because she has been doing too much of

Dub's coke lately and it doesn't really agree with her although judging by the amounts she does it is not true.

– I have to get up.

She reluctantly slides off me and tells me what an asshole I am in that cute St Paul–New York mélange. She throws the pillow at me and says . . . 'Well that's the last time we're ever having sex.'

This is, in fact, true. – *Cadumphff*

It is now 4.18 am.

The clock on the building says so. For me the end of time is probably nigh. Ed the Drunk is standing on the street corner and is waving to me. He is carrying a sandwich board with the words 'The End of Time is Nigh . . . Repent Now.' He smiles as I pass and I wonder has he seen some sign in the stars or something.

It is because he knows about the aliens from the planet Rongagen, in the Paxo Quadrant. – *Cadumphff*

The phone rings at 4.37 pm of a Tuesday and indeed it is Dub checking on my whereabouts . . . a stickler for time so he is. He quips that he hoped me and Becky were not doing anything that he wouldn't do.

– No Dub, we weren't.

– And we certainly won't again.

(Becky slamming the door and going in to do some more coke.)

– Right, listen up . . . here's the directions to get the stuff . . . listen carefully and do not write it down, do you hear me . . . that is very important . . . if you write it down, they can link you to the crime . . . you got that?

- Sure.
- Right ... kiss Becky on each cheek of her arse for me and then off into the cold Manhattan night with you. Wrap up warm baby.

But anyway.

The next time sex is involved, think of this one inexorable fact ... it could be your last time ever. Breathing ... something I am not mastering at the moment as the end of Manhattan looms larger with each street corner passed.

Anyway.

That was it. My last time. And I was watching the fucking clock waiting for Dub to ring. Imagine that.

And now ... guts hanging out ... life ebbing away ... and all the visitors to my trolley seem to agree ... ebbing away at a pace. And Becky was breathing beside me ... 'Just tell Dub to fuck off, why don't you?' ... and I wish I had.

- Go on honey ... tell him and then go pick up some Ben & Jerry's and we can eat ice cream and watch silly TV all day.

I should have done just that but I didn't and we now could be wrapped up in the *leaba*[16] eating Phish Food or New York Super Fudge and watching silly TV and that sort of thing ... instead I am just watching stupid TV.

---

[16] Gaelic word for bed. Danish term for astronauts who never actually make it into space. Planet Rongagen term for astronauts who went to Planet Earth and ended up in a country called Denmark. These terms can be used interchangeably in Planet Rongagen or in Denmark but not in Ireland.

36

regarding Francis Champion

I pass a shop called Peaches & Cream. I am quite near Fulton Fish Market and I have to be honest I am getting excited. I have no real idea why . . . maybe there is a sense of finality or whatever. I cannot really tell. I am going to stop . . . not the trolley for I cannot seem to do this . . . but stop in my head and consider the facts as they are.

The facts as they are: my trolley and its occupants . . . including the TV, the saline drip, remote control, pillows, bed sheets, the remote control, the saline drip . . . oh, you've said that, and Bruce Forsyth is beside me, holding my elbow in avuncular fashion and urging me to repeat the list of items as much as possible – oh, didn't he do well! . . . are hurtling through the streets of Manhattan at a speed greatly in excess of the designed maximum.

Another fact is that poor Santos – for you have to feel for him realistically – is now tearing his hair out frantically looking for me and the trolley. The trolley is insured but perhaps I am not – and he has not found me yet and he is unlikely to if he doesn't arrive before I hit the end of Manhattan.

But Santos is stressed which is not healthy. He is thirty-seven and he is nearly bald.

He will be completely bald by the time he hits forty.
– *Cadumphff*

God is cruel. This is not a statement relating to my own predicament . . . I deserve this and much more probably. Easy to be stoical when you have no blood left in you and not much else besides.

No. God is cruel because he is not just satisfied with making men go bald . . . that would be too easy . . . what he does is actually pull the hair out of their heads through the nose and ears . . . now that is cruel.

I have a full head of hair. People often used to look at me and say I had a full head of hair and they said it to my mother about me as well and look and me with the full head of hair . . . My dad said it to me once when I tumbled down the side of Vinegar Hill . . . and broke my wrist in a bazillion places – bits of fern and muck and grass lodged in my hair and he said as a way of comfort that that would not have happened if I was bald and that I was protected by my hair . . . and the no blood and the no stomach and I think that is funny . . . some guy from school that we used to bully . . . Francis Champion rolls up beside me on his skateboard and he takes a look at me and smiles caustically and says with as much bitterness as he can muster . . . 'I always said that Shern fella had no stomach for anything and now I am right.' If that is not bitter then the squeezing of a lemon above my wounds is bitter.

Francis Champion is his real name but it is somewhat of a misnomer, he is neither a champion nor a winner nor ever shared a place on the podium with anyone. He should have been christened Francis Nobody or Francis Egghead or Francis Bacon ... or King Francis the First Loser on the Planet.

Chimp that's what we always called him ... anytime we ever bullied, badgered, harangued, pushed, shoved, niggled, tickled, slagged or teased, that is what we taunted him with ... there goes Chimp and he's only a wee silly little thing.

He is back now beside the trolley and wearing the expensive suit and he is four feet taller than I seem to remember ... I kid you not, four full feet ... not a word of a lie ... and he has this aura of confidence around him ... it really is an aura ... around him it is the Aurora Boringbastard ... but he would not appreciate the humour. That was Chimp's fault ... he never saw our side of the humour as we dangled him by his shoelaces from the fourth floor window and only Cookie Callaghan's intervention would save his life ... and we would plead with Cookie that we were only trying to prove a few basic laws of the pulley system and the parallelogram of forces and Cookie would be real proud and let us dangle Chimp some more ... but there would be none of that dangling thing now and him with the extra four feet on top of him, no messing.

But the aura around him shimmers when he turns his head ... it is very impressive and it makes him look angelic and like some sort of a saint, which he could be considering what he put up with from the rest of us, God bless him. By the looks of those shimmering lights around his head it looks like God has blessed him indeed, and maybe put him down in the big beatification book where all the Holy Joes go ... Saint Joe the Hole ... never heard of him ...

But when I think of those beautiful nebulous, wispy lights around his head I laugh which hurts like hell because we always used to say that Francis Champion was light-headed and it looks like we were right all along.

But Francis Champion the Now Tall Brave Light-Headed Person is looking sympathetically at me. He pulls back the sheet gently and tuts tuts but not maliciously. There is not a malicious bone in his body ... in fact there are probably very few bones left in his body on account of that one time when his shoelaces snapped as we were doing the pulley system thing and he managed to bounce himself off the ground in such a fashion so as not to break everything ... it is still talked about how he managed to actually bounce himself off the ground ... it is no mean feat ... and Mr Callaghan telling us that the impact between Chimp and the ground would have caused both bodies to accelerate slightly depending on their respective masses ... and we did indeed have a respective Mass for Chimp to pray to Saint Holy Joe that Francis Champion would recover and come back because we had no one else to volunteer for the pulley system.

- So Chi ... Francis ... are you here to gloat or what?
- No.
- Really?
- I was hoping to help.
- A form of gloating ...
- No, a form of medicine actually ... I am the Head of Oncology at City Hospital.
- Head of ... at your tender age?

- Yep, last April.
- Go on . . . you mad thing ya. Listen . . . Francis . . . about all that stuff . . .
- Relax Shem . . . this isn't *Flatliners* . . . I am not some menacing visitation from the past come back to make your life a misery.

He uses the word 'misery' with a noticeable inflection at the end that sounds ominous to me.

- I am not here for retribution.
- But the time with the shoelaces snapping and the bones broken everywhere and . . . all that messing . . .
- They healed.
- I felt terrible about it.
- Believe me when I tell you that I felt worse. Anyway if I hadn't repeated that year I might never have made Med School.
- True, true . . . so are you here to thank me then?
- Don't push it.
- I've had bad dreams about it . . . the way you seemed only to look into my eyes in those few seconds as you were falling down but some of the other lads said they swore you were looking at them and it's like that famous picture with your one looking at you no matter where you stand.
- I wish I could say I did it deliberately but I don't remember too much . . . just the agonising sound of the shoelace snapping and then the slow motion effect of falling. It really is true what they say about your life flashing before you.
- Sure don't be telling me. But worst of all was Cookie prattling on to us, as you were lying on the ground and the ambulance not even rung, that the way you

were screaming on the way down was a classic
example of the Doppler Effect.

- Cookie . . . I wonder is he still around.
- He was here earlier . . . but then you probably know
that or don't know that or are part of this whole
weirdness thing that's happening to me.

Francis Champion shrugs.

- Yeah well . . . for what it is worth I am really sorry for
my part in the whole scheme.
- Accepted.
- So?
- So . . . Shem . . . do you want my professional opinion
or not?
- Give it to me Doc.
- You have a splattered spleen, damage to the
duodenum, lacerated liver, punctured pancreas and a
few other complications.

I note the alliteration in his diagnosis and suspect that
maybe he is having some fun at my expense, which would
be a deserved dollop of nemesis and me with the
alliteration as well.

- Okay Francis . . . I think I get the picture. Don't
suppose there is any chance for me at all?

His bleeper goes off . . . interfering with the TV.

- Have to be off Shem.
- Okay Francis . . . thanks for dropping by . . . I know
how busy you must be. Listen, if you see those
paramedics guys around will you tell them to stop
looking for me as I'm going to pop home to see if I
can see Becky.
- Okay Shem, I will do that . . . but before I go . . .
remember when you guys used to do all those

terrible things to me and I would go home to my
single widowed mother and cry for days on end and
then wet the bed constantly ... well she used to grab
me by the shoulders and shake me until I stopped
and look me straight in the eye and tell me ... those
little bastards are guttersnipes and useless nothings
and will never amount to anything. They are cowards
... yellow through and through, gutless, no stomach
for anything.

He lets a dramatic pause happen and I know not to
interrupt what must be a great moment for him.

- Well ... I have to say she was right about one thing
  Shem, and I say this to you honestly, professionally
  and without a trace of bitterness ... you are gutless
  and you have no stomach.

And he is gone.

37

Vee knows best

Francis is right. Now I do not have a full stomach . . . I have a partial one. Some of it is still back on the corner of 32nd and Second Avenue. Some of it is on the coat of that nice man with the cell phone who rang the ambulance. Some of it is on Becky's clothes and some of it is on Santos and other bits are in the ambulance and places like that and other bits are on the trousers of that Old Black Man who was standing at the scene staring at me with that weird look on his face. As Dub would often say to me, 'Jasus Shem, you're all over the fucking place, so you are.'

But I do still have a full head of hair . . . but not a full stomach. How come no one ever gets shot in the hair? I wish now that I had been shot three times in the hair. Permacide.

Should really try and send an e-mail to Aido . . . get him to make up one of those puzzles and the first three correct answers will each receive a commemorative piece of my tummy ... could be worth something in years to come. So that's the deal.

We are passing a Starbucks. The coffee is so good there it's not funny. Just one big cup of coffee and I could suck the frothy foam and leave the rest to posterity. There is a woman in the window of the coffee house eating a blueberry muffin and drinking a large frappacino.

This woman is Becky's mother. Purely a coincidence. She looks up momentarily. Yes it is definitely Becky's mum, Vee. I never found out if that was her real name or not ... Vee ... just Vee. She recognises me on the trolley and smiles. It is not a happy smile, not a sad smile ... more of a stoical smile. And then she nods her head ever so slightly as if giving her imprimatur to my plans to go to see Becky. Mums always know best. Vee knows best. I laugh at this in my head because that's what my own mum used to say to us when we had colds and the flu and stuff ... she would go to the magical medicine monstrance and bring out the sickly sweet smelling bottle of decongestant and shake it in front of us and say ... 'Venos best.'

This is merely a linguistic coincidence and no great significance should be attached to it.

One coincidence that is worth noting, however, is that Vee is reading a magazine and the paper on which it is printed came from a tree in the Trondheim. The tree that is currently beside Becky in Kylemore Abbey is a spruce tree that also came originally from the Trondheim. Vee is not aware of this, in fact, I am quite sure that she is not aware that her daughter is now an oak tree back in Ireland ... not a lot of people are ... just me, Becky and the Old Black Man, who seems somehow responsible for all of this in one way or the other. The fact that Vee does not know any of this is a shame because they have never been close and this link via the piece of paper is effectively the closest they have come in years.

Vee turns the page and forgets all about me. And there is good reason why she should. In front of her in full colour gloss for all the world to see is a picture of Becky's dad ... Michael ... also Vee's estranged husband. They had split up because he was having an affair with the Latino beauty who is now holding his hand, and his fortune, in the picture. Michael is not pretty to look at but he is loaded. Becky never wanted any of his money and even sent cheques back to him ... this is when we were selling stuff for Dub, so it must have been pretty hard for her. We could have used the money to get away and start afresh but she was very serious about it, so I never hassled her.

38

the facts about Michael Flanagan

Michael Flanagan came over from Ireland in the late 1960s and settled in St Paul, Minnesota. Some joked that it was the 1860s he came over in, but they didn't joke very loudly or very long. He was a skilled man, as his father before him, and he worked his way as a carpenter and a construction worker and anything else he could put his hand to. Often he put his hand to the left buttock of just about any passing female. He was a solid, upright type of man but had this one failing for the opposite sex.

Stan, the barman, once said to Michael in a moment of blinding prescience, that women would be the ruination of him. However, despite this he was no slouch and went to night school and became a bit of a whiz at electronics and formed a small little firm that specialised in making low power radio devices for switches and alarm sensors. Flanagan Wireless eventually became one of Minnesota's most successful enterprises and exported their products all over the world.

Michael still keeps tabs with the homeland and Becky told me of how he used to secrete monies away for the IRA and how he was regarded as a big man in local Irish circles. Some of them looked up to him as a shining example of what the Irish could do in America . . . and he would wear a Guinness baseball cap at the company barbecue and everyone thought he was great and Vee was no exception and she fell for him big time and they were happy and then Becky came along and he was getting richer and richer . . . and then Becky was a young woman just like that and Vee knew that he was having affairs and she turned a blind eye mostly and that really tore into Becky and then what tore into her more was when she came home from college with her roommate for Thanksgiving and Michael somehow ended up in the guestroom with Becky's friend from college. Becky left and never saw either of them again. And that is the truth about Michael Flanagan.

A small flake of brown paint peels off the ceiling in the coffee shop where Vee is and lands noiselessly in the frothy mountains of her frappacino. It blends in with the chocolate and cinnamon powder and she never notices it. A quick flakology calculation using the laptop shows an F value of 0.008.

Hmm.

There may be trouble ahead.

Let's face the music and dance.

39

the flight across to Ireland

The Old Black Man has been pushing me so hard that I have gained considerable velocity. Escape velocity. Down towards the end of The Bowery and onto Manhattan Bridge. Except that I never make the bridge. We are going so fast that I lift off before it. And what with him having the limp and all that. Amazing. I fly up in the air ... I seem to have been here before and the judges marks ... 5.9 ... 5.9 ... 5.9 shows that the practice has indeed helped. I look back and the Old Black Man is smiling and waving like some crazed actor in a cheap children's movie.

I get a great view of Manhattan. There are a few low clouds that cause the bed to rock a little but the trolley holds solid. The TV rattles but it has survived worse and the saline seems to be flowing better at altitude. Still, I grip the metal bars on the side.

Back in Dr Klinowitz's study there are <u>stress-strain</u> curves for the metal of the trolley that would put my mind to rest but I do not have access to these for the moment so my mind is not at rest. But the TV holds firm under the strain thanks to the Flanagan Wireless Conformal Coated Printed Circuit Board which was stress-tested at their facility in St Paul, Minnesota.

stress-strain

Everything has its breaking point. The measurement of the stress versus the strain will give a good idea of where this point is. Metal can be tested this way to ascertain how safe it is for bridges and things like that. Medieval kings also believed that people could be stretched and strained in the same way to find their breaking point, using a complex piece of high technology called 'the rack'.

Up, up and away I go.

I am flying now. To be honest it does not feel strange and exhilarating. I think the trolley is more excited than me and Brownian Motion of its molecules would probably lay testament to this fact. This flying thing is easy. It is also easy for the Airbus 330 that is now flying alongside me.

Airbus 330

Airbus Industrie's A330/A340 family of aircraft with a choice of two or four engines on the same aircraft fuselage, allowing them to optimise their aircraft choice for particular missions. CD player is optional.

They are supposedly working on a space craft that will enable people to go on pleasure cruises to the moon, at affordable prices. People have placed bookings already apparently.

A message from Air Traffic Control at Kennedy Airport comes over the TV's speakers.

- Trolley #2 please report position and intended flight path.
- Eh? ... I'm not sure.
- Trolley #2 please report your position and intended flight path.
- Eh, well I seem very high up and I only have half a saline drip left. (There is a long pause.)
- Thank you Trolley #2, you may proceed ... have a safe flight.
- Eh, thanks Control ... but if you don't mind me asking, what's with the #2 stuff?
- Trolley #2 copy ... you are the second this week to attempt flight without pre-clearance while using a non-US federal aviation authority approved aircraft.
- Sorry ATC but did you say second?
- This week ... affirmative. (pause) This is New York fella.

I am a little bit miffed by being second. I mean, come on, what does one have to do?

Once we reach our cruising altitude the TV automatically switches to the in-flight movie. Fuck. It is one I have seen before ... the one with Gene Hackman fighting on the roof with myself ... and it is getting quite cold but the wind is at my back so it should be a relatively short flight and the saline is magically full again which troubles me how that happens, but not enough to lose sleep over.

I am at 37,000 feet now. The little altimeter tells me this fact. It is reassuring to know. It is also very, very cold. Little shards of ice form on the sides of the Klinowitz trolley, which is now operating well outside the environmental specifications for which it was designed, so anything could happen really.

My airborne raggle taggle of blankets and saline drips and TV is flying alongside the much sleeker Aer Lingus jet bound for Dublin. It is amazing how cool they look from the outside and they also look like they are a complete aberration of all the laws of nature and how in the name of fuck do they actually stay up there in the first place . . .

I glance across to the pilot's cabin. The co-pilot is reading a book called *The Physics of Flying* and it is open on a page entitled 'The Truth about the Suck, Squash, Bang, Blow Theory.'

The air hostess is welcoming all and sundry aboard. *Dia daoibh a chairde*[17] and you are all very welcome on board.

Mary Higgins is in row 22A. She is looking out the window. She sees me, all wrapped up and trying to keep warm, in the trolley. I wave a wee wave to her. She does not wave back, so she doesn't. Mary hates flying you see. She hates it more than anything else in the world. Before the flight she took two Lexaton tablets, which are really valium by another name, and since take-off she has had three bottles of red wine . . . and she is smiling to herself . . . there is heavy turbulence and the seat belt sign is on and some of the other passengers have gone a little bit quiet and she is smiling and looking out the window. She is so thankful that she took the tablets and she doesn't care

[17]Welcome friends . . . basically Hello but with lots of religious stuff thrown in

if the plane crashes or not.because she is happy and she is looking out the window and she knows she is completely spaced and there's a funny little person in a hospital bed on an ambulance trolley flying alongside the plane and she thinks this is quite hilarious.

And Mary Higgins is right to have taken the tablets and the wine and to be now drunk because the captain of the plane and his co-pilot are playing video games up in the cockpit and although highly trained and skilled pilots this is of no consequence when you are basically flying one enormous big Pentium processor.

Alongside the plane I can hear the rattle and hum of the engines. It reminds me of rattle and hum.

40

why Becky adores Dub

Rattle.

Rattle and Hum.

The poster on the subway for U2 and their movie, album, CD, tape and DVD is impressive. I felt proud. Really proud of the boys. Our Boys.

Pride. That's what I felt.

It was 4 am . . . we had been in the city and were on our way back out to Sunnyside to meet Dub. I remember telling Becky all about how great U2 were and the way they could walk around Dublin and no one would hassle them except the American tourists . . . and the dig in the side she gave me . . . and how they could go into an ordinary bar and they would have their pints and no one would hassle them or even stare at them, in fact people in Dublin had developed a technique called Bonovision whereby if himself or any of the other lads from the band were having a beer you could actively look around the pub and your retina would paint in a digitised blur . . . like they do on crime-stoppers-type programmes where the person clubbing the cashier over the head with a piece of Wavin pipe is still technically innocent . . . and this Bonovision works great and they appreciate it and we don't feel like we're annoying them, because basically they are Our Boys.

I tell Becky also about the magazine *Our Boys* that we used to have in school that had short stories by the same person each week and the moral of the story was always the same and it was a veiled invocation to us all not to be touching our own genitals and I think maybe that Brother Froggy wrote the articles. Becky was buzzed, so she was following this conversation with a very interested look on her face and kept saying 'Yeah, yeah I know, yeah' repeatedly. She said that they would be mobbed in Minnesota and I thought she was talking about the Christian Brothers, who could well be mobbed anywhere, and maybe some of them used to appear in the *All Priests Show* . . . and I had to explain that to her as well, about how there was a show in the Braemor Rooms or somewhere every year and you could not . . . I repeat you could not . . . get a ticket for love, money or seven decades of the rosary and some of the priests would sing songs and dress up like Elvis and some of the brothers would do comedy acts . . . 'Did you hear the one about the fella who used to touch his own genitals?' And it was a rip-roaring success.

Becky and I were laughing at how fast we were both speaking and how everything seemed so crystal clear and lucid. But she said again that U2 would be mobbed in Minnesota.

U2 will never be mobbed in Minnesota.
They will be mobbed in Nebraska. Their tour bus will break down in the year 2010, when they are on an

Anniversary Tour. A farmer passing by will stop and help them out. This is the conversation that will ensue:

Farmer: Look like you gone blown your engine there fellas.

Bono: Yeah, do you know where there's a garage nearby?

Farmer: 'bout 70 miles due west of here.

Bono: Okay, is there a phone around here? None of our cell phones seem to work out here.

Farmer: We got no need for them cellophanes. Nearest phone is over Dan Struther's Feed Store. About 70 miles due north of here.

Bono: Look, we really need to get to a phone, we have a big gig tonight.

Farmer: Where you fellas from anyhows?

Bono: Ireland.

Farmer: I knew a fella from Finland once.

Bono: Eh, we're the band U2 and we really need some help.

Farmer: Yeah? What you fellas banned for then?

The conversation continues much like that until a bus carrying a high school cheerleader team passes by and picks the boys up. They will then be mobbed on the bus. *– Cadumphff*

Rattle of the subway carriage. Twinkly lights. Becky and I . . . both twinkly-eyed from taking a fair slice out of Dub's stuff tonight. Little bit out of this bag here and a little bit out of that bag there and we were all set. Sparkly, sparkly, little star, how I wonder where you are.

She put her arm through mine and entwined her fingers, combination style, into every possible permutation and each one sending a little twinkle, twinkle, tinkle up and down the arms. Our skin fused as if molten glass. No burning smell, just the smooth melding of our functions in one mass. Like <u>Siamese twins</u>.

291

<u>Siamese twins</u>
Name popularly applied to twins congenitally united
in a manner not incompatible with life or activity. The
name is derived from the famous twins Eng and
Chang, born of Chinese parents in Siam. Eng and
Chang were joined together at the sternum by a thick,
muscular ligament and remained united throughout
life. Joined twins are always identical. Surgical
separation is often possible. An operation was
successfully performed in 1953 on twins who were
joined near the base of the spine and shared the lower
intestinal tract, and in 1979 on twins joined at the
skull. Never get into a round with Siamese twins.

I thought the moment was right to air some things that
had been troubling me of late.

– Dub is getting out of control, Becky.

She is not really listening to me even though she is
probably tuned into four other conversations and a radio
station or two. The stuff we had taken that night was
premium grade class AAA, none of your Japanese rubbish gear.
And we were buzzing. I had 360 degree vision. This was a
new thing and I had never noticed it before and it was freaky,
but kind of nice at the same time and I was not complaining.

I could also smell most things around me and pick out
what people in the carriage had for their last meal though
this was not offensive smelling, it was more of a great
concoction of all the disparate cultures that make up New
York . . . I did not make that up, it was actually on a poster
in the carriage advertising the NYC Tourist Office and the
blurb from the mayor saying about the melting pot of
culture and the great concoction and I wish I had said it

because I think this is great and I am happy about it.

There is a very pretty Hispanic woman at the far end of the carriage and I can see that she is pregnant as if I was looking at a scan. Little foetus barely discernible. Baby would grow up to become President someday. I knew all this ... it was powerfully obvious to me ... and it was a burden knowing such a vast amount of information. My brain felt like Deep Blue or one of those super computers that beat <u>Kasparov</u> and made him throw a tantrum, and who could blame him.

<u>Kasparov</u>
Gary Kimovich Kasparov, world chess champion, who became the youngest world champion in history at the age of 22. In 1996 Kasparov competed against an IBM computer named Deep Blue, the first time a world champion has competed against a computer under standard match conditions. Deep Blue, operated by a team of IBM programmers, was capable of processing 50 billion chess positions every three minutes. Applying this massive computational power, Deep Blue won the first game of the match to become the first computer to defeat a world champion under regulation time controls. Kasparov subsequently defeated Deep Blue by a score of four games to two to win the match. There was no virus on the computer.

– Dub is all right.

It is Becky beside me. I almost forgot she was with me as you do when you are multi-tasking and sorting out chess Merediths and presidential hopefuls. She is staring at me full on and I know this means that she means what she says and it is not some casual remark.

293

I jump into the eyes and swim about and forget about life for a while. Backstroke, backstroke and then look directly up into her brain and see all the synaptic connections twinkling like the lights in the subway tunnels as we enter and leave them.

> - I think we should quit while we are still in his good books . . . you heard about Sean?
> - I heard.

We did not have to speak about the Sean incident because it started to play on the window opposite us . . . the glass illuminated in a full colour movie format.

There is Sean and Dub talking across a table. Late night in the bar and only some of the cronies playing pool, out of focus, in the background. Eight ball in the corner pocket.

Sean was nervous.

Dub was eating.

Sean was fidgeting and Dub was stuffing garlic mushrooms into his face. Dribbles of melted butter were running down his jowls and globules of it were glinting in that pathetic moustache.

> - So how's tricks Sean?
> - Fine Dub, fine.
> - You happy working for me Sean?
> - Of course Dub . . . of course . . . yeah . . .
> - Good . . . that's great fucking news altogether. We'll have a game of pool.
> - Lovely.
> - A few quid on it . . . maybe a twenty? For sport like.

Sean visibly relaxes and his hands stop their incessant fidgeting.

> - Sure Dub. I'll just grab us a couple of beers and let you finish your dinner in peace.

It is a deft manoeuvre and I think at first it is the flash of an out of sync tunnel light but the blur on the screen is due to Dub's extremely fast movement of his hand, as the garlic buttered-stained fork plunges into Sean's hand and skewers it to the tablecloth.

The table vibrates and one of the mushrooms falls off Dub's plate, pinballs off the salt shaker . . . ker ching ker ching . . . curves parabolically around the crumpled up serviette in a movement not unknown to bowling enthusiasts and nestles itself between Sean's index finger and thumb.

Sean's scream stops the cronies in mid shot. Close-up right in on Sean's face.

- Didn't I tell you never to fuck with the merchandise? Didn't I?
- I didn't . . . I . . . it was only for myself . . . sorry Dub, sorry . . . I didn't think . . .
- Oh, you didn't think full stop. But you are thinking now. Right?

Dub exerts more pressure on the already Uri Gellered fork.

- Yes Dub.
- And you'll never fuck with my stuff again?
- No Dub . . . I promise.
- Right then.

And just as quick as it happened it was over and he had the fork pulled out . . . and his arm around Sean, as if bosom buddies. Caring Dub wraps a napkin carefully around the bloodied hand. Dub living the American way . . . bomb the fuck out of you and then give you a Band-Aid. Good man Dub. *Maith an fear thú*[18] .

- Now, Sean . . . (and he slaps him on the back . . . friends

[18]Go on ya good man

again) . . . you know Dub does not hold grudges. Let's have that game of pool.

And Dub insists that Sean play a full game before he dispatches one of the lads to bring him to hospital (he has full medical insurance, Dub insists on it for all his 'staff') . . . and Sean has no choice. He is in agony taking his shots and he leaves splodges of blood all over the table and Dub is telling jokes and doesn't seem to notice.

- Hey lads, what do you call a Black man in a suit . . . wha? . . . the accused . . . wha? Good one that, isn't it, Sean? Emerald Eddie told me that one.

The cronies laugh. Sean is almost passing out with the pain and the shock and trying to hold the cue and the little inverse stigmata on the green baize and then the picture fades from the subway window. That was the Sean incident.

- Dub is a good person under all that.

Becky is adamant.

Even with all this serious talk and the Sean incident, I think this is hilarious. Becky is now dressed up like Adam Ant and the make-up across her eyes and everything and she is singing the Prince Charming song and dressed in the whole garb, but it is momentary and she is back to herself again which is a relief.

- He was very good to me. When I came to NYC first . . . I was fierce innocent.

I smile at the very Irish way she says 'fierce' and what with her Dad and all my friends it is a wonder she does not speak in a Cavan accent. She does not speak in a Cavan accent.

- I told you before about how I got mixed up with that Italian guy when I first came to the city. I never told you what really happened. Dub used to do some dealing with him and then the guy turned psycho and started keeping me indoors and hitting me and stuff, and accusing me of having affairs with other guys. He was fucking mental. I was scared out of my wits. I've wanted to tell you this before but there was never a time to do it ... so now here it is ... but Dub came over one day and told me to pack my stuff. He wouldn't take no for an answer and he told me not to worry about anything. I never saw that Italian guy again.

I was suffering information overload and I did not know what to say and I remember the Makem & Clancy song and 'Sure whatever you say, say nothing'. But this was the right time to tell me something like this, when we were in a subway carriage at 4 am and we are both buzzed from the *sneachta* and the bloodstream is super-saturated and there is a pleasant humming in my head.

Rattle and Hum. Deesiiiiiiiiiiiiiire.

- He ... well ... he helped me get away and start a new life here and got me working in the bars and some steady money and ... well I feel I owe him ... and he has never asked me for anything in return. Never.

There is a silence between us and I am trying to absorb this and she is making sure that she takes her fingers away from mine and there is that Readybrek shield around us that cannot be touched ... force fields to the power of ten and then I think I said the right thing.

- I understand ... I know what you mean. You're right of course.

And she slots the fingers back into mine again and we are one. One love. One Life.

Rattle.

Rattle and Hum.

41

at the abandoned warehouse

Abandoned.

That is the only way to describe the warehouse. Except for Louie and Louie's cousin, Rodriguez, who knew a guy that drinks in his bar, that knew someone that drinks in some other bar that perhaps maybe would be able to help them to shift their new-found bag of snow dust.

Santos is outside in a rented car waiting and actively losing hair from the worry. Inside Louie and Rodriguez are very nervous and when they meet the two strangers, as arranged, they relax a little. The strangers seem less intimidating than imagined. In fact, one of them is quite comical looking, dressed all in white except for a black shirt. He even wears his coat gangster style over his shoulders. And he keeps calling his helper Roaster, or Raster, or something like that.

Louie relaxes. He is carrying a black plastic bag and inside the black plastic bag is the original bag with the small Guinness logo which contains the merchandise.

Louie thought about swapping to another bag but he only had a few and he thought that the less they moved the stuff around the better. He also thought the harp logo would bring them luck.

In about five minutes from this moment there will be two muffled shots as Louie and Rodriguez fall to the ground, injured but not dead, and Dub claims back what he considers was always his in the first place. He cannot believe his luck and he also cannot believe that these amateurs would leave the gear in the original holdall bag. They should not play ball with professionals like him.

Then . . . the sound of Santos screeching away in his car and Dub and Rooster shouting and running out after him . . . white leather coat tails comically pavonine in the swirl of dust and smoke.

Santos gets away and keeps driving. He will not stop driving until he reaches the Canadian border and then he keeps driving until he reaches the town of Niagara. He stays there for as long as his credit card allows him to and then gets a job in one of the cheap souvenir shops there. He sells plates and lighters and ashtrays all showing pictures of the glorious Falls. There are even little souvenir ambulances with the Maple Leaf embossed on the side but he will not sell too many of them.

– *Cadumphff*

42

permission to come aboard

The pilot has been looking at me through his little window and he obviously feels sorry for me, sitting in the bed and playing solitaire on the laptop. Sad really. He waves me to come closer, so I do. He opens the little window and asks me where I'm headed.

- Back home to Ireland.
- Well don't stay out there man, climb aboard. Sure there's room on my horse for two. You have my permission to come aboard.

I am surprised that he is not sucked out of the window at this altitude but maybe that scene in *Goldfinger* was wrong ... remember the big fat baddie fella being sucked out through the tiny window. Sure you never know what to believe. The door cranks open and two of the hostesses help me clamber on board with the trolley.

- We'll have to leave you sitting in the trolley, I'm afraid, as all the seats are full.

- No problem, thanks for the lift. I don't suppose I'll get frequent flyer points for this?

They exchange looks and smile the corporate smile.

Unfortunately the only way around having me on the flight is if the hostesses use my trolley as the drinks cart. This is fun I must say as I get to meet everyone on the plane. I feel like the Pope being pushed around. A few people order Bloody Marys and I have to laugh.

Go on out of that with your Bloody Mary, says I.

One woman has an inflatable neck brace on and eye patches that say, 'I am asleep. Wake me at your peril.' The hostess shakes her roughly and asks her if she'd like a drink from the drinks trolley. She takes one look at me and faints. They'll revive her again when the chicken or beef comes around.

Another man we pass is snoring through his mouth ... opening and closing like a cat-flap so it is. He has gold-capped teeth and I wouldn't fancy sharing an apple with him.

Eventually when they give out all the drinks they find room to squash me up against the emergency door. Some of the passengers are looking a bit worried, so they are. There is nothing wrong with the plane, it's just that they can see the hostesses starting their journey with the food trays ... chicken or beef ... chicken or beef ... chicken or beef. The ones who have eaten before are afraid. Some of the newbie passengers seem excited. I look out the window and pretend to ignore them as they pass by. The woman with the neck brace starts to shout abuse when they wake her up again. She opts for the beef.

The TV screens on the plane are showing old comedy shows. There is one all about my own class in second year.

Jones the Messer is asking the half-deaf old brother in civics class if we can have a masturbate. The brother turns red with anger and his bulbous nose almost bursts with exasperation.

- What did you say Jones? I heard you. The dirty mouth on you.
- All I said Brother, was that we should have a mass debate on the issue.

The people on the plane with their headsets plugged in are laughing and tittering and bouncing up and down in their seats and generally giving the impression that we are going through some serious turbulence, which we are not.

43

games pilots play

I manage to get into the cockpit for a wee look. I think I was in the way so the hostesses pushed me in there. The co-pilot has a box of Silk Cut Purple on the dashboard . . . for that is the only word to describe the two joysticks and two computer screens in front of them . . . a dashboard.

- Oh hello Shem.

The captain is like some Biggles character with a handlebar moustache. I think the goggles and cap are a bit over the top but he seems like ever such a nice fellow.

- Captain, you'll have to excuse the trolley but I can't really go anywhere without it.
- No problem Shem.
- Thanks Captain. So, the two of you playing Doom when the plane is flying 'itself? .

They both laugh nervously. Har de har har.

- No, no Shem, it's not like that at all.
- Really? Two joysticks for a monster of a plane like

this. Where are all the buttons and wires and dials and things?

- Oh no Shem, old fellow, it's all fly-by-wire now.

- Oh yeah, and which wire is that now, exactly?

They both look at each other nervously again and the co-pilot lights up a smoke.

- So this fly-by-wire thing, I've heard a lot about it. Hope it isn't KAPTON wire.

Again the nervous laugh as they exchange worried glances.

- Actually it is FIFA 2000 we are playing.

The co-pilot speaks . . .

- I am Brazil and he is France and I was winning 2-0 before you came in.

There is a petulant edge to his voice.

- Oh sorry chaps, don't let me stop the game, please go ahead.

And they do. Up on the screens in front of them the football graphics beam up and they do the joystick thing. A smoke alarm goes off above the co-pilot's head and he knocks it off with impunity while conceding a rather nice overhead kicked goal from Zidane.

- Nice goal.

- Thanks.

- Listen, if you want to get to the west of Ireland we could drop you off.

- Oh right then . . . I thought we were going to land at Shannon.

But they were already engrossed in the game again.

- Sorry Shem, no time to talk now. Must concentrate . . . goal!

❑ KAPTON

The TV screen on the end of my trolley is showing a documentary called *Why Planes Go Down*. This edition is all about Clear Air Turbulence and the whole Kapton Wiring thing . . . you see they know the wiring is faulty but there are so many planes up there that to re-wire them all would be such an undertaking and it would mean that the price of flights would have to increase by about 50%.

The reporter is nodding her head and the guy from Boeing who says he is the Head of Safety is saying that he really does not have enough information.

The reporter reminds him that he is the Head of Safety again, but the guy just smiles awkwardly and repeats that he does not have enough information

The reporter knows that she is not going to get any more of the limited information and so she just signs off the interview and that is that . . . and the planes will keep on coming down and the people will have to turn up and identify their loved ones from a piece of a shoe, some torn clothing or the sodden piece of a book. ❑

I am escorted back to my seat by a lovely hostess. She is wearing leather gloves and she really is quite pretty. They have found a space for me and they leave me be. I get the sensation after a few moments that I am being watched. A few more moments and I know I am being watched because there are two people standing in front of me flashing FBI badges in my face. One of them is the woman who was wearing the neck brace and eye patches earlier on. She is still wearing the neck brace but now it looks like a bulletproof neck vest, which is quite cool actually.

- Sir, we have reason to believe that you are couriering drugs.
- What, me?
- Sir, did you pack the contents of your saline pouch yourself?
- Of course not. I was given it in the ambulance.
- Hmm. Likely story.

The woman now squeezes the pouch and looks at me with disdain. It's the man's turn to charm me.

- Sir, I have to inform you that you are under arrest and that by the powers vested in me by the President of the United States, I order you to hand over the saline drip and all its various attachments.
- Hold on a second there Mulder, I happen to be one of the attachments.

My voice is raised and we are attracting quite a lot of attention now. A group of fifteen large men near us are all sitting up and taking particular note of what is going on. I do not know it at the time but they are the Garda Síochána soccer team that have been off playing their opposites in the NYPD. The Irish team won 1-0 in extra time only because all the New York cops headed off for doughnuts after full time and the referee allowed the Irish police to score into an empty goal. The Irish police also won the drinking contest afterwards. One of them, Garda Maguire wanted to arrest half of Manhattan for late drinking until his colleagues explained the law over there. He plans to emigrate there next year.

- Sir, I would like to remind you that you are still in American air space and as such …

It was just at that moment when the captain's voice came booming over the PA.

- Ladies and gentlemen, we are now leaving American air space. So if you would like to look out the window and wave goodbye to the country then now is a good time to do so.

Mulder and Neckbrace were now looking slightly uncomfortable. They would have been even more so if they had turned around and seen the fifteen Gardaí, with folded arms and pursed lips, waiting to assert their jurisdiction.

Mulder was a little upset. He takes out his cell phone and rings head office. It is then that the boys pounce.

- You wouldn't be making a call on a mobile phone there sir, by any chance?
- Well, eh ... I was just ...
- You were just nothing. It is illegal to make a call without the captain's permission.
- Listen fellas, back off.

It was Neckbrace, asserting herself.

- And you madam, would you be trying to sneak drugs into our pure and simple island in that neck brace of yours.

What follows next is a melee with trenchcoats flying and cell phone scattering. The result is that there are two vacant seats and a group of Gardaí singing 'Two-nil, Two-nil' for the rest of the journey. The main guy in the Garda team looked like Great-uncle Donal.

44

a virus in the house

Okay.

It is time to own up.

All the hyperlinks and the intrusions and the interruptions with the story . . . they are my fault.

Here's the deal. I invented a virus and it is responsible for all the interruptions during my story. They should have been more factual and sombre but I could not resist. I apologise here and now . . . but I also must advise you that they are not going to stop.

I call him Brian the Virus. He is my invention and I am rather proud of him. I originally developed him to interfere with some of Dub's accounts and spreadsheets and things but I guess it all just got out of hand. He's been on my laptop for the last six months and he has seen and heard a lot of things that are not, let us say, strictly speaking legal in human terms.

The plan is for Brian to zap himself off on the last available e-mail out of here. Like some cheap sci-fi movie where the planet is about to explode and there is one last launch and the hero turns around to the one he's been trying to screw all during the movie and then he knocks her out and jumps on board himself and leaves her to die . . . that doesn't sound right.

Brian came to be here in the first place because of an e-mail . . . one that Aido sent . . . seemed harmless enough . . . an .exe file of some guy on a surfboard and the Guinness music from the advert playing and every time the guy fell into the water it turned into Guinness instead of water and I thought that was very funny.

If I die and he is still on the laptop and has not managed to hook an e-mail out of here then when the battery dies and the laptop powers off it is highly likely that Brian will never see the light of day again.

I mean think about it . . . if I croak it and they bury or cremate me and then maybe they give the laptop to my relatives but they don't know my sign-on password . . . and believe me they will never guess it . . . and thus they will throw away the thing or maybe not even take it in the first place such will be the grief . . . or Santos will take it for himself . . . if he and Louie ever manage to catch up with us again and bring us in to the hospital . . . or it may simply be discarded in some scrap-heap . . . or maybe some under-privileged inner city kids mess around with the electronics and stuff and someone will stick a soldering iron where they shouldn't and that will be the end of poor Brian.

45

another night in the Orchard

There was this night myself and Brendan were in the Orchard ... it was 3 am and we had sold all our stuff for Dub and we saved some for ourselves ... the dealer's cut . . . and we were in high spirits and up to no good. The bar was hopping ... and we should know seeing as we had supplied the half of them with *sneachta*.

Two girls from Donegal were talking to us. Seven years they'd been here and they were going back next Christmas for good ... no doubt about it this time ... sick and tired of working the bar scene and waiting for one of them fucking visas to come through and sure you were never even sure to get one of them anyways and that's not fucking fair sure it isn't ...

Brendan and myself half nodding and only half listening to half the conversation and that is only 25% attention, which doesn't really count.

But the girls, they were most definiiiitely going back, so they were. Christmas. Back to Onegal ... that's the way she said it ... the uglier of the two ... Onegal ... I was going to ask her where the D had isappeare to but thought better of it.

Brendan and myself were buzzed anyway so they could have been reciting Latvian mountain poetry and we would not have cared less. Brendan kept winking at me ... we were solicitous in the amount we had skived off all the deals tonight . . . Dub wouldn't notice unless anyone complained and they would complain to us first and no one ever did because most of them didn't know what the fuck we were giving them in the first place.

It was like selling candy to a baby.

Brendan called our portion 'The Angel's Share' . . . remembered it from a tour of the Jameson distillery and the girl talking about how some of the whiskey would evaporate through the wooden casks or barrels during the maturation process over the twelve years or whatever and this was called the Angel's Share by those in the know, and theft by those not.

And we were having fun at the girls' expense ... both of them were called Gráinne which they thought was a very good reason to hang around together and we kept calling them Gráinne Squared and they would giggle.

We joked that they had done the vectors option in the Junior Certificate and they hadn't a fucking clue or at least we thought they were stupid when in fact one of them alone would have browbeaten us under the table and she kept telling us bits of trivia about things and we thought she was reading these off beer mats but she was not.

   - Did you know that dolphins are considered to be more intelligent than humans?

Brendan answered for both of us.

   - I did not.

- Though I was talking to one the other day and he did seem to be up there for thinking.

And we giggled and Gráinne Squared giggled in their way.

Then in comes the guy with the newspapers under his arms and he is going around shouting *An Phoblacht* the Republican newspaper . . . and we are all sipping our beers in a bar 3,000 miles away and the little guy is shouting, 'Buy your *An Phoblacht*' . . . and all the boys reaching for their dollars and the barman nervously decides that he needs more ice from the cellar and he disappears and then Bren is slagging the wee fella.

Gráinne Squared buy one copy between them, which is considered mean but not a knee-capping offence, and they giggle at the cover which says something about the Troubles and how the Brits have been causing hassle for millions of years and there is a picture of a Tyrannosaurus Rex and a big red X through the picture and a guy with a balaclava on him.

They have his name underneath in a caption, which sort of spoils the suspense.

There is a Spot the Bullet competition, where you have to pencil in where you think the bullet is most likely to be. The picture they feature in this edition is actually me lying on a street corner. They have this great photo of me just about to fall to the ground and it looks like that famous photo of that Vietnamese kid being shot in the head. And Gráinne Squared giggle when they cop on that it is me . . . and I pull my jacket closed to make sure they can't see the wounds because they could probably work out the trajectory from the picture and that would be cheating so it would.

And Brendan thinks this is all very funny as he knows the guy selling the papers, who is not Irish at all ... his name is Chuckie and he sells this paper around the Irish bars every Thursday, some Timorese paper on Wednesdays, an Indonesian pamphlet of a Friday ... he is well tuned-in to world politics so he is ... fair play to him ... and Bren is talking to him and chewing the cud and he pays for the girls' paper and gives Chuckie a tip and Gráinne Squared are fierce impressed and they are more interested in Brendan even though my photo is on the front cover ... fame can be such a fickle business ...

– So Brendan, how do you know that guy?

– Chuckie? Oh, me and Chuckie go way back when.

And Brendan is tapping me on the foot and that means there is a setup on the way and like a good volleyball player I am to be ready to parry the ball up near the net for him to whack home the point.

– Chuckie is from the home country though you wouldn't know it to look at him ...

Chuckie is Chinese-looking though he actually comes from Hong Kong.

– And he is on the run from the Brits.

– Really? (the girls nod in unison)

– Oh yeah, terrible sad story. He was at the airport trying to come over here for a holiday and they were asking him his name and he told them his surname is Arlaw ... a bit unusual and the guy in the passport control was a bit deaf and he kept asking him to repeat it and so Chuckie gets all upset and eventually he shouts at the top of his voice ...'Chuckie ... you deaf bastard ... Chuckie Arlaw ... Chuckie Arlaw ... how many times do you want me to repeat it?

Chuckie Arlaw . . . Chuckie Arlaw . . . Chuckie Arlaw . . .' and he was dancing around and singing and shouting because he was having a partial nervous breakdown and the guy in the passport office is getting all worried . . . and well basically he hasn't been back in the country since.

Lantering Jasus, says Gráinne Squared.

And Brendan is in hysterics and I'm too far gone at this stage and I notice the little train that they have going around the top of the bar and it just goes around and around and there is also a blackboard with all the numbers and times of the flights to and from Ireland. I look at the train again and on one of the open carts there is an ambulance trolley and there seems to be someone in it . . . but when it comes around again it is empty . . . and then someone puts a song on the jukebox and it is the Waterboys . . . and I saw her crescent but you saw the whole of her moon.

46

a drop for Dub

Dub was a fierce man for the spitting while he was talking
to you. But no one ever said anything and that's just the
way it was. Once he was asking me to do a job. Well, he was
telling me why I wanted to do this job, more precisely.

- I need you to drive up to Buffalo for me.
- Right.
- You can take my car and you can take Becky with you.
- Lovely, she likes driving.
- Go to this address and ask for a guy named Pete.

Just on the saying of the word Pete, between the P and the
ete, at that momentary pursing of the lips, a piece of half
masticated cashew nut left Dub's mouth and traced out a
perfect parabolic path until it collided with the end of my
nose. I knew to wipe it away would cause Dub to get most
annoyed and you don't want to be doing that if you can
help it. I could feel the sodden piece of food slowly slide
right to the precipice. I thought gravity would do the rest

but a weird combination of Dub's frequent use of various stimulants and the particularly humid day that was in it ensured that the piece actually glued itself to my skin. I tried to wriggle my nose imperceptibly without drawing too much notice ... wriggling of the nose around people who deal in cocaine is not good business ... they either think you are diddling the stock or hankering for some merchandise ... so staying steady is the best advice.

The piece was hanging there and it seemed to me to have gained in size ... I must have looked like some harlot from a Roman Polanski version of <u>Macbeth</u>, a tragedy, and the witches always had these terrible growths on the ends of their respective noses, the poor crathurs. They wouldn't get a kick in a kick-shop, they were so ugly, so they took revenge on mankind with their spells and their potions and their tanks and their bombs and their bombs and their bombs ...

Macbeth

The principal source used by Shakespeare for this work was *Chronicles of England, Scotland, and Ireland* (1577) by Raphael Holinshed. The tragedy is a penetrating, concentrated and harrowing study of ambition. In the characters of Macbeth and his wife, Lady Macbeth, the play provides two strong roles long regarded as attractive vehicles for the leading actors of the world.

It is the only play of Shakespeare that uses a dog in one of the roles. His role is brief and Lady Macbeth cuts him down to size with the immortal words ... Out damned Spot.

Discuss the impact of this play on socio-economic

and demographic trends in Northern Europe in not less than 500 words.

But Dub would have killed me if I had said anything or nonchalantly tried to wipe it away and he now seemed to be staring at me a lot harder than usual as if he knew, and he probably did, because that was the type of sadistic bastard he was. So I decided that vigorous nodding and shaking of the head to Dub's questions was the only option.

- So you know where to go?
... nod of the head.
- And you know who to ask for?
... nod of the head.
- And you won't fuck up will you?
... shake of the head.
- Right then ... that's that then.
... nod of the head from me.

And he was up and about and away with the swirl of the white coat and he turns to me.

- Shem, you have something on the end of your nose, you sloppy fuck.
- Thanks Dub.

47

the Swiss Roll episode

Barry Deagan runs up alongside the trolley . . . he is
running very fast. Little circles of dampness are spreading
out from under his arms and they look like someone has
trickled tar into his armpits. He is panting.

– I got it . . . I got it . . .

It is a Swiss Roll that he has robbed from the cake shop
on Camden Street called Kylemore which has nothing to
do with Kylemore Abbey . . . or maybe it does but right now
I don't give a flying fuck which or whether . . . and the
reason he has the Swiss Roll is this: he wanted to be part
of Our Gang Our Gang Our Gang and to do that you had
to rob something from the Kylemore bakery because there
was an auld one who worked there and she could cut you
in two with a look and so it was considered the thing to
do for us twelve-year-olds. We called her 'The Face'.

If you managed to steal something and divided your catch
among the gang then you would be admitted. We were a
foursome at the time, when Barry Deagan asked to join.

323

We did not want to be five so we set him the huge task of getting a chocolate Swiss Roll . . . this was none of your currant bun rubbish, this was the Real Thing, about a foot long and as thick as a brickie's arm . . . and it was right in behind the glass counter and deemed impossible to get, like the gold watch at the carnival in those machines where you put in your coin and get twenty femto-seconds to operate a claw to pick up the prize, except that Barry Deagan, aged fourteen, with no criminal record and no gang membership, reached in his hand right under the nose of The Face and grabbed the confectioner's sacred roll and ran for dear life.

He is still running now . . . and we all doubted if he would ever stop. We refused him entry to the gang anyway as he did not share his spoils because he is still running . . . he runs by the trolley now and he has this crazed expression of wanting to be accepted and he casts me only the most fleeting of glances and says . . . 'I got it, I got it' . . . and in his hand is a putrefied piece of chocolate mush that has been in his hand since that day so long ago and the molecules of the chocolate and the sugar and the cream have coalesced with his skin and so he has brown and white patches on his hand and arm that look more like badly applied suntan lotion . . . and he keeps running . . . the boy just keeps on running.

48

the 800-lawsuit

Lawsuit.

It was only a matter of time.

A lawyer rolls up alongside my trolley. Bronzed and beaming he casts a scavenger look over my wounds and sneaks a peek at the chart on the end of my bed, which is blank as Santos had not yet filled it in as he was chatting to his wife shortly before I left him.

He seems to discern something from the chart anyways and purses his lips in annoyance.

- Hi, I'm Chad Brewer for Warstein, Winstein and
  Slaeygal, lawyers for litigation, marital break-ups and
  whatever. You're not married are you, Shem?
- No.
- Okay, okay . . . that's good, we can work with that.
  How did you hear about our services by the way?
- I didn't . . . you just showed up here.

He laughs . . .

- Shem, we never just show up anywhere . . . we are a

reputable firm of lawyers representing many major corporate and personal clients over many years and I can assure you we are no ambulance chasers.

I laugh and cry out in pain at the same time but he doesn't seem to get the joke.

- Listen Shem . . . we have to take this very seriously . . . this is a gross negligence case and we can sue the city, the State, the Governor, the Hospital Board, the ambulance driver, the paramedics and the makers of these trolleys. Please be serious. Now, can I see your medical insurance?

- Well actually the guy Santos, the paramedic, has it and to be honest with you it was a fake one anyway because . . .

He stops me in my tracks.

- I did not hear you say that Shem. Did you have anything in your possession when you were taken into the ambulance?

- Just this laptop and a hold-all bag.

- Ah, a hold-all bag. I see yes, a bag. And were there any defining marks on this bag?

- Eh, well I think it was a Guinness bag.

- Ah, a Guinness bag, yes, very good, I see, yes. And do you know what was in this bag?

- Yes, I do.

- Don't tell me . . . don't tell me . . . I do not need to know.

We go over a pothole and he nearly falls off the bed and he is almost excited.

- Those wounds . . . were they there before we went over that pothole?

- They are gunshot wounds.

- Is there anyone around to prove or disprove that?

I know a doctor in City Hospital. Owes me a few favours. Anyway, about this bag.

I cop it. He is not really a lawyer or maybe he is but he is not acting as one now. Dub has sent him to try to see did I rig up this whole affair and maybe I was in thick with the paramedic guys and maybe Dub would really like his bag of shit back.

Maybe Chad Brewer, if that's his real name, will probably sue me for talking gibberish. There is always a Babel Clause built into these conversations with lawyers. That's the way it is in the States, talk shite to someone and they'll sue the ass off you. And if you have no ass then the shite is likely to flow out even faster, they'll sue you for more and more . . . and the wheels of the train go round and round. This is a disturbing thought.

More disturbing is the fact that Chad seems to be evaporating right in front of my eyes. He is talking into a microphone hidden behind his lapel. A spaceship suddenly zooms down out of nowhere, well, one of the twinkling little stars in the Paxo Quadrant if the truth be known, and casts a rhombus of cold red light over him. He is speaking gibberish to his colleagues in the hovering craft. It sounds like Irish. I am getting quite suspicious. He keeps saying 'Shah, Shah, Shah'. He is either an inspector for the Irish Language Board or in league with some nefarious group of former Iranian leaders.

The rhombic shape narrows and he starts to digitise and pixelate. It is all very *Star Trek*. The beam of light becomes a funnel and Chad Brewer is essentially sucked up into the spacecraft. There is a swoosh noise and everything. Just before the spaceship hurtles away into the heavens there is a final word from Chad . . . 'Go nyree un boher latt.' Gibberish.

49

a little medical advice

Medical Status Check . . . this is flashing up on my laptop screen now in big red letters that would frighten the piss out of you . . . and it is saying . . . You Are Fucked . . . Press This Button For Advice . . . and there is a little green button with the word 'Advice' written on it in large shimmering letters . . . I have never seen this on my laptop before but nothing surprises me anymore . . . oh, except that my dad has just whizzed by on a motorbike and shouted at me that I was not to get into any trouble when I went to the States.

That was a surprise . . . I was not aware that my dad could drive a motorbike.

I press the large green button and a screen comes up with a beautiful picture of Kylemore Abbey and the lake and the trees and there is even a soporific soundtrack over all this . . . not that soporifics are really what I need right at this minute unless they come in liquid form and can be taken intravenously.

Anyways, there is the abbey and it is resplendent and I can see Becky . . . well the oak tree that she is now . . . well the embodiment of the oak tree that is now her. There is also a little GIF animation of a dog raising and lowering its leg repeatedly against another tree . . . nice touch that. The screen fades to a plain text screen . . .

Shem

There is not long left so it would be most useful if you sent an e-mail to your friends and family and even one to Becky . . . as there may not be another time to do so and time is running out and you are fucked anyways, as was stated earlier in the medical report.

The injuries and the gaping wounds are hurting like crazy now and there is little movement left in my arms . . . I think about it but do not press any keys . . . the screen changes once more and there is another flashing alert button saying that the battery is getting low and that I really should think about sending those e-mails now . . . again I do nothing . . . the screen turns rosy red and the alert button takes up most of the space.

Please Shem

It is vital for the sanity of mankind that you send at least one e-mail before the battery runs out and the world ends . . . at least my world will end as they will sell me to some huckster store down in the village and the laptop will be bought by some hobbyist and the memory where I reside will be burned or erased with some dodgy soldering gun and that will be the end of me.'

I realise now it is Brian the Virus trying to save himself.

It is funny the things you remember when death is looking at you full in the face . . . it is funny the things you remember indeed . . . Jake Cronin pulling along beside me and he still has that funny smug grin on his face . . . he apologised in public but I always suspected he was quite happy about the whole thing.

This was the whole thing: it was down at the annual family picnic in Wexford and all the extended relations were there.

Emerald Eddie interrupts and sticks his ugly head into the story.

- Did you know that Einstein's Theory of Relativity was right? Time does go fucking slower around your relatives . . . do you get it Shem?

- Thanks Eddie, now fuck off and die you sad cokehead. I am trying to tell a story here.

It was the football match after the picnic and most of my cousins played Gaelic football and they thought that giving someone the shoulder meant annexing the neighbouring county. They were basically bastards the lot of them and Jake pushed me into the river and that was the end of that so it was . . . I was up to my neck in slurry shite and everyone was laughing . . . and I was told it was a desperate thing to happen . . . and everyone was laughing and saying it was the funniest thing they had ever seen . . . and it probably was . . . and that was the end of that . . . so it was and there you have it . . .

50

St Patrick's Day in NYC

I remember St Patrick's Day in New York City . . . Becky was all excited because she wanted to see all the men in kilts. I was telling her to relax but there was no relaxing her . . . pushing through the crowd in an attempt to catch a glimpse . . . and she was rewarded when one of them threw his mace in the air and you could see his willy, although it was more likely a splodge of Clonakilty black pudding that someone snook over on the plane.

My trolley seems to be in the middle of the parade now and all I want to do is get back to Becky in Ireland but what with all this pedestrian traffic . . . it doesn't look too good. And then the trolley is the centre of attention on one of the floats . . . the parade passes by and the last one in it is the Old Black Man limping along because he couldn't keep up due to the wound in his leg. He was meant to be in the parade on the Southern Comfort float but they had to get someone else to take his part.

– You're a bit late.

I was angry with him ... I wanted to be on the way to Ireland by now.

- I know.
- What's the story?
- Oh nothing really ...
- Am I going back to Ireland?
- Oh yes, you most certainly are ... but I want to show you something before we go.

He has this great voice, which sounds like Richard Burton ... except he is not.

The video slots in somewhere magical in the TV ... must be one of those Narnia models ... and the scene cranks up. It is of last Christmas Eve night going home on the subway with Rooster and the boys ... the theme tune starts up ...

'... it was CHRISTMAS EVE babe ... in the drunk tank ...'

The Old Black Man whooshes himself up on the trolley.

❏ CHRISTMAS EVE

The camera zooms into a completely black fade and then we are whizzed out of a tunnel and into the vomity yellow light of a train station. There are four of us together singing ... 'An old man said to me, go on, sing another one' ... we sound like The Pogues except that we are crap and drunk and very out of our fucking bins ... the thing is that it is Christmas Eve ... and we are drunk ... Brendan, Sean, myself and Rooster.

Usual assortment of other characters in the carriage ... rhythm, sine wave, roll, rock, flicker of lights, Walt Whitman poetry and 'Dr Zinkmor will clean your pores' posters ... this city never sleeps and here on Christmas Eve we were so far away from home and the eyes in the carriage were on us, the four drunken Paddies.

All any of us wanted was to be home at Midnight Mass probably locked out of our heads as well but home nonetheless . . . and then Rooster singing brokenly like there was no tomorrow . . . 'So Happy Christmas, I love you baby . . . there's gonna be good times when all our dreams come true.'

Two Korean ladies stare at the floor . . . one spits and the other snorts . . . they might as well be joined at the hip. The camera zooms in to the globule of saliva on the off-grey floor and in it we can see the four of us reflected in some hideous Escheresque fisheye effect . . . it is quite impressive actually and the camera work is excellent . . . and then the Korean woman spits again and the camera zooms in on the face of Rooster . . . very close zoom in . . . too close for comfort if you ask me. ❑

The Old Black Man stirs uneasily beside me. He is toying with the saline drip feed and I can't help feeling that he wants to yank it straight out of the socket and wrap it around my neck . . . and that is easier done than said at the moment with all these other things sticking out of me. I feel like a piece of cheese in a cartoon where the mice can run in and around the holes and stick their heads here and there. I smell like old cheese as well, though the Old Black Man seems not to notice. He is too polite by far.

❑ The carriage also has two big guys covered in tattoos . . . one has swastikas all over his arms and the other seems to have the rising sun imprinted on his. It is hard to say for sure as his arms are so hairy. They both wear jeans and white tee-shirts with leather vests on them and they are holding hands. It is freezing but they seem to be inured to the cold by true love . . . there is no better way to keep heated up . . . they have the Readybrek shield of loooove. Good men.

Rooster has noticed them and he is singing the line . . . 'You scumbag, you maggot, you cheap lousy faggot . . . happy Christmas your arse, I pray God it's our last' with extra venom in their direction . . . he almost spits the word 'faggot' but they pretend not to notice . . . but I can see the grip of their holding hands tighten slightly as their palms become balmy with apprehension.

There is a poster for Dr Zinkmor who will clean up your pores for you. Put you on a strict seafood diet and charge you one hundred bucks an hour, thank you very much. Remember seeing it before on the train out to Belmont when I came out here first. The guy must spend a fortune on advertising. There must be big money in pores me lad. Fair play to him I say . . . the land of opportunity. No, no even better, the Land of OpenPoreTunaCity. I tell Rooster this flash of brilliance but he is no longer interested in what we are saying.

But that time on the train out to Belmont . . . two *fear dubhs* hopped on me and one of them stuck a bottle in my neck and there was some girl as well but I can't remember it too clearly now . . . I am not even sure any of that happened. Who cares, who can tell, this is heaven, this is hell, anyone for the last few pores closed now?

But the subway carriage in the Old Black Man's video.

Rooster is out of control. He drank himself into oblivion as usual and then did almost an entire eight-ball of *sneachta* on his own, the stupid mucker . . . and now he looks like something out of a wildlife programme, hanging on to the pole for dear life. The two tattoos get off and Rooster shouts 'Fucking Hershey drivers' after them and Sean laughs.

- Jasus Rooster, you are an awful man. Let's go for one in The Jaunting Cart.... they'll still be open. What do you think Shem, hah?
- Why not.
- 'It was Christmas Eve babe in the drunk tank.'

Rooster stumbles over as the train suddenly alters its periodic shimmy . . . a jolt of lightning, power surge in the cable, the mayor having to apologise to all the communities who actually celebrate Christmas and those that do not celebrate it are not to be offended.

Rooster's brain, even in its current state, had locked into the swaying frequency of the train and was using it as a beacon to know which way to adjust his drunken body in tune to the rhythm. But the unexpected shift caught him and he falls against a man sitting down near to us. The man leans down and helps him up.

- Don't fucking touch me you stinking *fear dubh*.
- I was only trying to . . .
- Yeah, well don't . . .
- Easy there now Rooster . . . come on, give us the rest of your song.

The man looks scared. He is in his fifties and he looks familiar. He is the Old Black Man.

Dr Zinkmor is still smiling but now there are pustules of skin on his face and he is not well by the looks of him . . . it is like Dorian Gray, all fucked up and forgotten and reversed and stuff . . . ❑

The Old Black Man, sitting on the trolley watching the video with me, is looking at me and waiting as if expecting me to say something. But I think the best policy is to say nothing ... and I think of Makem & Clancy ... and whatever you say, say nothing ... say nothing at all.

And I also think of Foster & Allen turning up on *Top of the Pops* dressed as leprechauns and they inadvertently turning back the cause of Irish emancipation ... dressed in green they were and I'm looking at the Old Black Man to see if there is a reaction but he just tells me to watch the video and so I do. He has that serious voice on him and I know he is a very fine actor, what with the full range of serious and not so serious voices he can do.

❑ Rooster is seething with anger and the Old Black Man is trying to look elsewhere. A little bead of sweat breaks out on his head even though it is sub-zero outside.

Bren trying to get Rooster to sing along ... 'And the boys in the NYPD choir were singing' ... but he does not want to dance or sing and the rest of us try to distract him but he is blinkered now and only has one thing in his sights. His drunken bulging eyes are nearly popping out of his head ... strabismus kicking in full throttle.

– Hey *fear dubh* ... you try to grab my ass, did you?
– I was only trying to help you up ...
– Don't you dare speak to me like that ya Black fuck ... I don't need no one's help. Especially not a fucking *fear dubh*.

Rooster makes a lunge for the man, fists flailing about at obtuse angles to his body. The nearest he comes to landing one is the perfect C that rings out when a ring on his finger wraps off the holding bar. The Old Black Man looks genuinely scared now and I would too if I was looking into Rooster's salivating eyes.

- Easy there now Rooster.

Camera pans around and it is me . . . I am speaking . . . I am trying to control Rooster . . . I am trying to be the hero. The Old Black Man's eyes lock onto mine and he passes about 20 giga bytes of information to me in that one brief, download glance.

Get me out of this please . . . use your control, use your power over this man and get me away from this safely, I beseech you.

I am not imagining this, as it's in subtitles across the bottom of the screen.

I know what I have to do.

Camera pans to me grabbing Rooster and putting one of his arms around my neck. I feel the dead weight of him and I try to distance him from the Old Black Man. We flicker in and out of a tunnel and the lights deaden for a femto-second but it is enough for my slurred reactions to falter.

In one deft manoeuvre Rooster has his switchblade out from inside his boot and flicked it open . . . the sound on the movie seems to emphasise this echo noise and plays it back in slow motion . . . in fact the whole screen switches to Peckinpah slow motion.

Rooster has the knife extended to its ugly length and has extricated himself from me long enough to plunge the knife deep into the Old Black Man's leg . . . he does it again and again . . . three times before I can spin him around and get control of the knife . . . Bren finally kicks into action and restrains him and Sean takes the knife from him, more as a trophy than the good Samaritan.

I turn to the Old Black Man who is writhing in agony
. . . no one else in the carriage moves . . . the temperature
has dropped a couple of degrees . . . I can see this on the
small temperature gauge in the top right hand corner of
the screen.

- Fuck sake Rooster, what are you at?

Sean is panicking . . .

- Come on Shem, we better get off.

I turn to the Old Black Man and try to tend to his wound.

He meets my eyes, full on, and says that he knows that
I tried to help.

- I am sorry mister . . . I'm really sorry . . . he's a prick
  . . . he doesn't know what he's doing.
- Come on Shem, we better go . . . now!
- Sean's right Shem . . . let's get this fucking dickhead
  Rooster off the train.
- I am sorry . . . can we get you to a hospital or
  something? . . . Jasus, you're bleeding badly.

I give him my scarf. It is a pure new wool one that my
sister brought over last Christmas, deep ruby and warm as
toast. He takes it and tries to staunch the wounds.

- You better go too . . . (it is the Old Black Man talking
  in his majestic voice)
- But I can't . . .
- Go . . . I'll be all right . . . just leave me alone.
- I'm sorry . . .

And the doors open and we run out and the TV screen
fades to snow. ❏

I am in a state of shock . . . normally with three gunshot
wounds, after having fallen out of an ambulance and all
that, a large dose of shock would be expected. No one

would argue there. But the Old Black Man is just sitting on the trolley and looking at me, but there is no malice in the look.

- I'm really sorry . . .
- I know Shem . . . why do you think I'm here?
- Were you . . . the limp . . . is it bad?
- It will always be with me but I live with it . . . it could have been worse.
- That's very noble of you. I don't suppose you kept that scarf by any chance? It was a present from the sister.

He actually laughs and I laugh too.

- You Irish. Tell me, what is a Far Dove anyway?
- Eh . . . it's a long story.
- A long story, eh?

And he smiles again.

51

at the abbey

The pilot was very funny. No really, he was. I thought we were landing in Shannon but we were not. When you are in Premier Class you expect to get sorted with anything and everything you can dream of . . . and I was dreaming about going to visit Becky.

This is not my fault, about going to Shannon. Most things that have happened recently are my fault but this is not one of them. Becky and the getting turned into a tree thing, well, that was her fault. She wished it and the Old Black Man just happened to be around to make it all happen. That's what he does . . . he makes things happen.

Ever since the subway incident with Rooster, when somehow I managed to be a good person for about twenty seconds in my entire life, the Old Black Man has had the power to do these things.

Gracious. That's what he is. Magnanimous. Magna Minous bo bo ba doobie . . . Magna Minous bo doobie do. Sorry about that. *Sesame Street* flashback. It happens . . .

hurtling through the streets on the trolley and suddenly you remember Big Bird, or Bert and Ernie, or Grover and you know you are well and truly fucked.

But the Old Black Man . . . he didn't have to do that. No sir, he did not . . . and after what Rooster did to him with the stabbing and all . . . Jasus, it is a weird thing to do to a man. Magnanimous.

They say if you live your life well and are nice to everyone and try to be a good person then you will go to heaven, whatever your own version of heaven may be. My theory is that if you do just one gesture that is truly good, important to someone else's life, then in that one deed is the essence of what you really are and what you really believe in. Darth Vader throwing the Emperor over the railings when Luke Skywalker is about to be killed. There is always redemption, otherwise it would not be called redemption, it would be called acting.

I will stop ranting now. There is too much saline stuff floating around in my system. I mean my own system . . . not the Rongagen System, in the Paxo Quadrant. George Lucas making a film of the guy on the trolley drifting through space spreading redemption like an ecstasy pill plague . . . call me Shem Faker or Bull Shitter or something I suppose.

I digress . . . it's the nerves . . . the thoughts of seeing Becky again. She has changed so much . . . this will probably be a bit unusual at the start . . . but starts never last long so we should be straight into the next bit after that.

The parachute is holding up well considering. Thought there would be problems but the stewardess was most helpful with the straps and the buckles and the light and the whistle. They don't normally give out parachutes but I am a special case and I was in Premier Class. She even tucked a couple of bottles of aeroplane bubbly under the blankets for later on ... and the big wink. She was a great girl for the big winks. Had a name-tag Daisy on her ... and sure she was great giving out the coffee and stuff. But I have a special parachute for the trolley and myself and I also have a life jacket, which makes me feel that bit better.

I blew the whistle and she frowned at me.

– They'll all want one now.

The captain ... God bless him ... drops me off just on the coast of Connemara, even though he lost 3–2 to the co-pilot, and I am drifting down now ... it is quite exhilarating ... pulse is up a few notches ... dangerous for the old wounds ... nearly dawn now and everything looks quite beautiful. I can see a map of the coast like one of those satellite maps that RTE use on the weather forecast.

The Winking Weatherman is on the TV now and he is talking his talk and winking as he does so. He is pressing a button in his left hand and all the fluffy clouds start to rain and then he presses again and they disappear ... and it is sunshine again and he gives the big wink and presses the button again, which changes the channel but he must press the correct button again because the channel switches back to him and he is apologising for the messing with the channels ... and the big wink again ... and more rain and fluffy clouds. This man makes the weather. The Winking Weatherman guy ... he is giving the big wink and saying that there should be nice conditions ... wink ... along the west coast ... wink ... for anyone trying to land a trolley ... wink ... and it should be smooth enough ... wink.

The landing.

Easier than I thought. Saline drip nearly falls off and

splashes about a bit. Used the little booster rockets under the trolley . . . originally designed for a moon landing. Dr Klinowitz was commissioned to do a lunar landing trolley in case any of the astronauts got sick and happened to have full premium medical insurance.

It was fun . . . minor adjustments to my gimbals readout on the TV screen and using the remote control as a joystick. All very interactive. And I am down. Pheeew.

I land in the car park of the abbey . . . still empty because it is too early and none of the American tour buses are here yet, so they aren't. Some of the Americans who are to take the coach tour to the abbey were on the same flight over and they were giving guff about me being allowed take the trolley on but then they saw the three bullet wounds and they were a bit quieter after that. One of them was very chatty to me.

- So, going home are you?
- Yes . . . well I'm going to see my girl.
- Oh, that's sweet . . . and where does she live?
- Kylemore Abbey.
- Oh really, how nice. When's the last time you saw her?
- Well she was beside me on the sidewalk screaming after I had been shot three times and I really haven't seen her since they put me in the ambulance but then they lost me going over a pothole when the doors sprung open and then she wished she was a tree and the Old Black Man beside me . . . did I mention him to you? . . . well anyway it doesn't really matter because he granted her this wish and now she is an oak tree and I am going to see her and I am really happy about that.

- Oh really.
- I don't mean to be forward but are you using your vomit bag because I think something has just slipped out of me . . . you know the way it is when you have extra holes in your body . . . well maybe you don't and believe me you don't want to either.
- Well . . . sure here take it anyway.
- Thank you . . . you are very kind.
- It's the least I can do . . . seeing as you have so little time left.

She regrets saying it already but I do not give a flying fuck anymore. She says her name is Daisy and if she can be of any help she will be.

There is an e-mail coming in just as I land safely.

To: Shem
From: Aido
Haven't heard back from you so I guess I'll have to tell you . . . you dunce . . . the next letter is 'E' . . . remember the puzzle from a while ago?
O, T, T, F, F, S, S . . . well it's one, two, three, four, five, six, seven, EIGHT . . . na na na na na . . . you didn't know it. Good one, isn't it?
Hope all is well, regards to Becky.
TTFN
Aido

Beautiful wooded area around the abbey where Becky is. The trolley seems to know this and heads towards a certain section of trees. The path is gravel-covered and this makes the going tough . . . it is spilling my insides . . . no really this is true. On the TV screen there is a poem . . .

'The Faeries' by William Allingham . . '. like the test transmission card with the little girl and the blackboard and the dog . . . and the poem is this:

Up the airy mountain
Down the rushy glen
We daren't go a-hunting for fear of little men.

The poem is from somewhere back in the way distant past with me and Little Bro reciting it and Dad driving us up through the mountains. We are singing this repeatedly and Mum laughing and Dad tapping the steering wheel in time . . . 'Up the airy mountain down the rushy glen . . '

There will be a rustle in the hedgerow . . . don't be alarmed now . . . it is just an armadillo. – *Cadumphff*

And there she is, swaying gently in the wind. She is tall and handsome and I never thought I'd ever say that about a girlfriend let me tell you. Her leaves start to shake as my trolley clambers its way along the gravel track. And then before I know it I am right beside her . . . touching her and feeling her and caressing her. I can feel that she is happy and that she is content and I am happy.

She unfurls her trunk. She is stretching out her cambium just like a role of film and she is trying to show me something . . . Becky was always trying to show me something or other and now she is using the very living cells of her body to show me what I am looking at . . . the cellulose thin layer is stretching for as far as I can see and the sunshine is illuminating it from behind and she is showing me a movie . . . it is a movie of a little boy in a zoo eating a Loop the Loop ice cream and he is letting some of it drip down onto his tee-shirt and he is aware that the funny little creature he is looking at is an armadillo with his funny shells and long nose.

There is a rustle in the hedgerow behind me and a foraging noise and I know this is Cadumphff and he comes out and looks up at the trolley and then jumps athletically up onto it and he nestles himself down into the blankets at my feet and watches the movie with me.

 - You didn't cop on to the signals I was trying to send you, did you?
 - That's true.
 - That's a pity.
 - Is it hard telling the truth?
 - Not for me.
 - Is Becky ... will she be all right here?
 - Oh yes ... a long and fruitful life is ahead of her. She is in the right place now.
 - And me?

Cadumphff develops a slight twitch.

 - Watch the movie.

And we sit in the grounds of Kylemore Abbey, the sun shining through Becky's cellulose sheets of cambium, as I watch my whole life flash before me and it is a beautifully warm experience and the blood and wounds feel warm and the sunshine feels warm. Cadumphff snuggles into my feet and they also feel warm.

The movie ends as quickly as it began and the cellulose snaps back into Becky's bark.

 - So is that it then?
 - Afraid so Shem.
 - Thanks for being honest.
 - It's my job.

The wind rustles the branches and leaves of the beloved oak tree beside me. I take one long last sigh and I am back in the ambulance again and it is a cold night in Manhattan and the paramedics are closing the doors and I think one of them is Puerto Rican or somewhere like that and they bolt the doors closed and then they attach monitor leads on to my chest and the little green line on the screen goes up and down in a saw-tooth and then the saw-tooth blunts and then . . . straight line.

Becky is holding my hand in the ambulance just as the line goes non-bumpy. I hear the constant piercing tone of the monitor and I am floating above the scene. I can see my own body and Becky leaning over it. I am floating free of the trolley now.

straight line
A straight line is the shortest distance between two points.

I land on Vinegar Hill. Dad is holding my hand tightly. I have an ice cream in the other. I can smell the nutty aroma of the pipe that is still smouldering in his trousers. Even on top of the hill on this cold day I feel warm next to him.

He is pointing at a church steeple far away. He bends down to afford me a better look. I trace the line from the end of his finger to the desired target. It is a straight line.

A few drops of rain start to fall and he silently guides me back down the hill.

epilogue

It is the year 2027.

The moon cruiser *La Lune* is so far from Earth that the planet is only a blue–green orb about the size of a football. The twenty-six passengers paying $40,000 a seat don't care what size the Earth is. They are more concerned with the size of what they are approaching.

They are all having a great time. The time of their lives.

They are among the privileged few with enough money to spend on this fantastic trip. There will be many others after them. But they are humbled to be on board. Even with the prices.

The tour operator is smiling smugly in the corner and savouring every minute as he thinks of how he can possibly even spend the interest from the money he is going to make. The cruise steward is smiling . . . happy to be on board working and giving out the zero-gravity-friendly sachets of champagne.

Everybody is happy.

Everybody except the pilot, that is.

He is not happy at all.

A little flake of paint from the roof panel of his cockpit has just fallen directly into his lap. The computer embedded into his spacesuit gives a tiny, almost inaudible, flakology alert. Some figures pop up on his in-visor display. Something bad is going to happen.

He checks all his read-outs and runs a diagnostic check. But he need not have bothered as it is the smell of something burning that is worrying him more than the flashing red lights and the alarms that are becoming more audible by the second.

He now has a fire in one of the nuclear reactors powering the spacecraft and knows that he has less than …

Cadumphff . . . The entire lunar craft, its captain, stewards, tour operator and moneyed passengers all disintegrate in a blinding flash of nuclear fission. It lasts a few micro-seconds and then it is all over.

Most of the passengers do not know what has happened. Becky and Shem most certainly did not as they held each other's hand and firmly grasped a sachet of gravity champagne in their other hands.

By a purely random fluke of fission mathematics and quantum uncertainties, this couple celebrating their 25th anniversary are coalesced into one searing fireball and shoot out in the direction of their home planet. Other micro-explosions and atomic mixtures are formed from the rest of the debris . . . each of them shooting off in random trajectories.

Such is the speed of the bullet-sized Becky–Shem–Champagne fireball that it breaks through both the sound and the light speed barriers. Cast back in time the fireball hurtles through the Earth's atmosphere . . . now no more than the size of a small hailstone. The rapidly cooling fireball is now liquefied thanks to the champagne . . . and heads straight down and lands on the forehead of a young man lying on a street corner in New York City.

The cocktail raindrop rolls down his forehead, along his ski slope nose and drips into his slightly open mouth. He is pleasantly surprised at how sweet the rain tastes.

And this is true. – *Cadumphff*